For the girl who chose to survive.

Altair

The glass splintered and rained across me as I sprung from my bed, catching the spear expertly vaulted into Vanna's guest room. I brandished my Grace to keep the glass out of my feet and reinforcing my legs with Autumns power, only to raise my head to meet a pair of frozen green eyes an inch from my face. Before I could muster a single spell in my defense, a sword ran through me, precisely running through my diaphragm and severing my spine. I felt my the feeling in my legs leave me, the Grace's power resolving from me, and feeling blood rise through my throat.

I opened my eyes, bolting up suddenly and clutching my torso. I wasn't wounded. There was no glass. The morning was as still as it was in my slumber, the gentle simmer of sunshine warming the window sill. I glanced over to find the dust dancing and settling across the amber summer air, my white night gown blending into the soft sheets still emanating the evidence of my unconsciousness. I turned to find the vibrant Azalea bushes outside, suddenly noticing a shadow trailing the walkway towards the window.

I shifted my glance up to find a long spear breaking the surface of the glass like the permeable surface of water, time almost slowing around the shattering glass webbing outward to the wooden frame

6

of the window. I leapt out of bed with expectant ease, catching the spear in midair and activating my Grace in tandem to prevent the broken glass from harming my feet. Had this not just happened?

Before I could cast a single defense spell- no, wait. Defenses. Activate defenses. I reached to activate my wheel of swords, 5 behind me and two entering my hands, forming an "X" across my body in preparation to catch the lunging thrust bursting through the still falling glass in the hands of slender arms poised in a trained alabaster grip. My swords parried the linear strike of her short sword, her black dress flowing behind her in her spiral strike, gliding through the air like an osprey gaining speed towards its prey in the water.

She was beautiful. Her tussled ringlet curls shined in the morning light a brilliant golden hue as her motionless pale face grew closer to mine; a pair of unblinking viridian stained-glass eyes staring a haunting and familiar stare into my face.

The first objective of this day, this new chance at life, was supposed to be *me* finding *my* past self in this timeline. This morning I was going to find the Chateaux and rally their resources to assist me in defeating the ghosts of my past. But I guess today was my lucky day. Because as I deflected the blonde assailant's blows, she motioned towards me a green ring of gravity magic intended to surround and crush me. As I disarmed the thought with a red anti-gravity spell, a look of ferocity crossed my opponent's brow. She had made this so much easier for me.

7

"Good morning, Wyvren." I said, the dissipating green enchantment hissing out of existence in the dance of my red aura. At the sound of her name she nearly displaced all of the space between us, beginning to summon her entire arsenal of rapturous blades in the workshop's spare room. I grabbed her wrist, displacing us with the azalea bush outside and tossed her into the air, using the sepia light of Autumn's power in my ankles to make a mighty leap towards her in the air, "you don't get to destroy that home," I said to her, wind whipping through my hair behind me as I approached.

All of our swords unsheathed themselves from their residing dimensions and clashed against the other's with precision and cruel grace. The lights shimmered across the freshness of our blades; every one of them brandished the morning sunlight and glistened across the shingles of the town around us. I had to get us out of here, there was too much collateral damage. I knew what this version of me was capable of. She would destroy this entire town before yielding to defeat, whether I was able to match her strength with my current alterations or not.

Before I could fully flesh out the thought of where to take the beast of my former existence, her swords began to move in their calculated rhythm; steeped in the movements of the mortals who once wielded them, programmed to clash with blades with the prowess of fallen masters. Luckily, my swords shared the same cursed fate. One of the things that made us so lethal was our swords relied on us to levitate with anti-gravity, but their movements were

8

rooted in two autopilot programs: sacred geometric rhythms, and kinetic memories of their former wielders.

As the gears of her war machine began to churn, so did mine. A swarm of blades, floating in the sky around two maidens mingling with the clouds. I'm sure to the ignorant eye it would have seemed like two angels dancing, fighting for the rights of feuding charges among mortals. But only one of us was close to the semblance of angel, my charge the innocents of this place.

I sprouted my wings, the halo burning around my neck as my light began to burn brighter than the great star now lingering fully over the horizon. My golden aura of heat and luminance blew the Wyvren back, spinning her out through several clouds. I combined the power in my legs with the gusting of my wings, screaming towards her as the friction of the air ignited against my already burning body.

I ripped through the clouds, blowing them out of even circumference as I closed in on my past life like an arrow. She raised her head, her body flying backwards towards the ground as I came upon her. She cast a gravity spell to resist the clutches of the trees beneath us and met my force head on, our swords entangled again, our fingers intertwining as our foreheads touched. Eye to eye. This would have been a stalemate, but luckily my steps toward liberation had not only granted me sentience, but the fire of a forge and the light of an angel.

I ignited my palms, the agonizing scorching of molten heat searing into the Wyvren's grip. In her best

9

attempts to resist the heat and divert the stress, she attempted a blue water spell that immediately resolved into steam. Bright orange cracks began to form from her wrists, splitting certainly and dramatically up her forearms as her magic became dust in my hands. Even her face began to burn as the heat of my forehead began to blister around her eyes and her blonde hair started to singe. I was winning. I was stronger than I used to be. Stronger than her. I could beat her.

Without warning, a stray sword flew from our steel gridlock and swung downward between us. The blade sliced through her wrists, severing her hands and thusly her from my grip. She pressed her feet into my abdomen and launched herself towards the ground, her hands still burning in my grasp as the air was knocked out of me. I guess up until now I the Wyvren had never been hunted by another of its kind. Her survival code probably demanded she lose the hands- March and Spring could always give her new ones.

I caught by breath, narrowing my wings and descending through her path like an eagle as I maneuvered through the branches of the forest that hid my prey. I felt my engine turn again, lusting for the blood of the monster in my pursuit. My legs met the ground and with a charging of sepia light, propelling my body forward with an unchallenged speed, a head of blonde ringlet curls in my sights before I knew it.

She turned, glassy moss eyes filled with something I could never have imagined across any Wyvren's face: fear. I gathered my swords, two in hand and a Mandela of blades spiraling in arsenal, dug my

10

stance into the ground and lunged an onslaught of steel into her like an army of starved locust. The heat of my palms inducted through the handles of my blades, sending the fire of my ardency through to the blade as it shown a vivid vermillion hue, landing true into the Wyvren's back.

Before my blade could completely pierce through, a tear in Space appeared before us, a bright white light emanating from the dimensional rift. A pair of velvet robed arms reached out, embracing the beast I was carving, pulling her impossibly fast from my impalement. As soon as my blades had impaled her muscular flesh, I felt her presence leave them, the rift disappear, and the hurricane of burning blades shred through the forest in front of me rather than the monster I was desperate to kill.

"Dammit." I whispered to myself as my blades finally lost enough momentum to stop their twister through the trees, sporadically landing through both the trees and the ground below. I should have know that he would come to save her before I could finish the kill. Spring existed outside of Time and Space, or at least he hid there. There were no alternate timelines for him.

Spring saw how much stronger I had become, he saw *who* I had become. It was only a matter of time before he scooped up his precious work. The unfortunate thing that worried me now is what alterations he could be making to this project on this timeline reflecting the past.

Time isn't linear. Thusly, Time travel also isn't linear. Time exists as a justification of Space, quantified

11

by light and how it travels. Time, inherently, at least for the purposes of our magical world, is light itself. When you leave one timeline, the light in that universe continues to move across the Space there. Light can't move backwards, so neither can Time. To be here, now, I am in a new set of possibilities. Surely there will be similarities, but there will be new truths, new events. Things that I have no way of foreseeing with absolution based on my informed presence of being from "a" future.

But now I am here. That Wyvren didn't have a face that was familiar to me. That was the Wyvren of *this* timeline, with no promised future of emancipation from Spring. That is what Karine meant before… she had come to each and every timeline, over and over again, looking for a Wyvren that exists in a scenario where both Irene and I existed, the iteration that would result in "Ren," and has failed more times than not.

"Karine…" I whispered to myself, thinking through the unforgiving passage of Time that brought me to this very moment without her. I felt myself start to cry, clutching the Clock Key secured by the yellow ribbon around my neck. I felt a warmth from it, then an ominous purple light flashed and illuminated my eyes.

I suddenly saw a vision present itself to me in hued blur, someone approaching me from behind, concerned and afraid, armed with a broad sword ready to strike me. As soon as my sight returned to me fully and the vision concluded, I turned reactively to the potential attack. Surely enough, there was a tall and brutish man coming towards me, frantic fear in his eyes

12

and a skilled aim towards my head. The Clock Key warned me somehow.

   With bright red sword still in hand, I tucked my wings and parried his strike, repositioning behind him as my burning footsteps charred the grass below. Even in this new form, my steps became an exhaust from the sheer heat this angelic power emitted. To that point, the man began to perspire immediately standing so close to me. To his human body it must have been like opening a furnace full of coal and dry pine.

   Before he poised another strike, I got a better look at his face- it was Gaultier, out of the cellar of the Chateaux. He must have sensed the Wyvren, whether it was myself or the blonde incarnation of me, that killed his daughter and sprung into action. His team must be nearby somewhere.

   "Gaultier, wait!" I said, dropping my sword and retracting my wings and halo. The temperature of the air around us dropped at least twenty degrees as my form regressed to a more human appearance. I raised my hands, showing I was unarmed, and Gaultier redirected his strike to land just beside me; a single lock of my long hair slivered off ever so gently as it missed my head.

   He retreated a couple of steps, smearing the sweat from his eyes and adjusting his view of me. He looked me up and down, turned and looked at the leveled path of trees my swords left in their wake, still visible and piercing through the path they left. Returning his cold stare to meet my level eyes he spoke at last, "how is it you chased that monster away on your own, young lady?" He snarled, his voice rough and dry from his sudden dehydration. "And how did you know my name?"

This was it. This was the plan- Karine was surely here doing it as well. I knew more than he did, at least for now, about the situation at large. He believed that the Wyvren was the big bad evil in the world, unbeknownst of the Seasons and Months. The Auspice had not yet been formed on this timeline. Hopefully Evelynn and everyone else were still themselves, beyond the influence of Spring and their identities in the Tower. I had to choose an identity and stick with it. I had to be the new me, not the monster I was before.

"My name is Ren," I began calmly, my voice surprisingly warm and soft. "I have come to find you in hopes to aid your cause in defeating the Wyvren that plagues this world." I lowered my hands as I spoke, "I have trained all my life in a land far from here to destroy it. It killed my friend and took what was left of my life away from me." I took a knee as I finished my abridged and partially fictional history, "please, allow me to serve you and your ranks. I will not rest until I have my revenge on that monster."

Gaultier stood silently for a moment, broad sword in the ground in front of him with his hands resting on the hilt. "Everyone, come out." He commanded in a raspy baritone voice. "We must assess this new prospect of our ranks."

Out of the bushes came Irene first, her long brunette hair and flowing across her red and white outfit- sleeveless fitted white top, fingerless and empty

14

palmed arm-length gauntlets fashioned from red leather that allowed her smithing, and durable pants fashioned from the same red leather that continued into boots; her various metals jingling as they were fixed to her belt and formed gently to the curvature of her back for storage. I tried not to gasp as I saw her standing there; graceful, powerful, and alive. I wanted to desperately to embrace and thank her for her sacrifice, but it would fall on an ignorant recipient and vainly blow my cover completely.

From across the way, Evelynn emerged from the foliage with her dark brown hair framing her olive toned face, met with rich and swirling brown eyes. In a similar outfit to Irene, black where the white was, and the red leather replaced with a dark navy blue material akin to canvas; her various liquids and vials jingling a higher tone that complimented Irene's. They really were a stunning pair to see side by side.

As quietly as I would expect Sabine emerged, her thick blonde hair tied behind her as she donned a simple blue dress. She held a sketch pad and charcoal in her hands to illustrate the thoughts and moods around her so that she may communicate her empathetic mind reading. She still required such devices to communicate her findings without her tongue, cut out years ago.

Simultaneously, Sara emerged from the trunk of a tree, having used her Fae Halfling powers to temporarily merge with nature. I remembered her brutal strike that impaled me at the Sinclair Estate and blinked firmly to resist the shutter of pain as I remembered it.

Her cunning slender figure instantly danced to Gaultier's side where she found most pleasure.

There was no sign of Constantine or Kyrie- they either weren't on this mission as they were too young or they had not yet been recruited or found by Irene and Evelynn. They all looked so alive and well, standing in the sunlit forest of a late morning in the summer; so different than how I remembered them before.

Before I could greet anyone, Sabine's eyes lit up at the sight of me. She frantically flipped through her sketchbook, turning the smeared charcoal pages between her nimble fingers to reveal a sketch of a winged woman, clad only in a nightgown and standing before a shredded forest with the sun rising in the sky behind her. She silently lifted her cinder-stained finger, gesturing across the remaining meadow towards me, eyes bright and alive with wonder.

Everyone's attention slowly shifted from Sabine and unified their gaze upon me, standing in Vanna's borrowed sleeping attire that I had truly forgotten I was still wearing. I stood between the two groups; Gaultier and Sara at one side, Evelynn, Irene, and Sabine at the other. Even the remaining birds in the still standing trees stopped their song in the oppressive silence steeping around us.

"Sabine, do you think she is the one Karine spoke of?" Sara finally spoke, breaking the silence with her charming and fluttery soprano tone. "Is she the Gravity Witch?"

I felt my throat grow dry and my brow intensify at her name. Karine was already here somewhere, and somehow knew I was coming. But how? The Karine I knew was… gone. This one should be trying to find and save the blonde Wyvren I chased into the maintenance room. Before I could formulate a reply, Sabine smiled a honeyed smile and nodded, her bright and psychic eyes filling with tears as if she had been waiting for me for eons.

I raised a hand to speak, gesturing towards Gaultier to address his authority again, only to be cut off by Evelynn behind me as she reached for a vial at her waist. "We barely know Karine," she stipulated to the group. "As soon as she returns to us, she is gone again; whisked away to the unknown missions she sees the rest of us unfit to join." She deepened her stance, readying a threat towards me. I turned my gaze to meet hers, feeling my eyes deepen as they rejected the light from glistening upon them.

Evelynn froze, a murderous aura emanating from my suggestive gaze. I spoke again, unblinking but addressing Gaultier, my eyes never leaving Evelynn or her aquifer grip, "Gaultier, I promise you I mean you no harm. I am at your service." I had an opportunity to show a bit of my hand in a meaningful way. "Karine and I, we had the same master once upon a time," I began, my eyes finally leaving and releasing Evelynn from their mortifying grip. "She must have thought me dead. We were separated, I narrowly escaped the Wyvren with my life. I have spent the last several years fighting my way back across this continent, searching for my friend." I almost lied.

17

Irene walked across the path to place a hand on Evelynn's, gesturing her to rebuke her threat. She turned to me, her green eyes and umber hair especially vivid in the light, illuminated by the vitality that I had taken from her in another world. She looked at me, determination and acceptance on her face. "We have all lost something precious, stranger, " she began, raising her leather clad hand to her heart. "It is rare that we have the opportunity to find those lost to us again."

Irene shifted her expression passed me and towards Gaultier, "we should welcome this traveler," Irene continued. "We need all of the help we can get if we are to keep the Wyvren at bay. It has not yet found its way to our small town before today."

"And you don't find that a coincidence?" Evelynn immediately interjected. "We have spent years without any sighting of that monster in our small corner of the world, the rest of the witches on the continent beginning to build a sanctuary beyond the veil, hiding from the beast."

Evelynn threw a look of sheer malice towards me, "and you come to town, suddenly able to beat it into submission when no one else has been able to for *eras*?" She accused. "If you are to come back with us, you should be placed under severe magical custody."

Irene came from a religious and forgiving background, trained and noble in charity and sacrifice. Of course she would be the one here to advocate for me. Karine had already empathized a visage of me to give me a foothold in Sabine, her power empathizing to the truth of Karine's intentions.

Sara would agree with whatever Gaultier had to say, and Gaultier would surely accept the help secretly and selfishly for his goal that only I knew amongst the standing group other than perhaps Karine at that point. Evelynn was the wild card here. She was guarded and held a past truly unknown to me. Whatever I had to do to get her on my side was worth the investment.

I placed myself on the ground, balanced on my knees with my hands in the air. "Whatever precautions you feel you should take upon me, I respect." I finally stated during Gaultier's contemplations. "I am an outsider, these are uncertain times, but you are right about one thing." I teased at their ears. "I am able to keep the Wyvren on its toes. I have learned its skills; its movements and its decision making pattern. I have lost many comrades in the process, almost losing my life as well…" I trailed off, the vision of Spring's arm thrust through Karine, holding bits of her spine in his gaunt grasp. I shook off the flashback and finished, "I know loss, as you all do, I'm sure. Bind me however you see fit."

The group stayed silent again for a moment, unmoving in their decisions except Evelynn, raising an unknown liquid from one of her vials and manipulated it forward, enveloping my hands and clasping them together in an aquatic shackle; sealing my hands completely, as my fingers interlocked in front of me within the depths of the mysterious waters.

"This water is cursed." Evelynn explained. "It is devoid of the life-giving vitality properties that most waters provide. It can only absorb; endlessly. Anything you try to cast at us will be immediately metabolized by my spell." She concluded proudly, going as far as to turn her nose up at me in a grin.

It was an impressive spell, one I was not in a position to test in the spirit of posing resistance. "Very well," I continued. "What should I expect you to do with me, now that I am at your mercy?"

Gaultier and Sara came to either side of me, lifting me from beneath my shoulders as my hands remained bound. "We take you back to the Chateaux," Gaultier decided. "If Karine can vouch for you, I trust her and her judgement completely." Irene smiled in celebration, folding her callused hands together pleasantly.

In true continued contrast, the black and blue clad warrior of water crossed her arms, continuing a furrowed and concerted stare towards. Sabine folded her notebook shut, taking a deep sigh of relief, probably suffering from being in the crossfire of so many contrasting emotions.

"Thank you for your consideration," I said. "I am excited to see Karine again." My words were a timid and confused understatement of fear and grief. Karine was dead. *My* Karine was dead. This version of her, this her that either existed on this timeline or was an iteration of her before she found me and died- the middle of a continuation I would inevitable escort to her death. Regardless of the unending possibilities, I was far from excited to see Karine. I was scared.

We all began walking through the unscathed remains of the forest towards the outskirts of town,

20

when suddenly from behind us called a bubbly and exasperated voice. "Wait! Ren!" We all turned, confused and surprisingly still guarded despite the warmth of the calling voice. "You forgot your dress!"

It was Vanna, running towards us, her beautiful yellow dress in hand, arms outstretched as she clumsily skipped through the forest. "When I heard the crash in my guest room this morning, I ran outside to see what was going on to see you fighting high in the sky! You were amazing!" She chided in a voice of spirited admiration. "You're really strong!"

She finally made her way to me, but seeing my hands bound by Evelynn's enchanted water she asked, "what's going on? Where are you taking my friend?"

"Vanna, you know this person?" Gaultier questioned gingerly. I guess housing traveling witches gets you in with the mystical halfway house that the Chateaux is.

"Absolutely!" Vanna affirmed in ardency. "She was in tattered clothes and in bad shape when she came to me last night- it looked like she had been fighting a sleuth of bears!"

Sara shifted her glance to Evelynn. "Release your spell, Evelynn." She commanded from Gaultier's side. "You know she can be trusted now."

Evelynn's face shadowed in disappointment as she waved the cursed liquids from my hands and back into her arsenal. I looked around, confused; Vanna's arms still outstretched with the delicate daffodil dress for me. I reached out, taking it into my hands, still glancing around for an explanation.

21

"Vanna's workshop is enchanted, Ren," Irene finally explained. "Since even before her mother took it over before her, the workshop is a resting place for traveling witches with the intent to do good in their hearts." She placed a hand on my shoulder, my body jumping as if shocked by her hands. "It is impossible for anyone else to find. That is proof enough for us." Her voice concluded, warmly and certainly.

I felt a warmth begin to teem in my eyes. I was a monster- *the* monster. I was the blonde beast that fled into the arms of Spring just moments ago before finding these people. I was the reflection of Spring's intentions, the will of his heinous and perverse debauchery upon this world. I *was* all of those things, once upon a time. But Karine found me. Irene found me. Scimariel found me. The martyrs of my forgiveness and the sacrifices for my sins, just beyond this world in the recent past of another timeline. And here and now, in a world where they got to still be alive, I, too, was able to be good. I was *good.*

I clutched the dress in my hand, wiping the tears away from my face as Irene tilted her head in concern. I explained, "I'm sorry. I've just been on my own for a little while now and I have only truly ever known one friend in Karine." I composed myself, taking a deep breath. "I'm not used to being affirmed by someone- to be vouched for or justified in kindness. Thank you, very much, for trusting me."

I turned to Vanna, taking her hands and bowing my head to them in my grasp. "Thank you for your hospitality and your trust, Vanna." My head rose to meet

22

her surprised and flustered gaze as my tall stature folded to respect the young woman I had known before as the kind older figure that fashioned me clothes in another time. "If there is anything I can ever do for you, I am at your disposal."

Vanna chuckled nervously, Evelynn's disdain shifting to surprise as she witnessed my humility to Vanna and the group for their trust. For the first time that day, Evelynn's gaze towards me softened. I thanked Vanna again as she saw us off, comforting me in stating that the workshop with its various enchantments had hidden itself again, fixed and brand new, concealed and waiting for the next magical traveler who needed her services.

We continued through the forest, walking through the dense and damp mosses, various glimmers and enchantments in place to subdue mortals and inexperienced witches from finding their way to Gaultier's hideout. At last, we came upon a clearing just passed the edge of the woods on the outskirts of town. I took a sharp breath as I saw the Chateaux again, the dilapidated building that housed the unlikely group of vagabonds under the direction of their secretly morose leader.

We walked inside to the dining hall in the main entrance, a fire burning in place and a seated figure in a chair by it, tending to some food being heated in the cast iron above the flames. Hearing our entrance, the figure stood to reveal a woman with darkened hair, turning to take the breath form my lungs as her cruel familiarity met my eyes. Karine.

23

"I see you finally found my companion, Sabine," Karine's knowing voice slyly rang through the great stone hall. She walked across the way to meet us, not looking at anyone else- her eyes only locked with mine. I was paralyzed. Her movements looked like they were slowed, as if the room was suddenly underwater. She was a dream, a mirage of my feelings swaying by the tables and furnishings of the room, a smile that told me she knew what I knew.

She was finally to us, opening her mouth close to my face; her soft and deep voice whispering my name for what felt like the first and thousandth time all at once. "Ren," she spoke, my eyes shuttering at the sound of her address. "It is good to finally see you again." She wrapped her arms around me, holding me firmly but not tightly, exactly as I remembered her embrace. She cradled my head, my taller body leaning my head into the nook of her shoulder as I breathed in the scent of her hair. It was Karine. It was somehow Karine. She was so… the same. As if the woman I saw die never did.

I finally raised my arms to meet her embrace, pulling her tighter to me, as if I wanted us to become the same person. I never wanted to let go- never again did I want her to be vulnerable to anyone else but me. I never wanted her arms to need anything but to do what they were doing now, her heart to beat anywhere else but here. I needed her to stay here; fragile, human, and alive. I wasn't like the other witches here. They had power, sure- but imbued in their frail human bodies.

"Welcome home." She whispered in my ear. I collapsed, taking her down with me to my knees as I cried. And cried. I mourned the Karine that was gone in the arms of the only one who could possibly know or understand my truth in the world, somehow in the embrace of the very spirit taken from me. I didn't yet understand what had happened- who she was, *when* she was. But she knew me. And she knew the name Irene gave me. Somehow, someway, this was the Karine I needed her to be. And for now on the cold ground, surrounded by confused strangers, that was enough for me.

Ephemeral

"So, 'sisters,' huh?" Irene questioned skeptically, forking another cut of beef and potatoes into her mouth. I sat towards the end of the table, Evelynn to my right, Karine to my left. I took a drink of water and looked around the room, Téo having joined the group from watching the ruined castle they stayed in with Karine while the others went on the mission where they discovered me. All of their eyes staring me down; staring *us* down. One eye on me, one eye on her.

"Well, *like* sisters," Karine responded for me, Irene turning her face from mine to hers. "We were both raised by the same person when we were younger. We grew up together." Karine sliced her meat with clean precision, a sharp squeak echoing from her plate. "Where Ren was taught spatial magic, our teacher taught me time." She turned to look at me, her deep blue eyes peering past my eyes and into my curious face. Same teacher? When we were young? Was she lying or had I met Karine somewhere before along the way?

"Um, yes." I clumsily responded. "That is how I was able to keep up with the Wyvren. Our teacher followed its movements and skills and boiled them down to a metaphysical move set he entrusted to me." I looked away from Karine, clearly receiving the message that I was supposed to have known this information already. "Time magic is beyond me. I have never been good at it at all."

Gaultier cleared his throat, cleaning his palette with cheap wine before stroking his rugged chin in response. "Ah, yes. Karine, you mentioned that your unique artifact is what allows you to see into the future, correct?" He commented. "That Clock Key around your neck?"

Karine reached into the collar of her dress, pulling out her most prized possession, dangling it in front of us all at the table on a delicate yellow ribbon, tattered and stained. Just how many times had she gone to get that yellow ribbon? "Yes. With this, I am able to see subtle phases of the past and the future. While not incredibly powerful, it gives me the power of precise foresight in short increments; just a couple seconds at a time.

I reached to my collar, feeling the "other" Karine's clock key beneath my daffodil dress I'd change into, remembering this morning when the Wyvren thrust her spear into Vanna's window; how I saw it happen to me twice. It was her key, it warned me about the upcoming danger. Karine knew I had the power of Space. In her dying breaths she was trying to give Time to me, too.

"But the truly impressive one here is Ren," Karine boasted, shifting the conversation from the Clock Keys each of us were twiddling in our thumbs. "My power is situational, Ren can keep up with the dimensional prowess of the Wyvren that has spurned all of our lives." She finished, chiding a look around the room with a complimentary gesture.

I looked around the dinner table, everyone's face becoming nothing less than morose. Each expression revisiting their own chapter of grief; the moment that hurt most as my past ripped their lives away from them. Without much surprise, Evelynn spoke first.

"I was three years old." Evelynn began. "The Wyvren came to our town, a small magical settlement just north of Paris." Her expression dimmed as she scoured her vague memories of my destruction. "The roof flying off the top of my house is my first memory," she reminisced, her deep brown eyes sifting through cruel nostalgia. "The next thing I remember was a maelstrom of blades spiraling through the night sky; enigmatic geometries slicing through the towns people- slicing though my parents. I can't remember their faces." She finished, her elegant face devoid of tears. Surely she had cried enough since.

"I found you days later," Gaultier continued the testimonies of the table. "I was following it- the monster. It had just left a town near here where my family and I used to live." Gaultier lacked the composure Evelynn maintained, having known the pain of loss more intimately with clearer memories. "It killed my wife and took my daughter from me." His opal eyes filled with tears, his Sara reaching to cradle his massive clenched fist with her slender nimble hands.

"I spent years chasing it." He continued, wiping tears from his wrinkled brow and eyes. His expression

28

changed to solemn consolation as he turned his head to Evelynn, her face smiling in return. "Luckily, as I followed the wreckage and carnage across the countryside, I came across young Evelynn, wandering through the remains of what would have given her a wonderful future." He chuckled with a paternal warmth as he concluded, "now she has only me to deal with. If not for Evelynn, I don't know what I would have done. The Wyvren may have taken my daughter, but I was lucky enough to find another one."

The room filled with a wholesome energy- the sentiment of found family ruminating through the table as the hatred for me and my crimes subsided to a reprieve of Evelynn and Gaultier's mutual salvation in one another.

"It was just the two of us for a while," Evelynn continued for Gaultier. She shifted her glance and smirked a sarcastic grin across the long table to Irene, "until we picked up this 'little cherub.'" Evelynn teased, imitating what must have been Gaultier's name for Irene when she was young.

"Yes, well, you know me," Irene replied in tandem tone to Evelynn's, "I can't *not* be relevant to the story somehow. Have you met me?" Irene gestured with immense grandeur. "Your life wouldn't have been nearly as interesting this far without a pleasant and delightful foil to your moody and sensitive character?"

Everyone laughed, Evelynn included. It seemed that the strongest relationship here was certainly between her and Irene. Bonded in sisterhood through tragedy and loss; a stitched together family that found

29

one another in the wake of an impossible calamity storming the world.

"They found me in a church," Irene continued, beginning her witness to orphanhood. "My father was a holy witch, divining and working with angels. My mother was a forge master; she used fire magic to manipulate and hone blades for magical warriors." She swooned back into her seat; avidly talking with her hands and proudly recalling her heritage. "They fell in love; the devout holy man and his peasant blacksmith maiden. The church welcomed her, and she began forging various weapons for them and their angelic counterparts."

Irene showed the first twinge of pain as she continued her story, a touch of recluse shading her previously dramatic story telling. "Our family was given an angel to protect us in thanks for the service of my parents. When I was six years old, the Wyvren came through our town of Lourdes. It was a holy place," her bright green eyes shading further into a viridian darkness. "A safe place."

The room grew quiet again. Irene spoke in such a way that commanded the space she was in. I knew how this story ended. I remembered this one specifically because of how the fires illuminated the bursting stained glass of the cathedrals that punctuated each street of that holy city. I felt the heat of guilt as the memory of those burning stone walls crumbled in my hands.

Irene finally continued, smiling as small tears escaped her confident face. "Our angel came, but was

30

simply not equipped to face *her.*" She remembered vividly, her eyes lost in a reliving rather than a memory as the evident trauma laced her gaze.

"After my mother fell protecting my wounded father, he used his holy magic to reduce our angel to energy and placed her inside of me." She paused for a moment. "That angel is still inside of me, but it is the only connection I have to my father's magic. I inherited the forging fire of my mother. Hopefully, one day, I can help create a weapon lethal enough to find the hands of someone strong enough to slay that demon."

Irene turned her glance to me, her face suddenly dry again as the tears evaporated off of her seemingly glowing face. "After what I saw this morning, I'm starting to hope that warrior will be you, Ren."

I wasn't sure what to say. I certainly felt unworthy of her praise, being responsible for the unfortunate events that led to those gathered here. But maybe she was right; it was even her in another life that gave everything to me so that I could maybe do the right thing. Maybe now I could help these talented people that I left in my wake. I could keep them safe. I could save Gaultier from the agony of losing his mind. I could save Irene from being targeted for her latent talents and skills. I could keep Evelynn and Téo alive as well, saving them from whatever cruelties Spring had in store for them. I could help them find the younger ones Constantine and Kyrie, potentially even saving them from having to join this group by protecting their families.

31

"Thank you, Irene," I whispered through hoarse words. "I found out today that I can keep up with it, but I am missing an edge that I have yet to find. Maybe you and everyone here can help me…" I trailed off, everyone now on the edge of their seats as I spoke, Sabine grinning a whimsical smile ear to ear as her magic felt inspiration swell within me. "… maybe I can help *you* all defeat the Wyvren. Together, maybe we can make this pain end." I looked at Evelynn who was as skeptical as ever as she rolled her eyes at my motivation.

"Evelynn," I spoke directly. She turned her dissatisfaction to cynical curiosity as she her eyes peered down her nose at me, arms crossed. "I am here to help you. I am sorry for what happened to you. But we have to work together. We have to trust each other. I know you don't know me, and I am an foreigner to your family here." I darkened my tone to a somber recollection of what I had lost not only to myself, but to Spring's devastating grasp as well. "I have lost something to this force as well. If nothing else, know that. Trust in my pain if you can not trust in me."

The room grew silent in anticipation of Evelynn's response. Seconds felt like endless moments suspended in the wonder of her potential acceptance of me. At last she spoke, "… Sara, it's your turn." She said crummily. "Tell us again how you came to meet Gaultier."

The disappointment of her deflection was heavy in the room, especially in the breaths I drew in frustration as I politely shifted my attention to Sara; the Fae Halfling that ran me through with ivy tendrils once upon a time. Her face was even more elegant than I remembered it through the lens of Irene's perspective; gaunt, narrow, slender- as many words to describe the thinness of her body, face, and fingers. She was pale, her ears lightly drawn into long points, purple irises gleaming against the luminosity of her own shimmering skin. She was fiercely beautiful, like a rapier adorned to the wall of a war room, ready to be drawn at the command of a powerful general and brandished into battle. Divinely feminine, formidably deadly.

"Gaultier didn't discover me as he did the rest of you," her gossamer voice evaporated from her tongue. "He was injured, having fled from just nearby after the Wyvren destroyed his home and family. He made his way through the forest that brought you here. And he came upon a seemingly abandoned castle-falling apart, crumbling under the passage of time." She gestured to the surrounding walls that housed us. "He had stumbled upon the former home of my mother."

Gaultier took Sara's hand, clutching it gently in his massive grasp as he spoke in return, "I stumbled, weak, starved; I was dehydrated and inches from death. When I finally collapsed, I found myself in a bed of flowers days later. My wounds were healed, my hunger abated, my thirst quenched as if I had never truly known the satisfaction of water before the magical dew that quenched me in her garden."

They took a moment to look at each other-Gaultier's impossible iridescent eyes enraptured in the delicate violet of Sara's. They were much more an evident item than I previously realized in my limited capacity before. Maybe without having met Karine and knowing what she'd shown me it was unrecognizable to my formerly beastly ways. It was special. In the silence of their mutual appreciation, I felt us not impatient at the pause but reverent at the artistry of their chemistry.

"We've been together ever since." Sara said, finally breaking away from the silent language that danced between their eyes. "I have done my best to be a good matriarch to the Chateaux, but we all know that Irene and Evelynn have their paternal preference." She pleasantly resigned as the group laughed. "My Fairy mother died after giving birth to me, my father raised me until he suddenly died in this place, too. I have never known why, but my Fae side allowed me to survive on symbiotically growing with the nature that overtook this ancient place."

Evelynn nudged Téo as Sara finished, his shyness apparent across his slender face. Unlike the linear prowess of Sara's features, Téo seemed sickly, tired, and weak. I remembered from before that his transmutation magic caused an abrupt rebound on his physical health, thinking back to his fiendish despair under the unbridled influence of Gaultier's manipulative influence. But he was far from that now, just a lean and famished young man. I wonder what happened to phase him into the warrior Dorian on the previous timeline?

"I… I met Evelynn coming back from a mission they were on a couple years ago." Téo's voice clumsily stumbled out of his mouth like a toddler's first steps. "I come from a bloodline of alchemists… my ancestors perfected the transmutative processes for the

34

philosopher's stone…" He trailed off, fidgeting uncomfortably in his seat as our eyes landed all over him. "While impressive… somewhere along the way it was incorporated into our blood. I'm… able to transmute things at will, but it impacts me physically. No single transmutation should kill me, but without having to adhere to the laws of equivocal exchange, my health is nature's consequence for my family's hubris in the past…"

Téo turned his gaze to Evelynn as he finished his story, "my parents died at a young age, and Evelynn came to my village's call to slay a demonic monster who happened to be my brother… he suffered the egregious side effect of becoming a beast in turn for trying to craft a new philosopher's stone from our blood in hopes to free us from our 'curse.'"

He smiled, looking at me as I was the outsider he was truly addressing. "I have not suffered from the same creature you all speak of, but I share in your bond of loss, stranger." Téo smiled at me. "And in that I know and welcome you."

Gaultier raised his glass at the end of Téo's statement, "well said, my boy. I propose a toast!" Gaultier rose from his chair at the head of the table, everyone following suit including Karine and myself. "Ren, you are welcome here, with us, by *all* of us," he began, slyly glancing at Evelynn as she held her glass up with us. "May you help the Chateaux be stronger than it was before, and may you help us make the magical community a safer place not just for us, but for those who need us. To the Chateaux!" He cheered.

"To the Chateaux!" We call exclaimed together. There was laughter, eating, wine; a true and humble celebration of an unlikely group, together in their commonalities and with one another. Slowly but surely, as I looked around the room and drank in the festivities of the platonic pleasures before me, I began to piece together in my mind and in my heart what it meant to be a family. To be *part* of a family.

I felt Karine clench my hand in my lap as she watched me smile in my keening observation. I looked over to her to find her gentle knowing eyes peering into mine with understanding, seeing something unfold that she had surely known before in another time. I still had so many questions for her- how she was here, why she was here, how she knew what I looked like from my previous timeline. I had to know if she was really the woman I loved and the woman I watched my creator undo.

But for now, I ate meat. I tasted wine. I made friends. I earned trust. In those moments, however fleeting, I was able to briefly exercise the gift of humanity so many had sacrificed to give me in real practice, without consequence, without strained performance. In their laughter and my naivety, I felt authentic. I felt real. Karine taught me the beginnings of the depths of love, but these people, despite their vicious pasts, were able to come together and find community in that pain in bereavement of their agony.

We finished dinner, brought the dishes to the shabby kitchen around the corner from the dining hall. The tall stone walls loomed over and around what was once probably a much more luxurious amenity to this place, now covered in mossy walls and leaking ceilings. Before, when I was the Wyvren, I never had need for comfort or rest. While this was not the cozy apartment I shared with Karine or the resting infirmary of the Auspice Tower, it felt a lot like what I would want to call a home.

"Before you all part your ways for whatever it is you may be doing this evening," Gaultier spoke, clearing his throat and pouring himself and Sara another glass of wine from a bottle that hadn't seemed to go empty for the duration of dinner, "we have a mission tomorrow. Evelynn, I would like for you to take Ren and Irene with you." He addressed Evelynn directly, almost suddenly as she sharpened her posture at a command. "You are in charge. Ladies, I hope you all get along well."

Of course. He suspects that Irene or Evelynn are going to be the next iteration of me after this blonde Wyvren dies. With me here, I could also seem like a potential candidate with my congruent prowess to the original Wyvren move set, despite my new fiery angelic additions. He wants to see how we perform together; Evelynn and Irene have no reason to suspect their adoptive father and savior of any kind of test or investigation. I should follow suit, exercising my skills fully to distract him from wanting to manipulate one of them against the other.

Hopefully, if we can destroy my past in this timeline, Gaultier can rest and know that his daughter and his past life as Zorne's mother can have closure; accepting Irene and Evelynn not as talented bait for the destructive engine of my core, but as true daughters. They can have a happy ending.

"Absolutely, sir." Evelynn responded, suddenly very formal, bowing her head and lowering her voice. "It would be my honor to take command and lead my sister and our new recruit." I looked over at Irene, her face twinged with the subtle disappointment of subordination.

"They Wyvren was sighted today, in our small town here." Gaultier began. "It was able to sniff out Vanna's safe house, surely honing in on the talents of our new recruit. That is a deadly event that has never happened before; without Vanna and her workshop, many of those who we take into our charge to remain safe could die quickly before making their way to us."

He turned his attention to the restless Irene, yearning to please her father in another way that didn't require simple obedience. She craved a task from him, something specific that wasn't diluted through Evelynn's command. "Irene," he finally addressed, her posture perking with excitement. "Evelynn is your older sister. She is meant to lead the two of you. But you are simply the hammer of this house." He boasted, knowingly complimenting her as it illuminated her face from disappointment to beaming pride.

He continued, having inspired her again with his informed words, "this is a combat mission. Evelynn is more assassin-oriented with her poisons and potions, but you will be responsible for delivering the kill with Ren." He stated, his eyes lowering into a severe stare at the three of us fully at his attention. "Tomorrow, you are going to draw out the Wyvren and do battle with it." He delivered grimly. "This day was coming, and Ren's arrival is a sign of opportunity for us." He justified hopefully.

The room remained silent in absence of a response to his dispatched orders. I watched the two of them as the others remained in the periphery of the dining hall; Evelynn's face paled with responsibility, her jaw evidently clenched in contrast to Irene's almost flickering expression of adrenaline at the potential of battle. Either one of them could have fallen victim to becoming my host, but Irene's innate strength and vigor to fight must have been fate's deciding factor to inhabit her.

The two of them finally met my gaze, inquisitive of any symptom of fear or excitement. But all I could muster to paint across my face was a strong and sturdy visage- one devoid of fear and tamed from violence. Before where I would have shown apathy to their lives, instead I chose to show strength and focus. I wanted them to know that I was not afraid. I wanted them to know that I was a capable ally to them. I fixed my eyes on Evelynn's, then Irene's, giving an affirming nod of confidence.

"I am a strong asset to these already powerful women, Gaultier," I addressed, my alto voice deep and robust with assurance. "Where you hold a keen mind and a honed blade, I will provide you and your daughters with an unrivaled strength. Together we can defeat this beast."

The room erupted with excitement. I never knew anything I could ever say would illicit such a response in people. But we all wanted the same thing, whether all of us understood it fully or not. We wanted it so, so badly. The ancient evils of this world had long since receded; Spring was the final threat of the magical world, having used me to snuff out all magical prowess both good and evil. They didn't know that Spring was the true enemy here, but if we could stunt him by taking his beast from his arsenal, it would greatly increase mine and Karine's chances of defeating him in the long run.

We finally dispersed, an anxious buzz hanging over everyone as we attempted to relax into a resting slumber. I looked at Karine, who had been the silent character she played for the Chateaux the whole evening. I wasn't sure how long she had been here, but to break that character now, even for me, would risk exposure to our arrival here. She returned my glance with a gentle abbreviation of the bright smile I remember her showing, a subtle and revealing light glimmering in her eyes as she silently assured me she knew me, and knew that I knew her, too.

With my quiet affirmation and my heart fluttering throughout my intercostals, Evelynn showed me to my quarters: a small room just large enough for a hanging cot and a small table, adorned with a makeshift window that was more of a glorified crack in the wall covered with a draping of canvas. I thanked her and walked into my new accommodations, intending fully to rest and remain to myself for the evening when I felt her cold hand grasp my forearm.

I stopped in my tracks, ferociously quelling the instinctual urge to turn and tear her in half at the imposition. Instead I slowly turned my head over my shoulder, feeling my eyes illuminate in a ghastly green. She stared me down, her face like stone in the moonlight that scattered through the torn canvas across the lithic gray room.

"I don't know who you are, Ren," she said. "But this is my family. I know that you are strong, and I know that if it came down to it you could probably kill me." Her grip on my arm tightened as I turned to face her, my height several inches above her head as I looked down on her scornful face. "But know that if you hurt these people, or dream of striking down Irene tomorrow, I will expend every effort in my bones to kill you or at the very least die trying."

Her words confused me. While I knew I wasn't being fully honest with her or the others about my origin, our goals aligned, both of our outcomes happy. Could she sense my origins? Even without knowing who or what Spring was, could she smell the intoxicating scent of his garden on me? I wasn't sure what to do. So I closed my eyes and calmed my defenses, relaxing my shoulders and taking a deep, steady breath before finally responding to her threats.

"I have never truly known what it means to have a family, Evelynn," I began. "But I know not only what it means to lose someone that means everything to you, but to be completely helpless and powerless to save them." I opened my eyes again as they returned to a calmer state, meeting a much more compassionate

41

expression. Not welcoming, not warm, but familiar in understanding.

"I understand what Irene means to you." I continued. "While my father was not kind to me, I know what Gaultier means to you, too." I hardened my face and furrowed my brow in sincerity as I finished, "should anything happen to you or Irene tomorrow, know that I will do everything in my power to save you from harm, or at the very least die trying, too."

We stood in the threshold of the door a moment longer before Evelynn finally released her grip on me, turning and beginning to walk away before bidding me something of a farewell. "Get some rest, newcomer. You're going to need it where we are going."

I didn't respond as she continued her departure down the corridor, finally turning out of sight. I closed my door, turning again to face my room. I walked across the stone floor, feeling the cold against my bare feet. As I peeled back the canvas partition between myself and the night sky, I saw a figure floating high above with a silhouette pinned against the atmosphere, illuminated by the backdrop of a glowing half moon in the sky and dazzled between the twinkling stars.

As I focused my gaze, I saw a robed figure with illuminated eyes, bright and blushing like freshly bloomed Azaleas against dirty blonde hair. Once his form became clear to me, Spring smiled at my realization of his presence before phasing higher into the sky, dissolving back to his dimension beyond the moonlit tapestry of the night.

I stared at that spot almost all night. He knew where I was. He always did. He knew where I would go, what I would choose. He knew Karine or at least a version of her was still alive. In his omniscience he was always there, and that night he chose to make himself visible to me. I could never truly escape him. Despite the joys and connections of this evening, regardless of my choice to do good and fight for a cause that would eradicate evil, wherever I went, so long as there was Spring, evil would follow me no matter what.

I finally tore myself away from the makeshift window sill and found my way to my cot, closing my eyes and holding my face. I wouldn't cry, not tonight. Not for this. He would not tear me down and I would refuse to be weak. Because tomorrow I had another chance to draw out my foe and stunt my creator. Letting him get the best of me now would be foolish. I had to stay focused. I had to be strong. One day, I would land the killing blow on him, and finally I would be free.

I felt the arrest of sleep finally take hold in the recesses of my mind, sinking me further and further into the resting safety of my dreams. Rest came surprisingly easy in my decision to remain unintimidated. Even as I rolled over and practically felt his presence embrace me from behind, cozying himself up to me in a threatening closeness, I chose rest. For some reason, I believed with all of my conviction that Spring wanted me alive, that he wanted his Lotus back in his garden. Maybe he thought that despite everything, he could somehow win me back.

43

Lucid

I rolled over, a gentle wind blowing through my hair as I felt my mouth run dry. I coughed, spitting up dust as I opened my eyes, leaning up on my arms and finding myself on the bizarre stone platform once again. I looked up upwards to find stairs appear as my eyes followed the celestial darkness from the edge of the dusty floor I was on, seemingly suspended in space as the higher level formed above me as it always did.

The sand began to fall from nowhere apparent amongst the mysterious stars above the higher level, the rectangular altar appearing just beyond the grainy veil. I rose to my feet looking around for more, as I had witnessed it before coming to this timeline. I still wasn't sure what this place was, previously I thought it to be Irene's mind palace as I kept encountering her here. After being imprisoned in my crystalline prison, I would find Zorne and Scimariel here, too; their ultimatums before me as I chose the righteous light the angel had to offer me, abandoning Zorne in her depravity.

My most recent encounter here entailed the great revealing of a much larger structure, seemingly endless and impossibly constructed; stairways lining the ceilings as they formed, windows to different galaxies dotting the sides of the structures, and most importantly, the rotary of doors controlled by the time dial at the base of the altar. As it all came back to me, I realized that it had only been just a short time since I was last here, having not been on this timeline very long. But all the same, it seemed that it had been years since my last visit. Time didn't work the same way here as it did in the waking world.

I walked briskly up the stairs, parting the cascading sands confidently as I knew they were not there to hurt me so long as no one meant me direct harm in this place. I came before the dusty brown altar, blowing the fine debris away from it in hopes to find the same clockwork that appeared to me here before. But nothing was there. I looked out beyond the platform as well, hoping to see the various floating passageways that formerly presented themselves to me. Nothing.

"I know you are here, administrator." I called out, remembering the charismatic voice that guided me to my decision to try the freshest timeline that ensured Karine's highest probability of longevity and survival. "I made it to my destination, why am I here again?" I spoke loudly, my voice finding no surface to echo from in the vastness of the artificial cosmos around me.

I turned my head and looked behind me, and to my surprise I watched the vision of surrounding structures flee from the periphery of my vision. I kept turning my head, quickly trying to chase the visions of the greater structure that I knew was there, that I had seen before. It was tricking me. It wasn't gone, it wasn't hallucination- it was here, all around me. It always had been. I was just looking for it in the wrong way.

I closed my eyes, walking around the altar to the edge of the higher platform. There was quite literally more to this place than met my eye. And I was trying to see something with waking eyes in a dreaming world. I took a deep breath and stepped forward, fully and confidently into the empty air in front of me, the other foot behind me immediately following suit in a clumsy staggered leap.

I kept my eyes closed, but instead of feeling the quickness of rushing wind across my face as I fell into the unknown darkness around me, I felt something beneath my feet. Keeping my eyes closed, I took some more steps forward, trying to make sense of the textures between my toes. I rubbed my feet off against my calves, dusting the sand off of them to find that the level I was on was smooth and cool like polished stone.

I reached my hands out in front of me, taking more confident steps but waving my hands about in hopes to find something I could hold onto. Nothing. Finally, in my continued adventurous decisions, I opened my eyes. A gasp of shock entered my chest as my eyes widened to the sight before me.

Rather than the mysterious sandy platforms I found myself in, I was surrounded by high walls hundreds of meters high with clouds in the ceiling, rumbling with gentle hints of thunder and sparkling arcs of electricity. The hall was bright, the floor a seamless white slab of marble that went on as far as the eye could see. I turned to look behind me, the veil of sand and meager altar nowhere to be found.

I turned back around to behold the rest of the room to find a pair of sharp pink eyes meeting mine, inches from my face with a sparkling grin. I lunged backward, assuming an aggressive stance and willing swords to appear. Much to my dismay, none of my powers seemed to work in this world. I kept reaching for weapons, for gravity, for elements- nothing. Nothing at all. Then I fully observed the smiling man before me to find that while he looked similar to Spring, he was not. He was different.

Everything was almost perfectly the same- the bright pink eyes, the sandy blonde hair, the sun kissed and freckled face, the gentle cinnamon sweet smile across his deceptively kind face. But it was certainly not Spring upon further investigation.

He was shorter, the Seasons towered well over seven feet tall but this man stood around my height, just over six feet. In contrast to the ornate robes Spring wore, he was wearing something more academic- a gray three pieced suit much like the more modern stylings, a slim black tie and a pinstriped white shirt underneath it all, punctuated with black patten leather shoes and a long black cane crowned with a silver handle.

In a familiar and charismatic voice he spoke loudly for the company of just the two of us, "my, my! It is rare that folks find the courage to take a leap of faith to find me here!" He bubbled, almost in a congratulatory exclamation. "Once people go 'behind the scenes' it sometimes is hard to make sense of somewhere to go, but you must be pretty sharper than I thought."

Of all of the questions I had, somehow the first one I finally formed was simply ridiculous in the midst of the enigmatic circumstances of this encounter. "Why...

47

are you yelling?" I asked initially, my eyes still adjusting to the brightness of the stormy white room.

The man's face went blank for a moment before he grasped his ribs across his body and erupted in laughter. Wiping a tear of amusement from his face he responded, "why, I'm just thrilled to see you! Do you know how rare it is for me to get company? If anyone even finds the Precipice they rarely have the courage to delve further."

"Where exactly did I 'leap' to?" I asked in my vulnerability. None of my magic worked here. I was in a clearly magical domain in the presence of the entity that had evident dominion over the space. All I could do was inquire as I had no chance of resisting the experience this being had to offer me.

"The is the Liminal, dear Wyvren." The character before me responded, presenting his arms above him as if to present something more than the vast nothingness across the tempestuous landscape perpetuated by rolling storm clouds above us.

Hearing someone call me "Wyvren" triggered a fear response in me that clearly struck across my face as my eyes widened with dismay. Seeing my distress, the boisterous character's face bent immediately from jovial host to empathetic caretaker. He rushed over to me and put an arm around my shoulder.

"Oh, dearest me. I suppose I shouldn't call you that anymore, should I, Ren?" He apologized profusely, still to my side as his sleeved arm wrapped around me. "Tell me, Ren. How can I help you this evening?"

I looked to my left, his charming face once again inches from mine and returning to its position of ludicrous excitement. I slowly removed my self form his embrace, awkwardly receding from his arm around me and facing him again. "I'm not sure what you mean," I weakly responded, confused by the question. "Did you not bring me here?"

The person laughed again, "Ren, you literally came here yourself. The Precipice appears to those about to take a jump towards something. You've been there several times before, right?" The man teased. "This is the first time you've yourself taken advantage of accessing the Liminal. So, I'll ask again: what can I help you with this evening?"

I stared blankly at my quirky and dapper host who bore the striking resemblance to my malicious creator. Liminal, as in "in-between?" Liminal spaces exist in the severed slices of reality between planes; alternate timelines and other worlds. This world wasn't supposed to be one congruent collection of all of the spaces between the planes of existence- the filling between Time and Space. This person was describing this place as if instead of between, it was all encompassing; a layer that encapsulated reality rather than separated its layers.

"You're the administrator, correct?" I asked, remembering his excitable tone and announcing nature.

The man smiled a crescent grin, his porcelain teeth perfectly symmetrical beneath his lips. "Why, yes of course! I the administrator, at your service." He took a bow, turning his cane up into his hands as he did into his hand, cradling it against his chest. "And you are the Wyvren, even though you 'aren't' anymore. I've been looking to meet you for quite sometime."

We looked at each other again for another brief moment of silence. "You need a way out, right, Ren?" The administrator teased in a precocious voice. "You are certainly the strongest iteration of your kind across all timelines; the Wyvren's power over space and gravity, Autumn's Grace now installed permanently into your legs, and an angel's light illuminating your power endlessly like a star that will never burn out."

He twirled his cane in one hand as he continued casually, "and now most recently Spring's Clock Key hangs around your neck." His smile darkened as he finished his descriptions, "you're practically a master of Time *and* Space if you can figure out how to use the assets before you."

"Wait, did you say 'Spring's' Clock Key? This doesn't belong to him, I got it from Karine- my friend." I defended urgently. Karine gave me the gift of her temporal abilities in her dying moments. I wasn't going to let this person twist my experience.

"And where exactly do you think a witch acquired such a power?" The administrator asked in a precocious and inquisitive way, trying to lead me to an answer I was already formulating but didn't want to believe. "Do you think the power of Time could be simply rendered by someone of Karine's dimension? *No, silly!*" The administrator bellowed, devolving once again into a laughter that was now much more sinister, echoing across walls beyond which I was able to perceive.

"Karine is a human witch, administrator," I corrected desperately. "There is no way Spring would have coordinated with a human-"

"*Oh, really?*" the administrator rebutted, cutting me off. "Was Zorne not a human he cruelly intervened with? Were *you* not once the incarnation of a human before you were implanted with the destructive seed of his higher dimensional prowess?"

I felt anxiety rise in my chest. "Karine isn't a monster like me- Karine is not a Wyvren." I defended again, my breath short in a rush of emotions I was not yet used to regulating. "Karine is human."

"Yes, Karine is human," the administrator confirmed, lifting a gentle portion of the weight off of my chest. "But she is in a debt she can't quite pay off." He chimed.

"What do you mean?" I inquired further, the fear of the situation driving my speech completely now. "What do you mean by 'debt?'"

The administrator appeared behind me in an instant, clearly able to phase at will through his domain. I turned quickly as I felt the breath of his answer tickle the nape of my neck as he responded, "just as Zorne reached out to receive the will of a god to be answered by Spring instead, Karine made a similar request." With the flick of his wrist and the wave of his hand, the administrator summoned a table and chairs, two glasses of wine set at the table before us.

51

He gestured forward, "I have the answers you seek, should that be what you need from me this evening." He offered his hand towards the table and turned his sly glance to me. "Shall we?"

I had no idea what to do. I found myself afraid, powerless, and most of all: curious. With no evident way out of this place, I walked towards the table. The administrator appeared behind my chair, pulling it out for me, and instantly appearing in the chair across from me. He took a sip of wine, and rested his cane against the ornate wooden table, clearing his throat and meeting my curiosity with an almost conniving tone of pleasure. "Let me tell you about your dear, dear Karine; the first of all witches to fall victim to the throes of the gleaming garden of Spring." He raised a glass, "cheers, my sweet Ren. Thank you for such an interesting beginning to my evening."

I numbly raised my glass, feeling dread begin to crawl and creep beneath my skin as the blood left my face in devastation and fear. I never asked Karine anything before. I never questioned her past, her power. I suppose I was still so young in my cognition, so naive to believe that someone simply encountered me and had the capacity to pursue and even love me. But she was not only connected to Spring, she had been since even before the night of my diabolical creation. I began to tremble as our glasses touched, the gentle chime of the crystal ringing through the great white hall; the only thing of clarity I had perceived thus far.

"Now, where to start…" the administrator contemplated through a sip of dark red wine as my glass held still in my hand; my fingers gently wrapped around the stemware as it rested on the table. Without looking at me I could tell that he was enjoying each tantalizing moment as it past by- the stillness of time in this place contrasted fervently against my anticipation.

"Perhaps the beginning, would be best?" I suggested, my voice still in loose footing like skipping through gravel.

The administrator grinned over his glass and met my eyes again, "perhaps the beginning is best, indeed." He set his glass down, more wine filling within it from a source unknown as it returned to its original volume. "Sit tight and get comfortable. This is a good story, certainly."

And so he began, and so I listened; completely and fully at the attention of his tale, "Karine Faust was a young woman, a daughter of the priestesses that worshipped a secret and old goddess they called Ashura. She had no known father, as the ancient convent only accepted women, often orphaned young girls. Young Karine showed great prowess, even in her youth. She was able to learn and cast spells without any effort, she was able to learn any language at the kiss of the tongue of another, she was mighty in both body and mind. Truly a savant of the magical arts, pioneering them even before most were discovered at large by others in later empires.

"Karine's mind was born and designed to learn and absorb- she craved challenge, though nothing was difficult in her hands as nothing was beyond her grasp. When she turned fourteen, she left the convent of

53

Ashura, pursuing new and compelling skills that her teachers could no longer divine from their goddess for her. Many believed Karine herself to be the incarnate of the goddess Ashura. Though they have now passed, her true potential would remain unknown to those who raised her, truly for the better.

"She made her way to the great library of Alexandria, tearing through the scrolls and books, bartering more time in the library by teaching the scribes new magics to record from her time as a prodigy of Ashura. To the shock and surprise of those attending the space, in a mere three years the young Karine absorbed all of the information the great collection of tomes had to offer.

"By the time she was twenty years old, she had traveled across the lands, chasing her potential and acting as an example of magical talent and teachings throughout the continents, fluent in all of the major languages, master of all known magics. In appearance, it seemed that she paid no price at all for the sheer breadth of her immense power. But everything comes at a price.

"As she turned twenty five, she began to fall ill; unable to catch her breath, aspirating blood and phlegm almost constantly in the mornings, using her knowledge of medicines and potions to keep her physical body as healthy as possible, but the wise young Karine began to realize that the price of her charmed life and unmatched usage of magical skills had ultimately come to collect its toll on her: her vitality.

"She began to search for the impossibilities of immortality; transmuting alchemical processes to attempt to add years to her life, consuming secret and forbidden tinctures and tonics to keep her growing illness at bay. She even returned to her convent and begged before the altar of Ashura to forgive her pride and take her magic in return for her life. But the cathedral halls of her youth rang with only the sounds of her pleas without any response from the sleeping goddess.

"She traveled across the lands, searching high and low for new knowledge, and as she reached her final destination in Rome, she felt her life begin to seep finally and fatally from her lungs as her heart slowed. In a desperate attempt to survive, she unleashed a burst of magic; a conglomerate of all of her knowledge, shining from her frail and dying body. Her light shown as a final distress beacon, trying in her final moments to reach someone or something amongst the divine to spare her and give her another chance; anything to help her turn the clock back."

I felt my body sharply inhale at the words the administrator spoke in a grieving realization, "Spring came. Of course he did."

The administrator smiled, omitting a response to my comment as he continued his story. "Spring knew that he and the rest of the Seasons only existed in the higher dimension as reflections of the human collective, observing them as passings of Time. This massive collection of concise human belief 'thought-formed'

55

them in such an exaltation that they became more powerful than any god this world has ever known.

"Spring, the most creative and initial Season, began to grow tired of existing as a mere reflection of humanity. The Seasons had become so strong that even if all of the humans in the world on every timeline perished, so long as the world turned and lived in their reverence, the Seasons would endure. This is in stark contrast to the other gods of this world- without their believers and followers, they would flicker out of existence.

"Spring saw humans of this world as frail and pathetic creatures at his mercy- he sent disaster after disaster in hopes of destroying mankind so that he could be free from the vague hold over his cyclical role in their minds. But when he saw that beacon of power- that pillaring tower of knowledge and unmatched prowess emanating from the world, he formulated an idea. 'If I could harness something like this- collect so much power and vessel it in a talented witch on earth, they would be my ultimate play at the end of humanity.'"

I interjected, "Karine was supposed to be the first Wyvren?" My question was almost redundant at the clarity of his implications.

The administrator grinned a sinister smile; the first symptom on any sincere malice since my arrival. Again, without a response to my question, he continued to elucidate Karine's cursed past. "He appeared before her, out of Space and Time in a place much like this, and made her an offer: immortality with a couple logistical steps. No matter how many times she died, she would have the opportunity to reappear and reform at a 'checkpoint' of her desire, so long as she did the necessary processes ahead of time.

"Spring fashioned for her a small trinket from a small green flower he plucked from his garden, something that operate the gears of a machine that was just beginning to be imagined: a wind-up Clock Key. He offered her this deal, and in her frail desperation for continuance she agreed." The administrator's eyes were practically darkened to a crimson hue as his excitement grew. "Why do you think you are only able to manipulate Space, Wyvren?"

"Because Spring already gave Time to someone else…" I realized, clutching the Clock Key around my neck. I felt nausea creep into my abdomen at the thought of treasuring something derived directly from the same material that ignited my dark engine.

The administrator's eyes lightened back to their bright fuchsia in joy at my response, "eureka! Correct! You really aren't as naive as I suppose I originally suspected." He praised with sarcastic patronage. "Has Karine ever fully described to you *why* she has invested so much in looking for you? *Why* she has spent literally entire timelines chasing you down and *loving* you so deeply?" The storm clouds above began to rumble tumultuously. "Could it be that she already has Time, and in her great pursuit, she is trying to harness Space as well?"

I felt cold all over. My depth perception began to sway the room in and out of focus. Confusion filled my skull to the brim while fear followed close behind. Karine was immortal? She had died over and over again? Did she know that she was coming back to this timeline? Was this her last checkpoint? Was this all an elaborate scheme from the first night she saw me manifest in Irene?

"You seem to have a lot on your mind, 'Ren.'" The administrator continued, recognizing my dismay but invalidating the severity of my experience. "What, you don't trust her anymore?"

"You told me to come here, administrator." I interjected, a brief moment of lucid clarity arriving in my brain while dodging his enlightened badgering. "Why tell me all of this, while knowing what you know about both of us, however that may be, and have me come here? Are you working with her? What exactly is your motivation?"

My mysterious host rolled his eyes, a smile still smeared across his enigmatic face. "You think I want anything from either of you? I'm simply here, in the spaces in between it all, trying to give all the players of this game the knowledge they need to participate as best as they can." He leaned in, emphasizing his previous statement once again, "knowledge is the only thing I have ever wanted for anyone, 'Ren.' I have always been misunderstood in the presentation of my gifts."

I sat in confusion, unsatisfied with his answer. "The only thing you want from me is my… awareness?" I pulled the Clock Key I got from the "dead" Karine from around my neck and held it up. "Then explain this to me- if Karine is able to just 'become' again wherever

58

she last left off, *however* that happens, how does she have a clock key that is just like the one she gave me before coming back to life in this timeline?"

"Oh, and here I thought you were learning something, silly girl." He responded in academic frustration. "Time is not a linear thing. The events that happened on that other timeline are, in their own respects, absolute. You can never go back in time and 'undo' something, because it has already been done."

The administrator took another hefty gulp of his endless wine, "that is the curse of the 'gift' Karine received from Spring. Just as the events you experienced on that timeline exist in your past, coming to this timeline didn't make you any younger, correct? That is because the future of that place is still your past here, because you are the light on the other side of it."

That was resoundingly dense. I foddered with that for a bit before responding, "so, you're saying that the somewhere, parallel to now, the Auspice Council has fallen apart, the magical world is in disarray, and Karine and the others are dead; all the while, it is happening at the same time as 'young' Karine making a deal with Spring for the first time; ALSO in the same moments as when Spring came to Zorne and created me?" I tilted my head, eyes wide with unpacking the metaphysical mess of understanding, "the timelines are lines, Spring simply gave Karine the ability to flip between the chapters, all the while everything is happening in the same book?"

"Call me Kieran," the administrator chose to respond with a prideful grin upon his delicate face.

59

"You've earned the right to know my name with that delightful conclusion you just drew." He leaned back in his chair, swirling his wine glass in his hand and gazing fondly into the spiraling clouds above. "Just flipping between the chapters in the same book... I like that a lot. I'll be sure to tell that to the next one that finds their way through the Liminal."

"Kieran... how am I here? I know you said something about a Precipice and the Liminal Spaces and all that, but the place with the sand, the Precipice; I've been arriving in that place since I manifested in Irene," I observed, speculating answers as I questioned for them. "Why have I never, in all my years, been there or here before?"

"Are you sure that is the question you want to ask me right now?" Kieran warned playfully. "The sun is about to come up in your waking world. You'll be conscious and away from here again soon. I'm happy to answer that question, but I'm not sure it is the most valuable information you could pursue right now."

The sudden addition of a ticking timeline around all of this inspired a brand new stress. I thought hard, my mind swimming through the rivers of information Kieran the administrator had just given me. He implied I have time for one more question. I had to think quickly.

"If we are all experiencing time, every instance, at all times, how are we not crashing into one another?" I gestured, clumsily assimilating as much new metaphysical information as I could. I barely understood Time before, now it was becoming somehow more clear and confusing at the same time. "Is there a way to observe the other instances without having to experience them? Without having to jump to that 'chapter' completely?"

I furrowed my brow, continuing to explain my thought. "When I first arrived here, I saw the other Wyvren attacking me before it happened, in absolution and clarity. Surely enough, those events unfolded and I was able to save myself. But that means that on that first timeline, in another chapter of this book, her spear impaled me and she killed me. I read that chapter; I read ahead. And so I chose to follow another outcome." I raised my confused face to meet his pleased expression. "Is there a way that I can be selective about what outcomes I see as they exist alongside the timeline I'm already on?"

Kieran raised his eyebrows, straightening his posture with an ever-cunning grin growing firmer and wider on his lips. He raised a hand and snapped his fingers. As the sound echoed through the vastness of the hall we were in, shimmering outlines of the two of us danced by us; possibilities of what could have been in loose outlines as if the particles that made us up were waiting to be solidified by our intent.

"Each of these are the 'Mights' that could have happened in this little encounter of ours. Hundreds of thousands of little culminations, awaiting our energy to pass through their potential and solidify into a story of their own." He pointed far across the way, our two buzzing outlines clearly interlocked in some kind of combat, "that would have been an unhappy ending for

61

you, seeing as I have full control over this place. You'd be dead and without answers."

He pointed to another direction, my vague collection of possibilities collapsed by the table, "this is you choosing to wallow in the despair of Karine's betrayal; giving into your anxiety rather than making good use of this time."

He held his hands up completely above his head, the room filling with countless outlines and chatter just inaudible enough to not understand; esoteric whispers swirling down from the clouds above. "In the Liminal Spaces- here 'in-between' it all, you can see everything that 'Might' have happened, and everything that has happened. What "Might" happen is always unfolding, just not on the chapter you're reading."

My jaw dropped, my eyes dazzled with the infinite wonder of possibilities dancing around us, filling the room with a crowd of my potential choices and the pasts and futures of others that would find this place. The impossibility of it all hurt my head a bit, but the beauty of a circular temporal experience rather than a linear one opened my mind to a whole new metaphysical understanding of the world.

Our eyes met again, both of us in glee; him of my new understanding and mine of the wonder around us. I stood up in excitement, asking him, "what can I do with this?"

Ternate

I winced as the sunlight danced through the tattered canvas and swooned across my eyelids, the brisk morning air scampering around the room from the remnants of what was supposed to be a window. It was morning. I was awake. Kieran, the Precipice, the Liminal Space- it was all gone from me again. But I was all too aware of the keen dream from that place; of all the things that were not there, she was here. Karine Faust. The only person I have ever loved, and potentially at my dire expense.

There was a knock at my door, Irene gently peering her way in to inspect my waking state as I lay suspended in the hanging cot of my room. "Ren," she gently called, much more loudly than the average timid call of an actual whisper but with all of the rasp. "Ren, are you awake? It's time for breakfast...!" Irene continued with childlike excitement. "Sara made *bacon.*" She finished with boisterous and ringing enthusiasm.

Once she saw my opened eyes she skipped away from the door. I put on the same yellow dress Vanna gifted me upon my arrival to this place, pacing back through the memories of the dream I'd just awoken from. Was it real? Could it have been just some crazy hallucination? I could have very easily been piecing together my fear of Spring, with the uncertainty of how Karine was alive, all centered around the mysterious dimension of sand and dust I keep finding myself in.

I walked down the hall, everyone obviously already awake as I passed each empty dwelling down the stairs. When I entered the kitchen, expecting a full group to mirror the setting form the night before, there were only Sara, Evelynn, Irene, and now the unexpected addition of Vanna, equipped with her energetic expression and warm chestnut eyes glistening with something to say.

"Ren! You're finally awake!" Vanna sang as she pranced from the table the other young women were eating breakfast at. She reached her arms out revealing a loosely tied parcel wrapped in brown paper and secured with twine. "I know you arrived to me without so much as shoes on your feet or a change of clothes! I've been informed the barefoot thing is some kind of heat-exhaust situation and is intentional, so I made some last minute alterations!"

I took the package out of Vanna's hands, her feet prancing in place with anticipation of my reaction. I gently untied the tender string and unwrapped the paper with care to reveal something of a uniform. Arm length black leather armor, bare-palmed with shoulder padding, and a cross strap across the clavicle. Matching leather pants, boots that strapped across the tops of the feet with open soles as Vanna described, all complete with a white sleeveless top to wear underneath it.

64

"Vanna, this looks just like…" I began to observe, holding it up to my body to see how it would wear.

"… just like what I made for Evelynn and Irene when they turned twenty-five!" She exclaimed with a squeal, "you're officially part of the team now!" She gave me a hug around my arms, nuzzling her head against my chest in sincere delight.

Vanna pulled away from me and looked up to me, "the others already went on another mission to try to run some support for you later. They didn't want to wake you because you seemed to be sleeping so restlessly." She turned and began to leave. "I know that today is going to be… well, quite frankly *deadly.* If you're able to draw out the Wyvren, one of you or all of you could…" She trailed off, her eyes following the heavy words she said as her eyes glanced towards the floor.

I put the outfit under one arm, reaching out my other to Vanna's shoulder in condolence. "Vanna, your friends are strong. And I am, too. We are all going to come back home to you, and so will all of the others they get back from whatever it is they're doing, too." I gave her one last hug, looking over her head at a watery-eyed Irene and a skeptical Evelynn still sitting before their plates. "We're going to be okay. I'm going to make sure of that."

Vanna pulled away one last time, wiping tears from her warm, sympathetic eyes before finally finding her way to the door and leaving the four of us. I turned to face the three senior members of the loose

65

association I recently joined to find an odd mixture of emotions to meet what I thought was an otherwise inspiriting response. It seemed that I was perhaps misunderstanding the human emotion "motivated," or everyone in this room other than me was absolutely scared to death.

"Ren, you do seem quite confident in our abilities, and after seeing yours I would feel great going into battle with you," Irene gestured with an air of encouragement. "But you do know what we are attempting to go up against today, correct?"

"Honestly, it's like you've never even heard of the thing, newcomer." Evelynn egregiously interjected before I could respond. "Besides, how do you know how *capable* we are, anyways? You've never fought with us." She stood up, hands on the table as she stared me down. "Don't speak to, or about us, as if you know anything. Because you don't." She sternly punctuated.

As if I was not in the conversation at all, mouth agape and prepared to participate, Sara chose this opportunity to comment her thoughts on the matter. "Today is the day you make up your lives to your father. Today is how you can begin to thank him for deciding that instead of becoming a broken man, he chose to be a father again, in the shadow of the death of his actual flesh and blood."

She spoke with a maternal authority that we all knew she had not earned, but an authority that Evelynn and Irene respected in the spirit of her devotion to their leader. She prudently continued, "Evelynn, I know you hate most people, and quite frankly most things, but you have to try to trust Ren. Irene, you've been very supportive of Ren's addition to the Chateaux, perhaps try to empathize with your sister about why she is so distrusting?"

She turned her magical eyes towards me with a much more hostly tone, the bubbly charm of her enchanting voice, "and you, Ren. We have only known you in person long enough to see your magnanimous battle skills and pragmatic aptitude for unbridled destruction. Sabine has been interpreting and divining your arrival from Karine for a while now, both of those young women we trust."

Irene and Evelynn turned to face me thoughtfully with their adoptive mother, finally making way for me to speak. "Well, I appreciate the warm welcome and the brilliant cynicism of my sudden appearance. But it is as you said- Karine knew I was coming. We were separated. We have fought for a long time to reach this day." I feigned a notion of discomfort, bashfully turning a lock of hair behind my ear as I continued. "I am confused why Karine didn't wait to say good bye to me before this, but I'm sure it was important."

Something similar to understanding crossed Evelynn's face as the naive Irene practically wept in response to my insecurity towards Karine. Sara's face remained unchanging, unblinking. "Go get changed, Ren." Sara addressed formally. "You should probably get going soon. It is almost the afternoon and Gaultier and the others have prepared your pathway to... it."

67

I left the room without another word. The place was steeped in a familial drama that was so far out of my depth that it no longer served me to really participate. One day, sure, I'd love to be friends or comrades truly with these people. But I had to focus on the objective at hand. I had to keep my eyes on the prize.

Karine and I had to stunt Spring by cutting him out at the knees; removing his true foothold in the world here. We had to kill the Wyvren, then we could be together and truly start a fairytale with this goofy lot of traumatized people. If she even really wants a future of any kind with me.

Kieran's voice echoed through my head again and again as I geared up for the embarkment; his face the spitting image of Spring, whispering insecurities directly into my ears. I slapped my face, choosing to pull my hair back into a high ponytail like Karine taught me, with the bright yellow ribbon Vanna gave me on this timeline. Karine. Trust Karine. She has given me everything, including her life through a painful death, immortal or not. Immortal or not… I watched Spring tear through her like a hurricane through a city. Even if what Kieran said was almost true, in that moment on that morning, I chose to trust that she loved me.

Vanna's armor was more than comfortable- it was surprisingly efficient. The leather that comprised the sleeves, pants, and boots were all densely enchanted with some kind of enhancement magic I was unfamiliar with, surely passed down through her seamstress witch bloodline. The sleeveless top that

68

bore no protection was also a bit of a rouse- the fabric itself wouldn't tear at all and was resistant to puncture; the fibers magically reinforced as well. I thought back to March's magical threads that reconstructed my body parts once upon a time and wondered if the processes were related.

Before leaving, as Irene and Evelynn awaited me outside, Sara stopped me, offering me some food that I didn't eat during the friction of breakfast before I left and imparted one final sentence to me. "Bring them home," she whispered gently. "Please, keep them safe for me. For Gaultier."

I thought back to the desperation of Gaultier, magical rot burning across his face as he hysterically maneuvered his "children" like puppets across the Sinclair Estate, exploiting their magical talents to do everything in their power to kill Irene, simply because I laid dormant within her. Looking into Sara's violet eyes I remembered her violence as she tore through Irene's body, forcing her to relent total control to me and ironically allowing the Wyvren cycle to continue.

But seeing this side of her, seeing the dynamics of this family all together, it somehow made sense. Sara's devotion to Gaultier's cause- perhaps she loved him so much, even at the expense of the lives around the two of them, she believed that if she helped him throw it all away, that maybe the two of them could have what they did before he became obsessed with my absolute destruction. I pitied the life I caused them.

"I will bring them back to you," I promised. "I will bring them back to both of you. Sara, thank you for your hospitality. I hope after all of this I grow to learn all about the delicious food you make." I enticed, flattering her domesticity.

To my surprise, she leaned up to me, kissing me on the cheek, and sending me on my way to meet the others outside. We were truly three of a kind; all clad in the similar silhouette of Vanna's designs. While not a fighter this was her unique contribution to the cause of magical righteousness. As Gaultier instructed, we followed Evelynn into the forest, staying close as she observed the enchanted cues that I immediately noticed began taking us down a path that did not return to the city we originally met.

Before us was a great stone face at the end of Evelynn's interpreted path; moss growing around the edges from the ground on either side of the balding stone, flourishing thickly from the base of one side to another in a lush green archway. She reached for one of her vials, placing an open palm above the mouth of the glass flask and commanding a silver hued liquid to rise from it.

She conducted the fluid across the vast rocky visage, casting the liquid in the shapes of various circular patterns and sigils that began to sink and stain into the rock. Irene raised her hands, her bright forge fire igniting in her palms. She walked in front of Evelynn, who was keeping her hands raised in her own spell casting and touched the stone as well, igniting the combustible fluid at her touch. With their combination spell of uniting two opposite elements, Fire and Water, the bare face of rock began to ripple in a gray misty phasing, unlocking a magical portal in the mossy archway.

The sister witches looked at each other proudly, nodding affirmation towards one another. "We've never done that on our own before," Irene turned to me, stating with dignity for the two of them. "Sara showed us this doorway years ago, but has always instructed us in how to write and ignite the runes. It requires two witches of two persuasions of elemental magics."

"Yeah, great work, Irene." Evelynn said, a sincere smile of gratitude and reverence on her face. "Now that we've done the easiest part of this journey, perhaps this is a good sign for our success overall." She finished with her usual sarcasm and doubt.

"That was remarkable." I commented, "may I ask, where exactly does this go? I assumed you knew a way to draw out the Wyvren, but are we getting ahead of a known path of destruction or…?" I asked with open end.

"There is a… gathering of powerful forces; witches, coming together on the other side of the veil, trying to instill a new form of government over the magical world." Irene explained. "They claim to be able to track the movements of the Wyvren."

"Our plan is to seek audience with the witches in this fledgling organization," Evelynn continued for her sibling. "If they truly mean to do well by us and our kind, they surely will allow us to assist in their vanguard in pursuit of the beast."

I took a careful moment to think before I responded. The Auspice. The Tower. In this timeline, I was in the chapter before the final formation and governing of the Seasons' open influence of this world. While this was generally advantageous for me, this also held a unique obstacle: the almost certain appearance of the Months. Furthermore, the last time I saw Evelynn and the Auspice at the same time, she was Isadora, not herself. There was a severe fear of the unknown built into this plan, somehow only inflamed by an informed perspective of what could be.

I remembered again, back to my dream just hours before, the word "Might" bubbling to the surface of my recollection. The possibility of what could be- a way to not only select the chapter you read, but to write the words of the story. The potential energy, the notion to not only see the future but to understand its influence. I thoughtfully clutched the Clock Key in my hand; if I could just pay attention and try to see through my inclination of Space to notice the presence of Time, I could keep Evelynn away from Spring's influence.

Then there was Irene- the unknown factor. The Council was composed of eight members: four Months, and their four witches. Irene was not present on that timeline, for whatever reason; the possibilities as to why could range from she was never chosen as a Wyvren, she didn't survive my attack in her youth, or she just wasn't as she was in a meaningful way to this "book and chapter" format the administrator seemed to be so keen about. Whatever it may be, she could replace one of the Auspice seats, which I couldn't allow either.

"Getting cold feet, newcomer?" Evelynn teased, nudging Irene to encourage her to join in on my ridicule.

"You seem awfully distracted for being such a keen warrior."

"Sorry, I was just remembering something." I apologized. "Something about all of this just seems familiar for some reason. I'm not sure why- I was just taking a moment to gather myself." I looked to Evelynn, "That's why you're in charge; I'm just here to swing hard and hit heavy, not think." I self-deprecated in hopes of earning some trust.

Evelynn audibly laughed at my expense, accepting my ridicule as currency to our potential acquaintanceship, "finally, you say something I know to be true." She turned to Irene, "You take up the rear, Ren will follow directly behind me. Close the door behind the three of us once we enter completely."

"Aye aye, captain." Irene said jokingly. She took a moment herself to be solemn with us. "Everyone, be careful. We don't know these people. No matter what, we trust each other, deal?"

Evelynn and I looked at each other, turning to Irene and saying together in response, "we trust each other."

Evelynn turned towards the portal, taking a deep breath and walking through head first. I immediately follow, instinctively holding my breath as well through the potential vacuum of the passing world. The portal was not instant, there was a long hallway of spiraling bright lights, complimented by the crashing sounds of white noise that presented like a rumbling storm.

Ahead, I watched Evelynn disappear on the other side of the long tunnel of inter-dimensional passageway. I remembered to my dream again, and instead of just looking ahead as I walked through, I turned my head and looked to my right. In shocking surprise, I didn't just see the white halls from my dream before, but a dapper and well-dressed gentleman, bearing the face of my creator. With arms folded behind his back, he paced beside me, just beyond the thin membrane of the linear path I was on.

He smiled, no aggression or signs of malice on his face or in his presence. He just walked with me, looking me in the eyes. We didn't speak, myself mostly out of the surprise that he was so present. I should have known though, seeing as we were passing through a Liminal Space I previously thought just existed as connective tissue between worlds. I wanted so badly to peel off from Evelynn and Irene to meet with him and continue our conversation from the night before. If I could master the concepts he spoke of, learn from him, I could potential hold a candle to Spring's power. I could perhaps perceive even his Might.

Instead, I bid Kieran a nod of acknowledgement and continued ahead, finding myself phasing beyond the veil to the magical world beyond, Evelynn awaiting me, Irene thankfully forming out of the archway almost immediately after me. I turned to see not a mountain face but two gently bent tree saplings, bound together in a gentle arch that complimented our entry way on the other side.

Before us was the framework of a small town; plots of land and concrete pads, all being slowly built with a consistent magical construct spell. Almost every row of buildings were a copy of the last, commerce buildings growing themselves in town squares and circles, residential districts slowly shimmering into existence in perfect lines and streets. At the end of all of it, beneath the rumbling of colorfully mystified storm clouds, spun an obsidian obelisk I recognized all too well.

"We are here to talk to the Council?" I asked, disbelief sinking into the pit of my stomach. I knew we were coming to meet someone in this place that had something to do with the Auspice, but I didn't realize how far along their new world order had come. I could see the refractions of the Seasons flashing in the clouds above. Spring was already here, his influence already spreading as he began to "help" the magical world. But Evelynn was here, not there. This place was just starting. There was an opportunity.

"The Council?" Irene asked, concerned with the severity of the word. "Evelynn, is there a 'Council' here?"

Evelynn shot me a scornful glance as she responded to Irene's question, "yes, the early stages of this government has already been set in motion. Gaultier assured me that was proprietary information. How do you know about it?"

"Karine and I knew this was coming, her temporal prowess showed us a corrupt Council using outer dimensional power to strong arm our people into moving behind the veil to hide away." I responded assuredly.

Evelynn's brow ruffled with confusion, "Ren, we are here to help them. They are the only organized force that has actually taken action against the Wyvren with any reported success. We have no other allies capable enough. That is why the rest of the Chateaux stayed behind; Gaultier to lead them, Sara and Karine to advise them." Suspicion steeped her gaze as she finished, "we are the only ones strong enough to help. That is why everyone left before us- Gaultier needed their magic to help send them a message to let them know we were coming."

This was it. This was how Evelynn was taken to be Isadora. She came here to ask for help, in some way for some circumstance, whether it was my original timeline when Gaultier manipulated her and she was seeking revenge on the Wyvren, or perhaps some personal reason somewhere else. Behind her stern and powerful facade, Evelynn was malleable. Mutable. There was something missing in her- I couldn't place it. I needed to find out what made her tick before we got too cozy with the Auspice.

"Well, perhaps things won't work out how I fear they will." I decided to say. There wasn't anything productive I could really produce that would have swaying meaning right now.

"That's the spirit," Irene said to me, trying to lighten to the mood. "All we can do is try, so let's do our best to show our worth to them."

We made our way through the sparkling constructs; loose impressions of buildings outlined in light as magic swirled around their infrastructures, producing a city room by room. It really was magical. Despite the evil I knew Spring had and would continue to perpetrate against humanity, this was gorgeous. The perfect distraction and justification to trust them. An unmatched gift that demanded gratitude in the form of obedience.

"Welcome to the three of you, Ternate of Gaultier: Evelynn, Irene, and Ren." A melodic and angelic voice spoke behind us from the the direction of the Tower. We turned, surprised that anyone was able to sneak up on us. Before Evelynn and Irene stood a stranger, before me I recognized the young face of Kyrie.

"Terribly sorry to startle you," the young boy said, raising his hands as his soft round face apologetically smiled. "My name is Alto, I was sent as the Council representative to escort you to our meeting. We understand you believe you will be able to help us in our cause?"

"You are absolutely *adorable*," Irene squealed as she reached a hand out to shake Alto's. "Yes, I'm Irene, and this is my sister Evelynn and our ally Ren."

"How do you do, ladies." Alto's soft voice offered in fervent respect, shaking Irene's hand and extending a bow to Evelynn and I. "Please, follow me. I will show you to our meeting place in the Tower."

We walked down the manifesting streets, passing through the enchanted town that lead to the

Tower. Alto explained to us that his witch representative partner, Hector, was able to replicate inanimate objects, and with the assistance of their new allies the Months, he was able to amplify his power exponentially. This allowed him to completely replicate full sections of towns and cities; rebuilding spaces that the magical refugees came from so everyone felt at home in the new community.

I remembered Constantine and his full promise of youth; now Hector, again. His power remained the same, now augmented by Spring. I was too late- they weren't in the Chateaux on this timeline because Spring knew that I would try to come for them here to dismantle the Council ahead of time. This told me two things: firstly, Spring was able to flip through Time just like Kieran described, which further inclined me to believe that Karine did in fact receive her incredible mastery of time from my creator.

Secondly, the members of the Council seemingly had to remain the same, otherwise Spring could have had his fair selection of anyone else to appoint to work with the Months. There had to be some kind of consistency across the board; there were some things that had to align in the webs of fate to tell the right story. Spring had to rearrange the chapters of the narrative in the right order to regain control of the situation; me.

"It's beautiful, isn't it?" Alto asked us, marveling at the work of his comrade. "All of this, steady work from his diligence combined with the gifts of the powers at be. We are able to make this world a better place."

78

"And what exactly are the powers at be?" I asked, quietly and casually. "They seem to have a lot of resources to be able to buff someone's innate magical skill this profoundly. Is he still working now, I suppose? Hector?"

Alto slowed to walk beside us, nestling between myself and Irene, Evelynn to my left on the glimmering walkway. Even in his youth, it seemed more perpetual than authentic, as if Spring made him into this version of himself at the age he was presenting as he met us. But something about this young man seemed... old. Wise. "Absolutely," Alto responded as he met our pace, "Hector is my age, but he has been given as much magic and power as he needs to complete the task. He will probably feel more invigorated than exhausted when he is finished!"

Evelynn looked at me, her empathy showing that she understood my hesitation while learning Alto's story; seeing that the Council is at the very least exploiting children for their labor. That alone was a red flag, especially to someone who grew up with nothing as they did. She turned her energy from me to Alto, "as my partner asked, who exactly are the powers at be?"

Alto shared a laugh that almost rang like a choir; everything about his speech had cadence, rhythm, timbre. I forgot that Kyrie, his true identity and the base of "Alto's" true power was based in music. Amplified to this point, his magic was seeping into every aspect of his young life. Almost like his Season-enhanced magic was the source piloting his body, rather than his own consciousness.

79

"The powers that have allowed us to get this far, and will help us all get even farther are the most divine of all- more than gods, but principles." Alto introduced his statement with the upmost grandeur. "The Seasons of the Year themselves have decided it is time to manifest in this world, and save it from the absolute evils of it," he paused thoughtfully, turning to look Evelynn in the eyes, "that we have yet been unable to defeat ourselves."

Even in my angelic body temperature I could feel Evelynn's rage boil at the condescension of her power. She needed to calm down. This wasn't about him or the Wyvren, he was going to take us straight to the place we needed to be and she needed to stay calm. She was much more unstable than I thought, even from my fresh new perspective of digesting human emotions. What was the problem?

Unsure of what to say myself and remaining quiet with the obedient silence of Irene, we walked the rest of the way in silence, the great black Tower ahead growing larger and larger on the horizon. As the colors flickered in the sky above us, every time that familiar pink flicker happened in the sky I remembered Spring's figure against the light of the moon, knowing that always, even now especially, he was watching my every move.

Alto raised his hands to the smooth surface of the glassy black tower, gentle ripples of blue, pink, red, and yellow shimmering from his touch. He opened his mouth, an impossibly beautiful resonance emitting from it. I couldn't understand the language but it was as if he

80

was channeling an entire choir, their melody commanding the Tower to yield to his entrance.

The seams of a door revealed themselves, opening to the moving platform that rose to the various resources the Auspice had to offer; the various offerings of the civilizations that the Council would receive as recompense for their salvation and asylum from the outside world. But here, in the fledgling stages, the hollowness of the Tower was all too apparent, even devoid of the luminous geometric shapes that would culminate the various locations available to the platform wielder.

"Here we are," Alto introduced. "The humble beginnings of our great kingdom. You should feel honored, truly, to see it in this frail state." He smiled at the three of us. "There is so much more to come."

We gathered on the platform, Alto singing his song once again to command it to rise to the top, passing through various empty slots, like bays awaiting ships to land within them, all spiraling by us as our ascent increased in velocity. Finally, we slowed to a stop, reaching the final level, the ceiling within clear view, a glowing door revealing itself before us.

Alto looked at us, beaming with an innocence that almost glazed over his eyes, keeping him powerful and happy. "Your lives are about to change." He announced. "Are you ready to meet your gods?"

Achilles

The familiar door slowly and steadily opened, its heavy obsidian weight dragging across the smooth floor as the stratospheric wind began to whip through the opening. We were so close to the rumbling storm clouds, the colors flashing more vibrantly than I remembered them; almost as if the we were truly at the primordial beginnings of the combined wrath of the Seasons entering this plane. The air was heavy with the mysterious presence of Spring's call, even then I could feel his sensual callings beckoning me back to his side.

The floating walkway manifested, step by step before us in congruent tiling, rippling like water while reflecting the crackling skies above. Alto stepped first towards the levitations bridge, the three of us naturally following suit without question. As we each fully crossed a tile, it would fall away, disappearing into the air beneath us and removing our ability to recede should we desire. An audience of absolution, devoid of escape.

We came upon what was being assimilated as the horseshoe court of the Council, the altar present but the thrones of the leadership incomplete. Frankly, everything here was still under construction; there were only six chairs fully assembled, the two alternating ones in the center absent but stacked with the parts to construct them. Alto and Hector, Kyrie and Constantine; their thrones were prepared, only awaiting Isadora and

Dorian to join their ranks. Little did they know how close they were to their eminent queen.

Then it occurred to me: *of course* they knew how close they were. Whether Alto designed this as a trap or not, Spring was always ahead of everyone, including us. This certainly had the potential to get disastrous quickly. I had to rely on Irene to make sure that no matter what, Evelynn had no reason to be swayed to the other side.

We made our way fully to the Council where we would hopefully seek a productive audience. Our objective was straight forward: ask to pursue the Wyvren by utilizing the resources they have incurred thus far to locate it, and I would use my spatial magic to take us to that location. Simple, concise, effective. As I finished my train of thought, four hooded figures appeared before us all bearing different colored hoods: blue, black, white, and red.

"Greetings, my comrades, dearest Months of the Auspice Council. I have with me a noble offering of skills and assets to assist in our expansion so that we may thrive further!" Alto announced, gesturing to us with his ever present smile. "I have before you Evelynn, Irene, and Ren, from the house of Gaultier in the mortal realms. They are victims thrice of the Wyvren's fury and would like an opportunity to pursue and dispose of the beast."

"And what exactly would inspire such a ridiculous hubris?" I heard a chilling voice challenge from the blue hooded figure. She stood in her small stature, pulling back her hood to reveal the short black hair I expected to see, her icy blue eyes darting across the room like knives. "We have only just figured out how to track the monster, thanks to the efforts of our parents." She finished, crossing her arms in an effort to make herself more intimidating.

"October, you have to stop immediately turning away those who wish to help us." The black cloaked figure accused, pulling his hood back to reveal the tender blonde head of September; my only remembrance of him coming to the rescue of October before I absolutely overwhelmed and devastated her apart on this very platform. "While we can find it, you yourself have been unable to defeat it."

She scowled at her brother a look of disdain for revealing her combative shortcomings. It wasn't her fault, we were cut from the same cloth, I just happened to be a much more formidable piece. No matter how many times I recall these memories, she is among those I hate most in this world. "That is not a fault of mine- no one of this realm can defeat that monster on their own."

"Well, your honorable presence, we would very much like to give it a shot ourselves." I interjected into their sibling skirmish. "I have done all but be born for this task, and I have found the appropriate support needed to complete this task alongside these talented young women. May we have a further conversation about the possibility of us supporting you or shall we continue to deny any inkling of success for all of us at large?"

Everyone present turned to look at me, the sisters in shock, Alto and the Months mirroring their confusion at my sudden impoliteness. In their silence, I continued in the spirit of trying to be solution oriented, "we have heard of your mighty skills, your great prowess, and your various resources. It would mean a great deal to us if we could make use of the tracking capabilities you have on our mutual enemy."

"And what exactly would you offer us in return for our resources, outsiders?" The white hooded figure asked, stepping forward and relinquishing their cover as well. "My siblings are September and October; my name is December." The severe and noble Month introduced herself, commanding the room without so much as raising her voice. As her name implied, as she spoke the temperature of the space dropped even lower than it was already; frost crystallizing down her cascading pitch black hair.

I stepped forward, matching the position of Alto in depth from the Council, "is the head of the monster not enough?" I inquired proudly, offering an indigent promise of success.

The red cloaked figure walked forward, warming the atmosphere back to its original stasis, "you ask us for a resource you wish to pay for later with currency unsecured? I think not." She lowered her hood lastly, revealing a short and precisely cut blonde head of hair, hazel eyes staring me down and heating the air between us. "My name is July, and I don't operate in situations of uncertainty. We may be willing to offer our services, but not without something of value first." She crossed her arms, mirroring the reservations of October across the way to her left. "So we ask again, what do you have to offer us."

I turned to look at the pair of witches that I came with, concerned as I watched Evelynn approach the four Months past Alto and myself. "We have power to offer you. In the house of Gaultier, we operate in services; if you have a task for us, as the leader and representative of our group, I am happy to provide you with a proportionate service."

Well, that is deathly close to exactly what I was afraid of happening. But there was no book, there were no signatures, and no one had spoken of or seemingly yet sworn any loyalties. But even still, what was Evelynn planning exactly to offer them? As I wondered through my eyes the thoughts of possibilities, Evelynn reached for one of her flasks and presented it to the Months.

"I have with me many enchanted liquids, some touched by nature's wonder alone, others blessed by the various gods that have joined my family through the generations." She opened the bottle, commanding the liquid to cyclone upward from its container, revealing a twister of images, words, and faint voices that somehow whispered from the bottle.

"This enigmatic fluid in particular grants knowledge unknown to whomever should bring it to their hands and hold it to their ears." Evelynn explained, mystery in her cunning voice. "The information granted is one truth alone, guaranteed to be previously unlearned by the listener. I am willing to offer each of you access to this gift, does that entice you as payment?"

The Months looked at each other, finally July coming to the conclusion to consult Alto for his opinion. "Captain Alto, what do you suggest?"

"I think the gift of knowledge is the most sacred of all, my work as the becoming Archivist of the Tower of Auspice being my personal endeavor and mettle to bear. With the rest of the Council's permission, I find this a fine compensation to allow them to risk their lives for us."

For one of the few times I had ever known October, a smile of delight spread across her small and narrow face. "I would very much like to go first, being the most capable of those present here." She suggested in a voice of ardent anticipation and misplaced pride; July and December's respective powers influencing the very energy of the room while she simply thrived in her hubris.

It seemed the rest of the fledgling Council had already become accustomed to October's shrewd behavior, as they all relented to her audacious request. Evelynn made her way to October, holding the bottle to her ear as the fluid swirled around her head in a loose colorful orb. October's excitement turned to an ominous awe as the information spilled into her ears.

Evelynn continued her Aquarian journey down the line to each Month, ending with Alto. Every Month seemed to truly gain something from the esoteric magic Evelynn provided them, however Alto seemed to be confused more than anything. When the flask left his ear and the swirling orb of fluid receded back into its vial, he posed a single question.

87

"Who is Kyrie?" Alto asked, his smile now more fragile than it was before. "The secrets I heard… were for someone who didn't share my name. Could there have perhaps been an error?"

This was bad. I immediately intervened before the equally confused Evelynn stepped in to try to defend her magics. "Sometimes," I began, hastily and without much tact, "at least, in my practices, some visions and messages from a mysterious source tell us not just information that helps us, but that could someday help others. Perhaps, in your musical talents, you are to one day come across someone or something that is named 'Kyrie,' as the music?" I gestured blindly, unknowing of what the flask told the young witch.

He pondered for a moment, the Months also beginning to share in skepticism of Evelynn's abilities. Suddenly a veil of ease faded across Alto's face again, the gentle smile returning to his absent eyes as he became instantly satisfied with my suggestion. "Ah, yes. That must be it. Thank you for your insight, Ren. The Kyrie is of most sacred sounds; I should indeed hope it is one day my duty to help someone tandem to that music."

I grinned cheekily, resisting an apparent sigh of relief. "Thank you for receiving my notions, Alto. You truly have been a gracious host so far." I concluded, taking Evelynn's hand and stepping back behind Alto so that he remained the escort of our party.

"Was what I offered you satisfactory?" Evelynn questioned, now very evidently concerned with her performance. Her self-esteem was fragile despite her vast and versatile powers. It confused me greatly.

The Months took a moment to converse with one another, speaking in something closer to sounds and harmonies than actual words; vocalizing tones of various agile harmonies and resolutions as if composing a symphony in real time. It reminded me of the harmonious and rapturous choir of the Seasons when they chose to arrive in chorus with one another.

Once their cadence concluded, July spoke for the standing Council. "We have come to an accord. We are satisfied with the gifts from your leader, and greatly thank you for sharing them." She smiled an adamant expression, "they have helped us to learn even more than we know now, and that is invaluable to our progression in the formation of the Auspice. Are you ready to accept our resources?"

The three of us looked at one another, an anxious excitement across Irene's face, a cold resolve on Evelynn's. I could feel determination flicker in my eyes as I turned to July and responded, "at your discretion we are ready to pursue the Wyvren." I spoke with as much stately depth as I could muster.

"For your gifts of knowledge," December whispered through the winds across the altar in her mysterious voice, "we in turn offer you the gifts of our leaders, the Seasons, so that you may seek the justice we all desire rendered upon the scourge of our time." She turned to September, "brother, please, gather the Seasons for us once more so that they may bestow their all knowing power to our righteous guests."

89

"Wait, you're calling the Seasons?" I stammered, my motivation breaking in discomfort. "I thought the Council was able to track the Wyvren's movements?"

Irene nudged my arm, concern across her eyes at my outburst. Alto turned to me and reiterated, "I asked you before we came to the Council's meeting place if you were ready to meet your gods," he implored, "it would be inappropriate to imply that the humble members of the Council be your lords. We are simply their envoys, divining and carrying out their great will."

October turned a conniving grin towards me, "is there a problem, witch?" She accused fervently, "are you afraid to seek audience with the forces that govern the world? How do you expect to do battle with the Wyvren when you tremble at the thought of meeting with those who are giving you everything to survive?"

"I'm sorry, forgive my ignorance," I quickly tried to recover, "I'm just not familiar with the Seasons. I notice you all, save Alto, have the names of the months of the Year, but I didn't realize that you drew power from the literal Seasons, as well." I felt my throat run dry as I tried to defend my apprehension. "I didn't know they were more than cyclical times. I didn't know they were gods."

September broke the tension with understanding, clearly the caretaker of October's outbursts, no matter how justified. "Sister, we can not expect the mortals on the edges of the world to be enlightened to our great way. Let us educate them;

90

show them the path to our way of life." He motioned to December and July as well, "they are ignorant to the powers at be, this is a grand opportunity to witness to them with the truth of our power."

The mood shifted to a pitying comfort towards my feigned ignorance, September continuing his ritual to call forth his and my creator and his siblings. With an open mouth, light of the four colors of the Seasons, Pink, Red, Yellow, and Blue, all erupted from September in that chilling chorus of stacked harmonies, burning the atmosphere with the mighty friction of their wavelengths.

As before, the respective lights beamed down, manifesting in their columns of light the sturdy visage of Summer, the cunning majesty of Autumn, the concise beauty of Winter, and the chilling omniscience of Spring. While they materialized, draining the colors from the storm clouds above, the platform rumbled and the present Months bowed with Alto before their masters. Evelynn and Irene followed their practice, but as I saw Spring's face again in this place I was frozen in the traumatic memories of my lovers blood staining his robes.

They truly were radiant, the four of them; especially together in their euphony of light. In her commanding fashion, Autumn was the first to fully form, her great flowing red hair cascading down her broad and muscular frame, accentuated by the loose wrapping of white cloth that adorned her.

"My children, October, September," Autumn greeted in a surprisingly warm but strictly maternal voice, "to what do we owe this great pleasure? Are we hosting guests?"

Summer phased fully from his bright golden light, tan skin and muscular body completely naked save for a similar draping of cloth tied around his waist that stopped above his knees. The great luminosity of the sun beaming from his white blonde hair and face.

"July, my strongest daughter," Summer chimed in a rich and lavish voice, almost cutting off Autumn in her greeting in their simultaneity. "You are looking as vibrant as ever with your lovely golden locks. Has the storm yet left your eyes?"

Spring and Winter assimilated into corporeal form, together and silently as they knew Summer and Autumn would be more vocal. Spring, reserved as always in his silent knowing, manifested in rich a lavish purple and red robes that were even more vibrant against his sun kissed hair and light skin, draping over one another in ornate and precise layers. Contrastingly, Winter's olive toned face was the only thing visible, save her hands apparent at the end of her white sleeves, adorned by a pale, almost translucent cloak that hooded her honey brown locks.

Though I didn't quite understand how the Months were begotten of the Seasons, they shared familial traits with their respective "parents;" divided in meaningful ways, true refractions of the energy of their higher representative. October reflected the tenacity of Autumn and her representation of the maturation of the Year; well in her demand for attention and respect. Differing but related, September showed the quietness

92

of an Autumn day, the first cool winds loosening the turning leaves from their trees. November had yet to reveal herself to me.

"We have some proud and seemingly capable candidates that wish to pursue the Wyvren in our stead, Mother." October boasted sarcastically, patronizing our endeavor with her colorful doubt. "While we know you all can't intervene in such an affair directly, and we the Months seem unable to complete this impossible task, these women would like to die to further our point."

"Enough, October." July commanded, a sudden spark of ignition lacing the steady gray of her eyes. "Father, Autumn; forgive our impudence. These warriors have granted us a splendid gift of knowledge in hopes to seek audience with you in their path of peace. Will you hear them?"

All the while, I could barely hear the conversations around the altar. The rest of the setting faded away around Spring as he conspicuously stared me down, the world dissolving around the Azalea garden of his eyes. I felt my knees begin to lose strength. I felt him reaching towards me, his presence commanding me to drag myself away from Evelynn and Irene and kneel before him. As soon as I was on the edge of giving into his dark pleasures, I felt his hold on me disappear.

He couldn't have me, not here. Here he was Spring, one of the omnipotent saviors of the magical world, conducting business with new recruits to the beginnings of a world order he would graciously head with no compensation that could ever truly mean something to his grandiose being. He was toying with me, somehow the other Seasons didn't recognize me, but he was able to see me; he knew that not only was I the Wyvren he made for Irene, but that I was from the timeline I had escaped. How was he aware of this but the others weren't?

I remembered Kieran telling me that time was not a straight line, and that Spring had the power to thumb through the "book" we were living, but was that a power not afforded to the other Seasons? No, surely not. Surely, despite Spring being the beginning of the cycle and knowing things the others never could, it couldn't be that he was simply that much more powerful.

Winter gestured an elegant hand towards December, who immediately rose to meet it in a clear revery of her court's processes. "December, my darling, shall we share such important proceedings with these new guests of ours?" Her voice sparkled as the words left her mouth, tracing each letter in a secret swirl of flurries and glimmering snowflakes. While the other Seasons seemed completely formed, something about her seemed entirely magical, as if her corporeal form was barely present as she existed only in truly ascending the end of the cycle as it returned to Spring.

Her ignorance of my form concerned me further. None of them knew who I was. It was then it occurred to me how cunning Spring truly was. Surely the other Seasons held the powers he gave to Karine and I; outer dimensional influences and manipulations of Space and Time above this simple third dimension.

94

But he was so careful, so ahead of the game he was playing, that the other Seasons had no reason to scan the other timelines. The answers were before all of them, laying in superposition, their potential outcomes and secrets readily available to them. But without interest in being directly involved, they had no reason to further investigate. There was potential in that, and Kieran told me the beginnings of it. If I could, at some point, find a way to follow the Might of those other outcomes in front of them, they would be onto him. I could turn the tables entirely.

"Mother, I believe that if they would like to deal justice for us and have no fear of dying," December spoke as solemnly and mysteriously as her mother, "then we should allow them the opportunity to fight for their world."

The three Seasons looked to their silent brother, Spring, who just narrowly broke eye contact from me and allowed my breath to enter my chest once again. He looked up into the clouds above, grinning his adolescent smirk and stroking his chin pompously in the most artificial query he could muster to almost literally spit my futility back into my face.

"It is a dangerous notion, wouldn't you all agree?" Spring's cinnamon voice warmed the room, fresh air dancing across his lips. "Sure, I think that if these young warriors want to try their hand at making history, we should allow them the opportunity." He turned and looked at me, specifically calling out to me. "You, in the black. What are you called?"

I felt a shiver go down my spine as he addressed me- a perverse pleasure to bow and address him with deified respect, kissing his feet as the Messiah he was to my creation. I choked, clearing my throat and responding, "Ren. I am the Gravity Witch." I finally mustered, feeling my eyes trace down from his eyes to meet the floor in front of me.

Spring sighed blissfully, folding his hands together and resting them against his cheek in adoration of my introduction. His lips curled as his eyes brightened to an even rosier color, "Gravity Witch, you seem to have a power uniquely formatted for this task." He began, "and the young lady with the fire in her hands seems like she could run excellent support for you, divine healing magic locked away in her wrists and crafting at her fingertips." Spring waved his hands, illusionary cuffs suddenly appearing and falling away from Irene's wrists.

"There, young witch, I've unlocked the healing powers of the angel inside of you. You're the perfect support for any distinguished warrior now; a true power house in your own regard- potentially the most balanced and utility witch of the century." He boasted in Irene's regard. I suppose that makes sense to a certain extent, she was the next chosen Wyvren once upon a time- the inception of my entire existence as an independent entity.

Then he turned his attention to Evelynn. "My dear, you seem wise beyond your years," Spring began, his voice much more hesitant in tone than when speaking to myself and Irene. "You have a lot to offer, but are you sure you are suited for the battlefield?" He put a hand to his chin, in a flash teleporting down to our level to float around Evelynn, looking her up and down while she knelt. Portrayed against her kneeling body, Spring's towering height was especially intimidating.

"You don't have the fortitude of the rest of your party, your general wit and IQ seem certainly higher, and you do have a lot of forced experience." Spring critically acclaimed. "Why are you forcing yourself to fight? You seem much more suited in a leadership role." He knelt down to face her, lifting her chin and causing the Months to gasp at his casual approach to a mortal witch. "Have you considered a role in legitimate leadership before?"

This was it- he was playing her like a violin; targeting her insecurities and maximizing the role Gaultier always entrusted to her, but somehow even making her leadership role a set back. He was pitting her against the natural talents of Irene, and very unfairly comparing her to the war machine that I was designed to be. This was the beginnings of Isadora. And I had no idea how to stop it.

"Evelynn is my sister, and while I appreciate your kind words, is the most capable witch *and* warrior I have ever known." Irene interjected, having raised herself from her knee and now standing above Evelynn and before Spring, palms burning with rage at the insinuations devaluing her adoptive sibling. "Without her, nothing about this mission will be a success. She comes with us."

97

The altar space was silent until Autumn's furious response ignited the meeting, "how dare you stand above my brother in your insolent observations of suggested inadequacy," she bellowed, physically shaking the levitating platform in the sky. "*Kneel.*" She commanded, her words of absolution forcing Irene to her knees, slamming her forehead against the ground.

"Now, sister," Spring said in his ever soothing voice. "That is no way to talk to our young guests. Was she not just defending her sibling in the same way you just defended me?" Spring vanished away from Evelynn, the seeds of his doubt planted deep in her subconscious to grow. He appeared beside Autumn, taking her hand. "I appreciate your devotion to our family, sister. But now is not the time to exercise our powers."

The deep and buoyant voice of the muscular Summer addressed us all, "Spring, it seems you approve of the group- save one." He looked to Evelynn, kneeling in the center of our formation. "Shall we allow two to attempt to complete their objective?"

No, that couldn't happen. We can't leave Evelynn here. It all made sense; her insecurities, her complex with Irene, hell even perhaps sending me to destroy Irene's family all those years ago so that Gaultier and Evelynn would find her. Could his plan to form the "Captains" with the Auspice Council to combat my potential resistance gone back that far? Of course it could of. When he chose Irene as my vessel outside of time before she was even born, he chose Evelynn to be her envy- pliable to his offerings.

"I think that if her comrades deem it wise to have her with them for morale, then we shouldn't interrupt their rhythm." Spring's voice swooned over us. "Should only two come back, I can rest knowing I did my part to warn them. Should any of them come back at all that is."

I could feel Evelynn's bowed head begin to flush with embarrassment and rage. There was little more I could do than ask a revealing question, "Seasons, if you are familiar with the movements and are against the actions of the Wyvren, why not stop it yourselves? You are all powerful, beyond anything armies of the most talented human magical practitioners could accomplish against the beast." I stared Spring dead in the eyes as I finished my enigmatic question. "Why let it rampage and send those you know will die in your place?"

Autumn began to emanate a neon orange rage, Illuminating something of a halo around her burning locks when they were instantly cooled by a brisk gust form the ethereal Winter, raising her free hand in another gentle gesture towards her sister, the other hand still grasped by December. She quelled Autumns rage and turned to look at me, her white blue eyes arresting me in their writhing winter.

"We are sustained by the ever present observation of humanity," Winter whispered the familiar tale to me again. "We are omnipotent- but not constantly. We exist by accident, powerful because of the consistency of the spinning world. So long as there are Seasons to see, Seasons for mortals to experience, we exist at the hands of your world."

99

Winter's chilling voice continued in gentle rasps, "that delicate balance- if we interfere with the continuity of humanity, it will cause them to deify us further, allowing us to not only influence the events of the world, but to alter and change them. We can not exist without you, and we can not interfere with you, should it throw the world into instability; fracturing existence not just here, but through out the multiverse at large." She steadied her effervescent existence even further, "we can not afford to interfere. Or we could vanish. Destroying this world and every other. An accidental symbiosis of beings- us, and you."

That was probably mostly true, at least from Summer, Autumn, and Winter's perspective. but Spring was able to intervene all he wanted. He was the beginning. By principle he made whatever he decided flourish and grow. He secretly had that edge on the other Seasons- even the direct feeder than sends everything back to him recycled and ready for rebirth, Winter.

"We understand," Irene said, raising her head from the ground to reveal a bruise already forming around the lite bleeding the impact caused. Testing her knew power, she raised her hand to her head, healing the wound without much effort at all. She smiled at Spring, who was ready to return her enthusiasm with a gentle wink. Disgusting. "Seasons, please, allow the three of us to embark. We are ready." Irene finished.

"Very well!" Spring's voice range. "I have the ability to know where every living thing is; as they enter the world I am able to follow them step by step- even

100

the three of you." He spoke warmly, comforting to others but devastatingly true to me. That's how the Seasons justified the whereabouts of the Wyvren to the Months and Council. Spring just "knew," not because the Wyvren was running off of his programs, but because of some farce reason about being the "source of all life" or whatever.

Spring raised his robed arms over the young obsidian tablet that constituted the Auspice altar, swirling a finger above the structure to form a concentric pink light. Within the circle appeared a swirling slew of images, coming together in various parts of the world, scanning for where the Wyvren might be hunting. Finally, the images stilled as the Chateaux came into view, burning, surrounded by Téo, Gaultier, Sara, Sabine, and Karine. From the rubble emerged my predecessor; the fury of my past, swords swarming around her, waiting to find their homes in our comrades.

"Oh, dear," Spring said, pity in his voice, "it seems while we were chatting here our mutual nemesis found its way back to your home." He smiled at me as the rest of those present looked on in horror of the devastation. "Shall I send you back home now?"

"Yes, yes please send us there now!" Irene screamed, clutching her throat in despair. "I'm begging you, send us now!" Before she could continue to plea, we were swallowed by the ring of light, the passageway home long and luminous again. In the bright white hallway, the three of us ran as fast as we could towards the horrific scene, the death of the Chateaux members approaching yet again. I felt my run slow, Evelynn and

Irene covering more ground much faster. Suddenly I was simply running in place, the two siblings exiting the portal completely as it closed, leaving me in the white hallway again.

I looked around, searching for the exit they took now completely out of my view. I looked up to find spiraling storm clouds and turned to to see a round wooden table. Two chairs, two glasses of red wine. I turned away and kept running. Did I fall out of the passage somehow?

"Going somewhere?" Kieran's voice appeared behind me, his form appearing and tapping my shoulder as I ran in place again, going nowhere.

"I have to get back to the Chateaux!" I screamed, "I have to go back! I have to-"

"Walk right into another one of Spring's traps that he not only set for you, but built a passage to take you to?" Kieran sneered at me, taking a seat and sipping his wine. "Are you sure that portal even took you there?"

I stopped running, relenting to my knees. With a snap of Kieran's finger I was seated in the chair across form him, "no need for theatrics, we are on the same side here." He said, snidely trying to calm me down.

I couldn't think of anything else to say, "why do you look like him?" I finally accused. Why do you look like Spring?"

He cocked an eyebrow at me, taking the wine glass from his lips. "Because he is an inheritor of my story, 'Ren,'" he smirked, setting his glass down. "I made him in my image. All of them, but him first."

He leaned back in his chair, setting his feet on the table. "I am the administrator; I run this place. Inside and out." He stretched his arms behind his head, leaning back and propping the chair off the ground, balancing it underneath him, "or as you have so keenly observed, perhaps I should be called the 'author' instead."

"Are you... god?" I asked, dumbfounded and confused to even hear the words leave my mouth.

A violent and boisterous laugh left Kieran's mouth, almost throwing him out of the chair gingerly balanced beneath him. "Silly, silly girl. 'God?'" He asked, gesturing his hands wildly above his head. "Which one? There are so many, all with their own ideas of creation, all true in their own right." He slammed his balanced chair down, placing both of his hands on the table, reaching for his wine again.

"I am the Truth, Wyvren." He said sternly, in a voice I had yet heard him use. "I am the culmination, the original light. I am Knowledge." He took another full sip of his wine. "I am the Year."

Arcana

"What are you talking about?" I said anxiously, "You're just supposed to be this all knowing force that hangs out in people's dreams and between the cracks in reality?" I looked around, standing in outrage against his grand proclamation, only to be thrown by the force of Kieran's power back into the chair across from him. Whether I wanted to escape or not, I was clearly at the mercy of his power.

"I just told you we are on the same side, didn't I?" He said, resting his chin on his hands, fingers intertwined with themselves. "The vision Spring showed you all was an illusion. None of it was real. Right now they all just appeared at the Chateaux, confused and aggravated as to why they were tricked."

"Why would Spring do something like that? In front of the Months and the Seasons and Alto?" I pressed further, my chest tightening with worry. There were so many variables at play and the longer I was away from them, the more I felt them slipping out of any influence or control I could have dreamed to have over them.

"He will later justify it as a test," Kieran responded plainly. "He can easily say he was trying to keep you three out of legitimate danger while testing your resolve. There is no way he is going to let his Isadora go." He sipped his endless wine once again.

"She is necessary to his success. The four of them are, every time."

"That's what I thought!" I exclaimed, determined and encourage by his validation. "But why? Why do they have to be in place every time?"

"Téo, Evelynn, Constantine, and Kyrie," Kieran began to explain, his finger now sliding idly around the singing rim of his glass, "they are all special, in their own ways. They come from particular magical bloodlines, all orphaned intentionally by you at his command. Being from those bloodlines, they each hold magical genetic memories from their ancestors. Those memories and skills are important to him and the cause of the Auspice. Téo's family is usually murdered by you, but his proud brother saved you the trouble."

"What do you mean?" I leaned across the table, trying to stand but feeling the command of his will forcing me in place. "Because of their blood, they hold potential for him? Their ancestors are literally survived by their own blood?"

Kieran chuckled, rolling his condescending eyes once again. "Of course they are. That is why Irene is important as well, just in a different way." He raised his hands as if to present the room we were in for the very first time. "It is because of Irene that you have access to the Precipice, which of course ultimately leads you here. It was once a holy mind temple visited frequently by her ancestors. She has the potential to gain access to it in her lifetime as well, by way of her clerical father's blood in her veins," he sipped his wine again and chuckled. "Unless you kill her again, that is."

105

"That's why I appeared there first," I speculated in the beginnings of remembrance, avoiding a response to his jab at my morality, "when I first entered Irene, Scimariel must have wrestled me to that dusty place, knowing she could trap me in glass the way she did."

"You know, for someone barely a year old, I'm glad you can keep up, little one." Kieran teased. "Yes, Scimariel, being an angel inherited from that side would be very familiar with this place." He pushed his hair back and wiped his brow in an exacerbated sigh. "I can't keep you here for very long, not without them noticing. I could suspend us in Time but that would cause complications not worth discussing right now. You're asking questions that you clearly already know the answer to. Ask better ones."

I thought frantically. This is exactly what I wanted, what I needed. Ever since the short period between now and last night all I could think of were different ways I might be able to get back here. Now was my opportunity, and so long as he was "on my side," I had to take advantage of that. I had no idea how an entity like himself worked as far as allegiance and loyalty was concerned.

"How do I kill Spring?" I said, directly and flatly. He was right, I had to use this time wisely. As curious as I was about bloodline memory magic or whatever he was talking about, if he really was the source of all of the Seasons and embodied the abstract ideas beyond them like Knowledge and Truth, surely he had the capabilities to answer this question.

106

He turned his lips into a conniving crescent and his bright eyes darkened to a bloody hue. "Now you're playing the game, songbird." He said, his voice boasting my praise in a dark and sinister pride. He leaned back, for the first time finishing his entire glass of wine without miraculous refill, and set it down, staring me down like a bird of prey across the table as if I were nothing but an unsuspecting field mouse; or at least, that was certainly how I felt beneath that malicious gaze.

"You can't," he said, his voice ringing in a lower octave. "No one can. Not even myself."

The clouds above us began to part, a vision of the Irene and Evelynn in the sky looking around, checking their comrades over head to toe to make sure they were alright; everyone present except myself.

"You can't send me back yet," I pleaded. "Everything can die- everything *has* to die." I implored. "Nothing can live forever. Not even you."

Kieran let out a deep, bellowing laugh that shook the table and room around us. "Nothing at all HAS to die." He laughed bitterly at my inconspicuous ignorance to the nature of mortality. "The only thing that has ever had to happen is change. Spring can't die- not by the hands of anyone or anything, no matter how mighty."

I felt the rippling of understanding begin to rise in the recesses of my mind; his riddled response assimilating possibilities in my brain. Instead of devastation at the futility of my endeavor bloomed something new, something that I never thought possible at all.

"I can't kill Spring," I began, slowly as the rift in the sky beckoned me back to reality. "Spring is a concept- an idea. Something so above the existence of humans but attainable by something of his own understanding; something like me."

Kieran silently bowed his head to me, closing his eyes and snickering darkly. I suppose as a being that has never had to yield to something like tact, he had always been this free to express himself. Without looking back up at me, he raised his closed hand palm side up, and flicked his wrist with pointing with is index and middle finger. This gestured sent me flying upward from my seat, abruptly and shockingly towards the rift in the sky. Before I could even orient myself to which way the ground was, I was being spit out of a portal that mirrored the structure of the one Spring formed.

"Ren!" Irene rushed to my side, kneeling down as I laid there as I was unable to land on my feet. "Ren, are you okay? What happened?"

I gasped for air, the lunge from the ground to the artificial sky of Kieran's domain fresh in my stomach and sore against my ribs. I coughed, clenching my abdomen. "I… I don't remember." I lied. I kept finding myself lying to these people. "I was right behind you, then suddenly I found myself running in place. I was trapped in the same spot for a while until I was finally able to push myself forward towards where I saw you two exit." I looked around, playing the part of the unaware as adamantly as I could. "Where is the Wyvren? Were you able to defeat it without me?!"

108

"The monster was never here." Evelynn responded, coldly with frustration. "I don't know why, but the Council and their 'Seasons' lied to us, sending us away and back home. How disrespectful."

"Why would they deny our help?" I asked, feeding the fire of antagonizing the Auspice at large. "Were our lives not valuable enough to send for their 'noble' cause?"

Sara and Sabine helped me up, taking us all back inside. While I was gone for more than just a few short moments, it seemed that Irene and Evelynn trusted my story, not questioning me at all in front of the group; even expressing concern for my wellness. Once inside, we told them everything. Irene and I took most of the lead in expressing the details. Evelynn, now evidently insecure, stayed quiet, interjecting only when asked or to clarify details.

"Over seven feet tall?!" Exclaimed Téo, his surprised and loud response unexpected to say the least- just last night he seemed so shy and quiet. I guess he just needed to see my face more than once. "How are there gods like this that are so powerful without any direct followers? I guess people have been worshipping gods that are *related* to seasonal things for centuries, but how are they so strong?"

"I'm… not really sure," Evelynn responded to Téo, "but I would like the opportunity to speak to them again. I feel that the Chateaux and this 'Council' could mutually benefit each other in a lot of ways."

That response was difficult for me to hear. I knew that Spring's words were echoing in her mind, persuading her to seek power with or from him. I had to figure out why Kieran mentioned genetic or blood memories, why the ones Evelynn and the others had were so special, and what exactly it had to do with his influence on the world, having absolution over Time and Space and the other Seasons fooled into his righteousness being at the beginning of their cycle.

Karine sat beside me at the table again, everyone around us trying to make sense of what could have been the reason for spurning support. Evelynn would make it a point to return, I was sure of that. The teasing from Spring was all too delectable to her self-inflicted inferiority complex to Irene. She was bound to make her way back, I just had to figure out how to stop her from going alone. I was desperately trying to strategize something further, but I could only feel Karine's knowing eyes glancing down at my hand on the table; holding it gently with her intent. It was driving me crazy.

"Perhaps Evelynn and I should go alone another time," I proposed. "I don't trust them. They made it clear that they deal in mysterious ways. They took her offering and sent us on a wild goose chase." I turned and looked at Irene, "I would love for you to come, but perhaps if we let Evelynn take a more offensive position, they wouldn't scrutinize-"

"They sent us away because I'm weak." Evelynn interrupted me, looking down at the table, fists clenched beneath her indigo-stained leather armaments. "They sent us away because I don't have the vigor you and Irene have; because I'm not a real fighter."

Gaultier responded from the head of the table, "daughter, you are fierce and capable. You have gotten each and every one of us out of dangerous situations with your wit and abilities." He tried his best to further console her "just because you aren't necessarily the heaviest hitter doesn't make you invalid or weak. A strong blow is only effective if it lands, and you always make sure that it does."

Evelynn stood up, turning away as tears began to well in her eyes. She stoically walked away without a word, turning up the stairs. We heard the door to her room slam, causing Irene to stand up, looking up at the ceiling, her sister's grief beckoning from the floor above us. Irene always seemed to be at the disposal of Evelynn, but it showed that perhaps there was a lack of reciprocity in their sisterly relationship.

Gaultier and Sara went upstairs to try to intervene Evelynn's somber state, Téo and Irene leaning to one another as they tried to think of ways to cheer up their adoptive sibling. Sabine remained still, quietly sketching in her book, slightly detached from the situation entirely. I stood to walk out of the room to get some air, to my delight and anxiety, Karine followed me shortly after I found my away outside.

We walked across the yard to the forest's edge outside of the house, out of conspicuous sight of the others and the crumbling windows of the floors above. I faced the forest, my face contorted in a solitary misery as Karine reached out for me hand, firmly grasping it and taking it in both of hers.

111

"I'm here," her soothing voice whispered from behind me, making its way through my hair and to my ears, her very words inspiring a sensation across the back of her neck. I had only been here two nights and two days, the fragile reality I accepted with her standing on end. Everything I thought I knew turned around completely as the doubt of her sincerity crept into the chambers of my heart.

"How," I practically choked after a moment of silence, finally squeezing her hands in return, still facing the seemingly infinite forest before me. "I watched you die, but I can see in your eyes that you are the same woman I love; the one I watched my creator run through with ease as if you were no obstacle at all." I finally turned to her, my face hot and flushed, my cheek wet with tears I didn't know I was shedding, "how did you survive? I need to know how you are here…"

I met her hand holding mine with my other, looking at her fingers interlocked with my own while trying to avoid her beautiful eyes in knowing that whatever they decided to tell me I would accept as truth. So long as the words were coming from the mouth I knew so well, I was at her mercy. Her hand followed my arm, up my shoulder and neck to my chin, lifting my face to the sight I was so afraid to face.

"I haven't told you everything about me, Ren," she said, her eyes sapphire eyes dark with mystery and guilt. "I didn't have the time, ironically. We were so close to living our life together in a way that mattered in the 'other' timeline. I didn't want to ruin it."

112

Karine stroked my cheek, her face now wet with shameful tears as my face continued to tremble against the confrontation. "For the first time in so long I was happy, Ren. Even if just for those fleeting moments, I was happy. Is it a crime that I lean into that humanity, my darling?"

I felt my face rush with blood as my heart became invigorated with her persuasion. "I want… I want so deeply to trust you, Karine." I whimpered, my hand rising to my own face to meet her hand, cradling it now to my cheek. "I know what happened to you. I know where the Clock Key came from." I spoke, my voice burning out into a crackling whisper as I finished, my eyes closing hard to blink out more pain from my eyes.

We stood there in silence, the setting sun burning through the vibrant green leaves as the forest illuminated into a warm summer twilight. I kept my eyes closed, not angry with her for her origins but furious for her withholdings. If anyone could understand her, if there were anyone in this entire world of possibility she could share with in the misery of her futile situation; being in the debt of a cruel omnipotence, it was me.

I heard the grass between us begin to crush and press beneath her feet as I clenched my eyes closed even still, feeling her warm approach and her other hand leave mine and meet my other cheek. I relaxed my brow, smelling her breath against my lips as she leaned in to kiss me. I didn't resist. I didn't want to. No matter how confused, angry, upset I was with her, ultimately she was all I ever wanted. Beyond my autonomy and the

113

entombment of Spring and his conquest, she was the only thing I had ever known to desire.

I wrapped my arms around her, giving into her. She was the same, regardless. Even with our lips pressed to one another's, arms around each other, swaying in the gentle innocence of a pure love, I heard Kieran's warnings in my head. *Has Karine ever fully described to you why she has invested so much in looking for you? Why she has spent literally entire timelines chasing you down and loving you so deeply?*

Despite the fear and doubt sewn in me, I remembered the fear and doubt sewn in Evelynn by Spring. How far exactly did the apple fall from the tree; Kieran, the "Year," bearing and granting the image of Spring, surely had his own investments in how he delivered his information to me. I had to make a choice: trust Kieran, or trust Karine.

I pulled away, looking at Karine's face, solemn with guilt but comforted by my touch. She was so beautiful, truly. By no other standard had I known to revere elegance of any kind until I learned the gentleness she had to teach me. "Karine, I have to know." I gestured, taking her hands in mine again.

"What is it, Ren?" She asked, her voice soft and dry from tears.

"I know Spring gave you Time, and you know, now, that I know that," I meekly interrogated. "And you know that Spring gave me Space. Tell me the truth, right now." I stared a firm and desolate stare of sincerity and desperation into her eyes, practically blurring everything in my periphery with focus. "In your endless pursuit of

114

knowledge, power, and magics, am I your final frontier? Am I your trophy? Am I your asset in which one day you are able to control Time *and* Space?"

Karine's eyes widened, the bluntness of my statement clearly a touch overwhelming. I saw something that rhymed with fear in her eyes; not any kind of peril, but an echoing of regret in knowing her secrets. In her abbreviated shock, she was only able to ask, "when did you find him?"

"Last night, he came to me in a dream. Irene, her connection with the divine took me to the Precipice, and I took the leap of faith to find the Liminal Space." I fully and honestly explained. "Kieran met me there. He told me a version of what happened to you... I believe most of it." I weakly said, ashamed to admit that I distrusted her. "But I can't believe that you would use me. The only thing that would incline me to believe it would be..."

Before I could finish, Karine let go of my hands, raising her arms beside her head and closing her eyes. I felt the collar of my Left Hand respond to her Right Hand command and with a snap of her fingers, the binding of her influence shattered from around my neck, the light of her Right Hand power over me fading instantly.

"The only reason I ever did that was because I knew that Spring would always try to exercise his influence over you," she explained, lowering her hands. "I only ever paired us like this under Dorian's system because I wanted to be able to pull you back if I needed

115

to. But I won't ever do anything like that again," she exclaimed ardently, "not if it means you don't trust me."

She cradled my face again in her hands, kissing my forehead, then kissing my lips again. "I need you, yes, but not in the way Kieran described. I need you because I love you. And I need you to love me, too. And you can't do that if you can't trust me."

I was shocked. Pleasantly, over the moon with joy shocked, but completely caught off guard. In an instant, she heard me, responded in a way that meant everything, and didn't discount my fears and doubts. In the blink of an eye she was able to diffuse Kieran's hooks in my psyche. But now that left me with even more questions; if Kieran meant what he said, and meant for me to believe it while this Karine existed, how could he ever claim to be an ally?

"I'm... sorry I," I began to apologize, Karine's finger rising to my mouth to silence the rest of my statement.

"Don't you dare apologize. I wasn't fully honest with you. I was going to tell you everything, one day," she said softly, her voice even quieter against the initial rumblings of the summer cicada in the forest. "I'm sorry you didn't hear the truth from me. If you'll hear me, I'll tell you everything, right here and now."

I nodded, eyes wide with her finger still against my lips. She giggled, sitting down in the soft grass and offering my head to rest on her lap. I laid down, my long hair draping over her crossed legs as she stroked my head. As she ran her fingers through my hair, she recited the story almost exactly as Kieran had told it to me before.

"Way back when, when I first heard of the Wyvren and its command over Space, I admit: I did seek you out originally to try to defeat you." She said, her gentle hands removing any air of murderous intent that would have otherwise been implied towards my vulnerable state. "I thought that if I could take that power from the Wyvren, I could become strong enough to defeat Spring; able to work on all planes of his power."

She paused briefly, long enough for me to look up at her and find her lost in her own memories as she relived the story she told, "when I first found you, we fought. Hard. Long. Furiously. There was so much collateral damage. And when I finally thought I had an edge on you, we reached another stalemate." She explained, her hands now still in the locks she held.

"I kept resetting the battle, over and over again, trying to go back in time to figure out a way to defeat you. Until I realized that we were the same. I fought to defy the will of Spring, you fought because you had no choice but to follow that will." Karine took a deep breath as she rooted herself back to reality, no longer reliving the tale but again recounting it. "I decided that I wanted to kill you, not for your power, but for your mercy. No one should have to live forever like me, under the thumb of the true monster behind it all."

Karine continued, "I followed you, over and over again, through all of your incarnations as I would never age, fighting you again and again, sometimes dying,

117

always losing. Finally, I came to this collection of timelines, where Irene would be your host." She let go of my hair and clenched her fist against her chest, starting to weep gently, warm tears spilling down across my forehead as I looked up at her.

"And then *you* happened." She said, smiling and giggling through her tears, wiping her eyes and clearing her throat. "After that, Irene would always die, and you would do battle with Gaultier, eventually fighting your internal battle. Sometimes giving into Zorne, where I would have to fight you again and reset everything, but sometimes… like this time…"

"You have endured me as myself and as a monster, again and again- even after my break away from Spring." I wondered aloud, impressed and devastated by her commitment to me. "Why keep torturing yourself again and again?"

She closed her eyes for a moment, returning to stroking my hair, opening them again to look down at me and say in a voice more sacred than any hymn, "I would endure a thousand deaths, a thousand times. I would relive a thousand atrocities, a thousand calamities; again and again, as many times as I had to, so long as the chance of finding my way back to you ever remained possible." She finished, closing her eyes again, finding resolve in a statement I felt she had said to me before, but not in this life.

We stayed there with each other by the edge of the forest, the frogs joining the now roaring cicadas as the sun fully left the sky, only the low hanging moon and stars illuminating us to one another. Karine stood,

118

offering a hand I took to stand with her, entering another embrace before we returned to the Chateaux to greet the others.

"Why not tell the others about us? About how we truly feel for each other?" I asked, desperately not wanting to return to a platonic charade as we walked back towards the Chateaux.

"If we tell Téo and Evelynn the nature of our relationship, we could potentially be telling Dorian and Isadora each other's weakness in one another should we fail to save them in this timeline." Karine explained, ready to answer my naive request.

Knowing she was right, I kissed her one last time under the cover of night before we made our way back inside, ignorant to the proximity of Evelynn's window just above us as she peered through her own tattered canvas, watching the long lost "sisters" find pleasure in each other. In all of the oversights I would make in this life, little did I know that one small and simple kiss would be so devastating to my future.

Saint

It was getting late, even the symphony of wildlife was beginning to relent into the good night of rest and the rumbling heat of the fledgling summer skies. We creaked the door open and tiptoed with fleeting steps into the foyer before the dining hall of the Chateaux. With a parting glance, Karine made her way down the hall towards the staircase that lead to her room and I began to climb my own.

The eerie halls of the broken cold stone fortress became even more mysterious in the frozen shimmers of moonlight that slithered through the cracks in the stone walls. I dragged my hand across the withered expanse of the hallways, feeling the eroded stacks of granite beneath my equally ragged fingertips. This place was old and broken, but full of a warmth that came upon it years after it began to truly fall apart. I was recognizing a sense of nostalgia within myself in relation to the old bones of this aching place.

As fatigue truly began to pull itself over my mind and eyes I decided to reminisce further laying in my cot. Hopefully I would have time later to observe the nuances of this place and those who called it home, but tonight all I could focus on was how fast everything in my life always seemed to move, and if trusting Karine was really the absolute truth and resolve I had to cling to. Sure, she made me happy and of course she had all of the answers to all of the questions I seemed to want to know. But since talking to Kieran all I could be was suspicious. I hated that feeling.

I turned into my room and shut the door quietly, pulling it to the the frame with a gentle click as the hinges settled. I felt something different in the room, even in my unfamiliarity with it there was a presence, a warmth of some kind. I turned quickly and scanned the room, shortly and decidedly coming to my answer as I found a figure sitting with their legs strewn over the side of my cot, swinging childishly in the wind as if impatiently waiting for my arrival.

"Goodness, you stay up late," Irene's voice chimed through the darkness as she leaned to light a candle on the meek table beneath the canvased window with a sparking pinch from her fingertips. "I stopped by to check in with you and thought maybe you went to get some water. I didn't realize you were one to roam the night. Not that if you often do that it should surprise me." She looked down at her legs as they stopped swinging. "You're mysterious, Ren. And somehow… it feels like I really have met you before. I came here because I want with all of my heart to trust you but I have to find out for myself if I can."

My unease went away when I saw the gentle light of the candle dance across the kindness in Irene's eyes. "It's fair that you speculate my intentions, Irene," I responded, my voice low and hushed in a deep whisper. "Can I come sit with you?" Irene slid over on the cot and tapped the vacant slack in the hanging bed beside her.

I made my way over and sat down, my long brown hair intermingling with hers as it rested across

121

our respective hands. I never thought truly to myself why I never cut it shorter after becoming "Ren," but I believe it was because it reminded me of Irene; perhaps if I left evidence of her life sprinkled throughout mine, I could do good by remembering her in my victories.

"Irene, I know that you are a good person. You're kinder than you realize and stronger than you give yourself credit for," I began, turning my head to look at her in the mixing warm and cool lights of the flickering candle and the observing moonlight. "Against everything I have been told to do, I feel in my gut that I have to tell you the truth. The whole truth."

I felt her eyes narrow with curiosity as I watched her mind begin to race with speculation and wonder. She lifted her legs and crossed them in the humble bed, facing me with the utmost attention. Of all the times I did my best to relate myself to Irene, in this moment I found her akin to me; I remembered waiting for the words of revelation to fall from Karine's lips in the last timeline we were on, hanging on every word for clarity, wanting with all that I was to just know the answers to my questions.

I lifted my legs and crossed them as well, facing her with my full intention in return. "I'm telling you this from a place of love, protection, and trust, Irene," I prefaced, taking her hands in my own. "I'm not asking you to believe me, but something tells me that you will. No matter what, I need you to promise me on your guardian angel and your parents' graves that you will not tell another soul what I told you; not even Karine."

She gripped my hands back and returned my severe gaze with a hopeful and determined pursuit of knowledge, "please, Ren. I know you're here for something important. We watched what you did to the Wyvren; I truly believe that if we all work together we can be victorious against that monster." She didn't blink, only becoming more vigorous with each word, "I swear on all that is sacred to me to keep this conversation between the two of us, until the time comes that you can trust the rest of us with whatever it is you have to say."

Once I started I couldn't stop. The words spilled from my mouth like a river that wouldn't run dry even in the hottest of summers. As each word left me Irene's presence seemed to pull the next from my lips with no effort at all. I watched the wonder and horror, the suspense and despair ripple across her face. All of it.

I spared no detail of how I came to be, how Spring built me to take root in Zorne, how I was the very beast she watched me fight and pursue in the forest upon my arrival; how the only way I was able to create the supernova of heat that ignited my power. I told her about my deal with Scimariel to reach her, and ultimately her deal with me to defeat her adoptive father.

"That's one of the reasons I chose to come back to this part of our story, Irene," I consoled as she started to lose composure. "Now that I am my own person, I can do my part across not just this timeline, but as many as I can. Spring has made so much evil in this world and I'm one of the only forces that can begin to stop him." Irene was doing her best to receive the information in stride, but to her this was a living nightmare. In her kindness and in her service, she endured much better than I could have ever expected.

"If I can rewrite as much as I can, with Karine's help, little by little we can help create a world where Gaultier never has to suffer, where Evelynn doesn't have to suffer." I took her hands and looked into her teeming eyes, "a world where *you* don't have to lose everything, either. I know that my existence… my past, is the cause for all of this hurt and chaos. But because of you, Irene; because of you and Scimariel I was able to set myself free. I can never thank you enough for your sacrifice, even if it was another 'you,' it was still the heart you hold even now."

She lifted her left hand to her eyes and wiped away the tears that finally began to fall from her face. "I'm not crying for me, so much as I am for you, Ren," she responded in a strong but hoarse tone, the tension in her throat from holding back tears making friction in her words. "You were given a chance to be free, even in my sacrifice and at the death of my entire family, you were given an out, but instead of running away from your past, your sins…" Irene lifted her right hand to my cheek and gently caressed my tired face, "you chose to fight to atone for a life you never even lived."

"Irene, don't cry for me. Like you said, this is the least I can do. And what's more, I mean it when I say I'm going to fight across all of Time and Space to snuff out Spring and every Wyvren that has ever lived to kill." The candle was burning through faster than it should have been as we continued our exchange; probably due to

124

our mutual body heat being much higher than that of normal people. "No matter what happens, at the very least, I'm going to make sure you survive. I will do everything I can Irene, even if I have to rewind this hell a thousand times."

Irene smiled and looked away for a moment, taking in the entirety of the perilous tale I told her. She was truly divine; even more angelic than Scimariel in her grace and attention. She was selfless and powerful, truly a warrior of justice and a commander of peace. This world deserved her as their savior, not the bastardized weapon that was my identity. If only my power had come to her instead of the other way around.

At last she broke the suspension of dialogue in the air, "Ren, I want you to promise me something." She said quietly, still watching the dancing shadows that mingled in the gold and silver lights.

"Anything, Irene. Whatever you want, I will make sure it happens." I responded, leaning in with sincerity and almost desperation. If there was anything I could do for her while she was alive I would not let the opportunity go by.

Irene took a deep breath, slowly turning her head towards me, her eyes staggering behind as she peeled herself away from her focused glare at the wall. "If Spring really is as powerful as you say, and you are cut from that cloth, you will probably be able to survive a battle with him…" she began, pursing her lips as she continued her evidently uncomfortable train of thought.

With another exhale Irene continued, "when you battle him, I will be there with you. I know he will be the one to try to enact his plan again, over and over as you described how your past's dark incarnations proliferate across the multiverse. If there comes a situation where he is about to turn me into the Wyvren again, as it would seem I am destined to become…"

I took both my hands and placed them on her shoulders, our silhouettes mirroring now more than ever in my resemblance to her. "That won't happen. It can't. I'm going to kill the Wyvren on this timeline. It's never been done, a Wyvren has never been slain. But I know the program well; once it dies it can't find a new host on its own. It will die if it is outside of a host for too long, just like a virus."

"Ren, please," Irene responded, a holy fire burning in her brilliant green eyes and fiercely illuminating with her magic. "If there is a situation where Spring is about to turn me into the Wyvren, please kill me instead. I would rather die a martyr than be corrupted as a monster." She met my hands on her shoulders with hers across her body, "please, don't make me fight my friends. My family. Don't let me become a senseless monster, Ren."

The candle flickered out in the early summer heat and Irene's burning words, the smoke now rising in the remaining pearlescent moonlight. As my eyes adjusted to the night, my heart calibrated to her conviction. "I promise, Irene; I won't let you become the hateful beast of my past and tarnish the future you would have lived. Should Spring find a way to mitigate the Wyvren's death after I kill it, I promise I will make sure you are liberated from that fate."

126

Irene sighed in meaningful relief. "Thank you, Ren. I know that is a lot to ask for, especially in the pursuit of your redemption. But know that I will know that your mercy is welcome to me, and that my spirit will be with my family again should we part ways on the battlefield."

Irene stood up from the cot, snuffing out the candle smoke completely with a licked fingertip and walked towards the door. As she grabbed the handle, she left me with parting words, "please, no matter what. Save my family. They are the most precious things to me." Before I could respond, she opened the door and left me with my thoughts.

I reflected on our conversation for what easily felt like hours after Irene left; my lithic ceiling hearing my every rumination as they almost physically wafted towards the atmosphere. Every plea and every wish imprinted itself upon the bare vaulting above me.

I could feel my heart beat; my sinister gears turning and gnashing against themselves as they sustained me instead of the monster they longed to let thrive. Irene's words churned in my engineered ventricles as she spoke of me like some kind of savior. The guilt began to rumble in my chest and throat as I started to believe that perhaps I was of better use to Karine and the entire world dead. Gone.

That wasn't quite right, either. I never wanted to die so much as I wanted to come up for air. My hands didn't wish to choke out my throat as much as they did to just cradle my head and rest; rinsing and wringing out my battle scarred mind, bleaching and pressing the

127

memories I wish I could throw away instead of ceasing them forever. But instead they clothe every happy recollection of sunshine and dust in tawny hues, staining my bliss with sepia claw marks of what happened between now and then.

I knew peace would never fit quite right in my arms, always trying it's best to sink into my marrow as my body rejected it like a sickness. I never meant to resist the gentle release of a simple day. I never wanted to call the tempest to a head in the silence of a simple night. More than anything I craved the simplicity of a summer night; roaring with the songs of wildlife that didn't distract me from my heavy cross but lifted my soul into their sounds.

It was as if every part of me would rather break my bones and heart than to submit to the finality of peace, as if in tranquility I would find my idleness dangerous. I stared into that ceiling and wondered if in the whispering harmonies of an uncomplicated life I could even find purpose.

Would it be enough to be happy? Could I ever learn to find pleasure and satisfaction in spring hydrangeas and to not regret their splendor as they died in the heat of July? Could I find enough time to do everything that needed to be done to clear my consciousness to enjoy the solace of a tranquil amity?

If I continued to become more; to become something that could conquer my creator, what would that ultimately look like? What would I become? My evolution is just that- one of struggle. Spring didn't design placid genes in me, but ones that would always strive for survival. I'm supposed to rip and tear away at myself, again and again, until I carve this rough stone into the perfect gem.

As I felt my body finally sink into sleep, every reminiscent reminder of what I wanted pooled around my closed eyes. I finally began to surrender to the calmness and stillness around me. Those earlier prayers precipitated from my ceiling and came crashing down across my face in my dreams; hail storm kisses reminding me that I am not, myself, enough to survive what I needed to. I was too fragile, I was too weak, I was not yet enough. Before I could ever begin to know "peace," I must become first become "more."

More.

Act V

Smoke

"Where did she go?" Irene's voice startled me out of a deep slumber in my hanging cot, practically tossing me to the ground as I swung in my surprise. "We have to find her, how long as she been gone?"

"We don't know that she is in danger, Irene," Sara advised, trying to quell her daughter's nerves. "She could have gone for a walk; you know how she shuts down when she isn't feeling well."

I hurried downstairs, clumsily putting on my armaments in the event we were to suddenly mobilize. I knew that Evelynn didn't particular care for me, but she was an ally. More importantly, I promised Irene I would help to protect her family. She had shown me nothing but kindness and trust, even after learning the truth about me. I had to make sure I was the one to give everything should it come down to it, not her. Not again.

"So?!" Exclaimed Irene, clearly becoming a bit hysterical. "She went *last night.* She should be back by now. How do we know she didn't run into trouble?"

Karine appeared in the room, instantly and mysteriously as always as if she had been there the whole time, holding so still that we didn't notice she was there. She promptly glided on steady steps across the room to me, taking my arm and turning the corner from Irene and Sara before I could comment.

"We have to go. *Now.*" Karine harshly whispered under her breath. "It happens like this every time. We have to stop her." She looked me in the eyes, severity and desperation igniting her gaze.

I held her shoulders, keeping her in place as she practically vibrated in place with initiative. "Karine, what is going on? If you know something, we should tell someone." I narrowed my eyes to her, "at least Irene. She deserves to know what is going on. Can you share with everyone your insight without giving away anything potentially 'telling' about how we know it?" I asked in a shallow mutter.

"You really have been too kind, Ren," Karine assured, closing her eyes and rolling her neck in attempts to loosen her tension. "If we tell Irene what is going on, we risk her life." She touched my cheek, tilting her head in persuasive affection. "The two of us can survive what happens next, should it come to that. The only thing that will ever await Irene is martyrdom; sacrifice in death." She clutched the Clock Key around her neck and emphasized, "I've seen it time and time again."

"What are you two talking about back here?" Irene interjected boisterously "I know you know something, at least one of you do." She cut her desperate eyes in my direction. "Please, please tell me," she begged insistently. "If you don't tell me, I'm going to follow her steps on my own anyways. Whatever you're hiding, I will enlighten myself to it eventually. Please… we're friends, right?" She finished shakily, tears in her eyes as her lip quivered, her noble hands clasped in prayer.

Karine cut her eyes at me, knowing that the crumbling girl before me would melt my heart in her forging hands. I looked back at her, my eyes now sharing in the tears and my face contorting in pity for the angelic blacksmith. She didn't deserve to die, but she didn't deserve the indignation of abandoning her friend and never knowing what happens to her either.

"She went back to the Council. Last night." A voice rang from up the stairs, steady footsteps following behind their resonance. The three of us turned around to find Téo walking down the stairs. "She told me to tell you after the sun came up. She left just after midnight."

My eyes widened as I turned to Karine, knowing what was going to come of this. I looked to Irene, hands over her mouth in confusion and shock, "why would she go back there without us? What has she to gain from talking to them? Surely she isn't going to pursue the Wyvren alone."

"Worse," I said, the words leaving me before i could truly check myself. Karine and Irene turned to me, the contrast of their faces almost comical at my commentary. "I think… one of the Seasons got to her yesterday. The pink one?" I speculated aloud. "Irene, has Evelynn ever shown any signs of insecurity? You're the closest person to her, right?" I calmly asked, seeing Téo wince at the comment out of the corner of my eyes.

"Evelynn has always been the leader," Irene said, looking down at her hands as if they would reveal the answers to her. "Sure, I have always done most of the heavy lifting, but without her direction I haven't contributed very much on my own." She raised her head to look me in my eyes, the same ones she gave me in another life, "we have always been a team. I couldn't imagine why she would feel insecure about our family."

Gaultier's mighty steps resounded from the basement staircase as he ascended to join his family in this conversation. "Evelynn is my pride and joy," Gaultier began, his raspy voice chalky in morning words. "She would never turn her back on this place; not on me, not on Irene." He implored. "Whatever it is you're worried about, it is an impossibility. She is on a walk, clearing her head. She will be back."

Téo didn't speak again. While everyone else sat down to start breakfast, he returned to his room upstairs. I looked to Sara for answers, my eyes asking the question clearly enough without phonation. She shook her head, choosing not to respond to my gesturing inquiry of her son. I knew that Evelynn saved Téo from his fate, one outside of the Wyvren and without the guidance truly of Gaultier. Perhaps he felt indebted to her. Loyal not to the Chateaux, but to Evelynn herself.

The five of us tried to eat, all sharing in Sabine's meek silence while doing little more than skirting food around on a plate. Gaultier and Sara went back downstairs, leaving the four of us with our thoughts and the culinary mess to clean. We were washing the dishes in the kitchen, Irene and I, still silent, when we heard the crashing of porcelain and clattering of silverware from the dining room.

133

We rushed in to find Sabine, almost floating with toes on point, back arched and eyes rolled back completely to a ghastly white. Her tongueless mouth was agape as her fingers twitched, her arms jerking sporadically and suddenly in random directions until they found a rigid stop once gain. Karine ran to the end of the table, grabbing her sketch book and charcoal and flying back across the room to put them in her hands.

Before Karine could place the art supplies in her hands, she was blown back from Sabine's psychic force, the sketch pad and charred willow remaining in the air in place. Sabine raised a twitching hand towards them, configuring them in the air in front of her where the medium smeared itself in response to her vision. None of us had ever seen something so intense and violent hit Sabine in this way, Irene averting her eyes from the contortion of her dear friend.

The sketchbook ripped out sixteen pages, all aligning themselves in a four by four grid in front of her as the charcoal struck and blended a massive scene on the messy papers. Finally, when there was nothing left to draw with, Sabine's visionary fugue state resolved itself, causing her to become completely limp. As the remaining consciousness left her eyes, she went limp and fell to the floor with a morbid thud. As the papers began to fall, Irene and I rushed to Sabine while Karine gathered the artistic debris, assimilating them across the long table in the dining hall.

"She's alive," I said, checking her vitality. "Irene, can you use your new angelic healing power to try to revive her in some way?"

"I... don't think so." Irene said. "There is something that is telling me, my intuition maybe, that her mind needs to recover. I've never seen something come to her violently, much less in such a miserable way." She said, holding Sabine's hand.

"Ren, come take a look at this," Karine called in a level, monotone voice. I walked over to the table, Irene naturally following suit after moving the broken pieces of plates away from Sabine's face and hands as to not cut herself in the remains. It took a while for the image to make sense and come together amongst the chaotic scrawling that surrounded the periphery of the grid, Irene saw it come together before I did gasped, covering her mouth in shock.

Sabine's terrifying vision, rendered into visual ballad, showed Spring standing above Evelynn's dead body on an altar, while abstractly pouring a woman from several bottles and flasks from Evelynn's arsenal to form a woman sitting upon a throne, sharing her visage.

I felt the color leave my face, realizing that the severity of her vision was because it was not a possibility of the future; Sabine couldn't divine the future without Karine's insight. This was a prophecy; an absolution of outcome, forced into this witch's poor mind surely by Spring himself. He wanted us to know that no matter what we tried, it was futile.

"What does this mean?" Irene asked in a voice she was barely able to produce. She was a mighty warrior, but clearly her friends were her weakness. Between Evelynn's disappearance and Sabine's pitiful state, now capitalized with a mangled foretelling of her sister's mortality, I couldn't begin to imagine what Irene could be feeling. Based on her expression and frozen eyes, I don't think she could either.

"It means that we have to go. Now." Karine said, already changed into her battle gear; a floor length black coat, black leather armor the covers her chest and torso, extending fully in a lean chainmail that continued to her waist, where more black leather armor continued down her legs to her sturdy dark boots. She brandished metal gauntlets on her arms, a dimly hued steel that had a mysterious blue luminance to them. In her mastery of time, I believe perhaps she was briefly able to freeze our perception of her- there is *no* way she changed that fast.

"Ren, go prepare yourself. Quickly." She said, turning to Irene, trying her best to be sympathetic to her sense of duty for the only family she had left. "Irene… Ren and I are almost quite literally built for things like this. It would be best if you-"

"I know you know things, Karine." Irene, interrupted, stopping my tracks up the stairs and looking back at her. "I don't know how you know them, I don't know why you know them. While I'm more brawn than brain that doesn't mean I'm stupid." She stood her ground, her face now dry from tears and in their place a deepened leer of conviction.

"You've always been mysterious and aloof, but on every mission you always seem to come out of it unscathed, somehow saving me from situations it would have been impossible for you to see, even with your 'limited' perceptions of the past and future. I don't

136

believe that, especially not now." Irene accused in confrontation.

"I know that you are going to go and do something fantastical, and I'm sure you've done something like this with Ren before," Irene continued, "there is no way this impossibly powerful witch just fell out of the sky one day and knew exactly where to find you and who to ask to get there."

"Irene, I-" I began, reaching out and walking towards her before being interrupted again.

Irene held a hand up, stopping my words, "I don't need an explanation. Now isn't the time for answers from the two of you. You can tell me about yourselves later," in her interjection, she shared a lucid glance with me. Her defiance clearly a facade against our conversation the previous night. "But right now, you're dealing with Evelynn in a vulnerable way. And no one knows my sister like I do. Please, let me come with you to do whatever it is you're going to do. I can *help* you."

Karine and I looked at each other for a while, the tension pliable in the air between the three of us. Karine broke the silence at last with a response to her pleas, "Irene, you may come with us. But the *moment* things start to become to dangerous for you, I'm going to ask Ren to use her spatial powers to send you somewhere safe. No questions asked."

Irene nodded, an expression of certainty on her face. "Whatever compromise you are willing to share with me I will accept. All I can do is try. If I become a hinderance to protect, please, cut the slack and send

137

me away. I'm not too proud to accept that." She stepped closer to Karine, embracing her armored body suddenly. "Please, just help me bring my sister home."

Irene and I went upstairs, quickly suiting up in our custom matching armors from Vanna before heading back downstairs to Karine. Before we made our descent, something felt wrong. I turned to Irene and held my hand out to her, silently motioning us to halt. I looked around, listening intently to our surroundings. "Where is Téo?" I asked, tension and fear laced across my words.

We opened every door upstairs; every room, every closet, every trunk. Nothing. Téo was gone. We looked at each other and understood immediately that I was right to believe that he was loyal to Evelynn. He had followed her to the Tower. He was probably there now, almost certainly, to meet with the formations of Isadora. He would become Dorian again soon. It was all happening too fast.

We rushed downstairs, the moment I told Karine our discovery we were out the door, running full speed through the forest to the bare stone face that lead beyond the veil to the forming magical haven. Before Irene could begin to ask how to open the door without Evelynn's water magic to be ignited by her fire, I manifested the scythe I forged from Karine's dual swords I imbued with dimensional magic, Karine following suit with her temporal blades still in their original form.

"Wait!!" A sudden and frantic cry came from behind us; out of breath and nearly too late to reach us.

The three of us turned, adrenaline pumping through out bodies as Karine and I poised our weapons instinctually towards to source of the plea. Much to my surprise, it was Vanna, clumsily running through the forest towards us.

"Wait!" She cried again, her breath even fainter. She must have run all the way here from her shop in town. "Something woke me in the night and I saw Evelynn come this way. It was late and I was to afraid to come out on my own, but once I saw Téo follow her steps suspiciously this morning I thought I should come to investigate."

"Vanna, we really have to go. Evelynn and Téo are in danger," Karine said firmly. "I appreciate your concern for them, but this is something we have to handle. We have to save them, they are going to die if we don't get to them in time."

Vanna's flushed and sweaty face immediately turned cold and clammy. "What do you mean? Why would they willingly go somewhere alone if it was that dangerous?" Confusion swept through the seamstress's chestnut eyes as she began to teeter in place with anxiety.

I interjected before Karine could continue, "Vanna, please. This has to do with the beast that came a couple of mornings ago… the blonde woman?" I tried to subtly remind her without saying the word of our shared species.

"The Wyvren," Vanna said, eyes even wider, "are they going to find it? Why would they do that? Isn't the Council supposed to handle fighting that thing?"

139

Karine and I shared a glance, but before either of us could come up with an answer, Irene briefly demonstrated her knowledge of the esoteric information I shared with her the previous night. "Vanna, the forces at hand are very persuasive. The Wyvren isn't the only thing that we have to worry about, and the Council might not be the most trusting force either." Irene put her hands on her friend's shoulders and reassured her. "We are going to be alright. We are going to save Evelynn and Téo, and when we get back, you're going to have to design the five of us a brand new set of armors and outfits. Okay?"

Vanna fell apart into ugly crying, concerned tears wetting her cheeks. "Please, please don't die. You're always going off and doing dangerous things to protect me and everyone else- please come back." Vanna wailed, turning her sobbing eyes to Karine and I "No matter what, please bring my friends back."

Irene gave Vanna a parting hug and wiped her tears away. "There is nothing Evelynn and I can't handle together. When we get to her and Téo , with Karine and Ren's help, there is nothing we can't accomplish so long as we have each other."

With that, the two of us dug our blades into the stone, slowly rifting a portal at three points of impact and forming a portal in the shape of a triangle; the energies of Time emanating from the two points at the base, my concise domain of Space controlling the destination at the crowning point. Without question but with an expression of brilliant surprise, Irene turned a final wave of farewell to Vanna as she faded from view

140

and followed Karine and I into the portal, running full speed towards the other world where Evelynn and Téo were.

I looked around the colorful passageway, frantically checking for any evidence of Kieran, but there was no one to be found. Karine noticed me searching the in-between spaces and took my hand, pulling me along faster. She looked over her shoulder, smiling at me with a wink, and before I knew it we were out on the other side of the two bending saplings. Irene and I shared a sharp inhale at the forming town. It was drastically further along than we had seen even the night before.

The buildings were practically complete. There were circles for commerce and city squares of organized government, long rows of residential neighborhoods, stacked apartments and townhomes; all having sprung up completely over night. Irene and I gazed endlessly across the vast progression of this world, Karine breaking our trance.

"Time doesn't work quite the same way here as it does in our world- events ebb and flow in this place, not always faster than the passage of time in our world, but relative to events that we share." Karine explained, or tried to explain I should say. Irene and I looked at each other blankly, turning back to Karine to nod as if either of us truly grasped her rationale.

"We have to hurry," Karine urged, putting her swords on her back. "We have to get to the Tower."

We ran through the dreaming city, passing through the lights that promised potential witches with nothing at all a chance at a new life. I felt a strong guilt again at the idea of dismantling this place, only to remind myself that it only exists because Spring exists; there only needs to be a safe haven because of the danger that is assimilating this haven in the first place.

We reached the edge of town, just before the pathway to the threshold of the Tower stood the four Months we met with Alto the day before, all charged and practically crackling with magic. July spoke, baking the grass on the edges of the pathway, "our deepest apologies, we can not let you proceed any further." She martially commanded. "We are initiating new recruits as we speak. It is a delicate process." She reached her hand out by her side, a wisp of pink and green flames coming together to form a chain-link blade of fire that snaked down her side. "You understand, surely."

Before Karine or I could speak, Irene sprang into action. She dashed forward, arms outward to her side and calling various layers of steel to them, forging them into matching short swords in either hand. July coiled her flaming whip sword, releasing it in a fiery snap towards Irene. She evaded in a forward flip, landing squarely on the ground in front of her with a great deal of momentum ready to spring from her feet.

As Irene leapt full force with her blades towards July, she pulled her whipped weapon back, sliding across Irene's back and singing Vanna's thinly woven armor. Luckily, Irene still had plenty of metal resources on her person to shield her from various blows, including her back. She shed some weight with her forge fire palms from the short sword in her left hand,

142

rendering something closer to a dagger, suddenly tossing the still burning armament straight at December.

As July pulled the whip fully across Irene's flank, Irene used her now free forging hand to grasp the burning chain weapon, heating her fire so hot that the constitution of the ethereal weapon was disrupted. It snapped and sparked apart at her touch, giving way to Irene's innate mastery of fire.

December caught the dagger rather than dodging it. Despite the smoldering heat of the freshly smelted weapon, it cooled into a frosty dew, cracking to pieces at the sudden shift in temperature. Before she could interfere with July and Irene's skirmish, I removed the space between her and I, bringing her closer to me instead. Before December could orient herself to her changed surroundings, I had nine swords waiting just beyond our plane waiting for her.

December turned, beginning to manifest a handle of dried wood and sparkling blue ice, only to be stopped immediately by my swords literally tearing through the fabric of the reality the Auspice ruled, finding their home nestled in her throat, torso, and limbs. She turned a devastated look to me, blood spurting from her otherwise silent mouth, falling to her knees.

I turned all of the swords one foot counterclockwise, shredding her body while freeing my weapons from her. It was perhaps a bit of a disproportionate response, but I remembered August telling me the Months were functionally immortal. I'd rather her be immortal in pieces.

143

September crossed his legs and closed his eyes, his body not sitting on the ground but rather remaining in he air and his feet left it. He brought his hands together, palms touching and fingers extending upward towards his chin in front of his sternum. With a single inhale and exhale, he opened his eyes, creating an entire forest among the remaining six of us.

I ran forward, attempting to weave through the trees to catch up with Irene and help her destroy July, only to be met with icy darts from above, firing from the tree tops and following my path like a sniper. September's forest seemed to be a charming compliment to October's more nuanced abilities; concealing her in the trees while she exercised her precise assassination skills. Little did they know that just days before, I rendered a forest to mulch.

I reached inward, summoning the star fire of Scimariel's sacrifice and began to burn with angelic fire; the contradiction of the Wyvren resisting her goodness inside of my churning, creating even more fire and increasing my propulsion. Autumn's Grace ignited its sepia flames in my ankles and legs, burning the bottoms of my feet in exhaust to match the forging fire in my palms. Wings sprung from my back and my burning hallow spun around my throat. Like a small sun I erupted in combustion, burning everything around me within a ten foot radius.

I flexed my wings and launched myself upward, now soaring high above the tree tops, making my way to the edge of the forest. I could see Karine looking up at me, knowing I was aiming to disarm October as the

144

biggest combative threat in this scenario. She stunted the time around July and Irene, swooping in and extracting our ally to the outskirts of the forest.

Once time returned to normal and I saw Karine and Irene's retreat, I reached an even higher altitude before closing my wings around me, culminating even more heat and energy. In the sky I burned brighter than any constellation, igniting my fury as I began to fall, spiraling like a phoenix towards September's enchantment. I reached higher velocity, spiraling faster and faster, my trajectory a slight angle towards the forest's edge.

Just before I drove myself straight into the ground, I opened my mighty wings and forced all of the spiral energy forward, myself include, ripping through the canopy with the ferocity of a starving eagle. I ripped through the trees in their entirety, feeling the resistance of October's body caught against my pinions as they scorched the remnants of her corporeal body, rendering it to ashes.

September's focus broke in the carnage, falling out of the air through the short distance to the ground. He coughed in the smoke, grasping his throat and staying close to the ground, desperate for oxygen. I landed, my burning soles kissing the ground with an unforgiving char with each step as I approached the struggling Month. I raised my hand, calling only three swords, and impaled him through his head, chest, and abdomen. Even if he recovered, he was now pinned to the ground, unable to levitate which seemed essential to his spell craft.

145

I slapped my neck as I felt something like a mosquito bit lick across my neck. I looked around in confusion, there was no way an insect could have survived the inferno of my descent. When I finally turned to find July whipping at me with her enchanted fire sword spell, I laughed, audibly cackling as sparks left my mouth from the engine of my chest. Her fire was so meek in comparison to mine, I mistook her for a pest.

"Do not mock me, witch!" July roared, her heat influencing the forest fire around her. With each word, the flames near her were harshly augmented, "just because you are powerful does not mean you can dispatch my siblings and I! We are the *Months of the Year*. No matter what you do to us, we will *never* DIE!" She decreed, forming another chained weapon to her free hand.

"While I know I can not kill you in a way that matters," I spoke as the shimmering white angelic flames of my body licked across my teeth, "I can certainly put you in the ground as many times as you cross me. I will be your fate, Month." I threatened, calling a sword to my outstretched hand. "You may not ever know death, but I will be what makes you beg for its embrace."

July ran at me, both weapons poised like scorpion tales before me. The poor thing never stood a chance. In my spatial domain, and in her weakened state against my immense power, instead of removing the space around her, I removed the space within her. She stopped in her advance, frozen in pain and confusion as she looked at me across the burning forest

146

at the base of her gleaming obsidian stronghold. Out of her chest protruded the sword I was holding, in my hand I held her still beating heart.

She reached out, as if to take it from me to reinstate within her ribs, falling to her knees and leaning forward, unable to collapse fully as my blade propped her up. She wouldn't die, but she certainly wouldn't be a threat again anytime soon. Not until she found something to reconstitute her circulation anyways. With the least amount of ignition I could muster, I charred her heart with a cruel fire before dropping it to the ground. Before I walked away to meet Irene and Evelynn, I made sure to step across it. No matter what July ever did again, she would remember what it felt like to have the most precious part of her decimated beneath my burning feet.

"That was a bit dramatic," Karine chuckled as I dulled my flames and folded my wings to a tolerable level of heat. "Dramatic, but honestly pretty hot." She joked, laughing more at her pun than meaning her compliment towards me.

Irene looked at me in awe. "How... how did you become this powerful?" She asked me, her eyes glistening in the dying fire around us. "I have trained for so long to be a capable warrior, but I have never seen anything like you before."

I pushed my hair back, tying it back behind my head and out of my face. "There is nothing worth this power of mine." I said frankly, my eyes level with hers. "No matter what, nothing will ever justify this strength. I don't have this power by choice, but while I do have it I

147

will use it to right the wrongs I know are in this world. That is the only way I have learned to live with myself."

Irene bowed her head to me, "regardless of the circumstances of your creation, you are more than where you come from." She finished bowing and met my eyes again. "I truly believe that while we are responsible for our pasts, it is how we choose to move forward that defines our character."

She ignited her palms so she could take my hands. "The angel inside of me warned me the moment you appeared in the forest a couple days ago. But I told her that I could only see goodness in your eyes. While your sins are evident to the eyes of judgement, no such standard exists in my heart." Irene smiled and relaxed her gaze into what must have been my soul. "Ren, let's do our best together. I'm not afraid of you."

She knew what to say to me, almost as if she was speaking directly to the heart she sacrificed to beat blood through this vessel. I looked at Karine, desperate for something to say back. I turned my head back to Irene, who let go of my hands and walked back towards the path to the Tower.

"You don't always have to return niceties with words, Ren." Irene said, watching my flounder for a response. "Just keep me alive and make sure Evelynn and Téo come back home with us, okay?"

"O-okay!" I said, stammering again. Karine smirked at me, walking towards the path as well, myself following once I realized we were mobilizing again.

The dark obelisk of glassy stone stood before us, looming and shimmering in the surrounding flames of the fallen Months of the Council, leaving only Alto and Hector as functional members of Spring's new Auspice government. Karine raised her Clock Key to the base of the obsidian structure, the seams of the door forming instantly to its touch.

The great threshold opened inward, scraping against the illuminated floors inside. The contrast of the Tower had never truly stricken me until that moment- nothing but magical chromatic light constituting the innards of an otherwise sinister structure. Despite everything, the Auspice Tower was beautiful. We stepped inside to the levitating platform, looking up to see the geometric shapes returned to their spiraling and erratic constructs. The Tower had gained more floors and assets as it had before.

Karine commanded the platform to rise, causing and abrupt and swift rise from the ground as we passed through several floors of unknown value and purpose, offered by magical civilizations in recompense for asylum in this magical town Hector was constructing with Spring's enhanced power. The platform slowed to a rigid halt as we reached the top of the Tower, unknown conflict awaiting us on the other side of the of the doorway.

"We are here," Karine said, almost whispering it more to herself than to us. "And they know we are coming. Irene, you are here to talk to Evelynn. Téo will follow whatever direction she takes." She emphasized to Irene again. "If nothing else happens today, make sure your friends stay who they are. The Council wants to change them into other people; other personalities. We can't let that happen."

"I don't want it to, either" Irene responded. "Karine, I hope that you'll feel comfortable speaking to me in full truths when we are done with all of this."

"I'll tell you anything you want to know when this is all over," Karine promised her, smiling in affirmation. "Let's just get in and out as ourselves, everyone alive."

Karine raised her Clock Key again to the space where the door formed that lead to the Council in the sky. The seams of the door whipped open immediately, the winds stronger than I had ever experienced them in my few times enduring them. At the edge of the levitating pathway stood Spring above the stone altar, Evelynn laying down with her vials and flasks situated in a circle on the ground around her.

Spring looked up, smiling as if thrilled to have guests for his show. Alto and Téo stood at the farthest point of the horseshoe of the Council's platform behind Spring. As the clouds began to churn and a dim pink light shimmered through them, the Season greeted us. "Good evening, children," Spring's daffodil voice fluttered in gentle sweetness. "Have you come to watch me make a *real* witch?"

Truth

I moved faster than I thought I ever could. Every magical circuit, every muscle, every power at my disposal mobilized within me. Almost without realizing that any of the magics in me had fired, a glow of sepia light trailed behind my burning path as my wings launched me with maximum prejudice towards the malevolent father I never asked for.

I felt every sword in my disposal make contact with him, his smiling face completely still as my blades ripped through his image, only to phase completely through him as he became intangible to my onslaught. There was a burning in my chest, something indescribable as I opened my mouth, unleashing white hot fire into his face.

He displaced himself from his position beneath my blows with Karine. Before I could react to her placed in the way of my harm, I saw her burn and smolder beneath my flames. I practically bit my tongue off trying to stop the flames, turning to find Spring wrapping his insidious arms around Irene, finding his way to her neck and ripping out her frail human throat, twisting her head off as it rolled across the floor.

He then switched places with me- floating above Karine as she desperately tried to recover from the burns of a star's heat crashing against her immortal skin. He reached down, through her body to reach Evelynn, still laying down on the altar. Spring swirled the liquids from her flasks and vials, encasing her in iridescence.

Evelynn's eyes opened wide as the light of her spirit left through her mouth, lifting itself through the colorful waters she was submerged in. In a crushing tide of voluminous impossibility, all of her magical resources crashed down into her, filling the vessel of her body through her eyes and back through her gaping jaw. This was how he did it; he removed their souls, and replaced their consciousness with their magics instead. Isadora wasn't Evelynn brainwashed, but Evelynn replaced by her own powers.

As soon as she was assimilated, she rose from the altar, her eyes glistening with the sentient waters of Isadora's new mind, finding its way through Evelynn's body and familiarizing itself with its new home. Few things were able to appear grotesque to me, but in this perverse replacement ritual I found myself gagging at the wickedness of Spring's work.

"Ren, focus," Karine said to me, snapping me out of my dissociation. It happened again; a vision, the truth of ultimate possibility coursing through me from Karine's "other" Clock Key on my neck. If I charged him now, full force with the intention of his destruction, I was still leagues away from success. I had to think. I had to stay calm.

"Irene, stay close to us," I said, looking at Karine. Karine returned my concern with a nod. She saw it, too. As it stood, there was no success in sight, not as far as a combat strategy went. We had to rely on Irene to call Evelynn home and save her from whatever she thought Spring promised her.

"Evelynn," Irene cried from the edge of the platform, taking a step forward towards the levitating walkway. Karine and I both reached out immediately, each of us grabbing an arm. "Sister, please. I don't know what's wrong but come home. Whatever it is we can solve it as a family."

Evelynn remained still, her eyes closed and head rested against the reflective black stone. Was she unconscious? It seemed she was at least lucid in the vision Karine and I just shared. No, it was something else. She spitefully adjusted her shoulders against the altar behind her. She could hear Irene. She was ignoring her.

"Téo, please, help me reach her," Irene called out to him on the far side of the horseshoe. "You came here to help her, right? To bring her home?"

Téo stood still and unresponsive. He clenched his jaw and turned away from us, unable to raise his head and look at Irene. This was worse than I thought.

"She chose to come here," I said, choking on my words under the heat of my own flames beginning to swell in my chest. Unlike the vicious flames of rage I stoked in my most recent vision of charging Spring, these were flames of something much more bitter. I had of course heard of it over the centuries of my life but never had I yet in my conscious living seen betrayal in the flesh.

Irene turned and looked at me, the bitter flavor I was experiencing reaching her tongue as she realized

153

the same thing I did. She turned back, tears in her eyes, and screamed at her adoptive sister. "Evelynn, come here now!"

Evelynn raised her head, sitting up on altar, jaw agape with a sarcastic expression of exasperation, "and why should I go back with *you*." Evelynn snarled at Irene. "So you can steal something else from me? I figure if you want everything of mine so badly, you can *have* it."

Irene stammered, confused and insulted, "Evelynn, I don't know what you're talking about. What have I ever taken from you? I have done nothing but obey you, nothing but *love* you?"

Evelynn released a sigh, standing up and wiping her face in a superior air of annoyance at the presence of her sibling. "Everything was perfect. Gaultier and I, we had it all. But one day, we found you." She sneered. "Poor, innocent little Irene; same circumstances as me, just fresher so I suppose more important to my father."

"Evelynn... I was barely older than a toddler when the Wyvren killed my family," Irene gasped in response. "You think I wanted to lose everything so I could weasel my way into the lives of people I never met? Evelynn, you aren't making any sense. You're sad, you're hurt; let's go home and talk it out-"

"And after you took my father's favor, you showed just oh so much promise, didn't you?" Evelynn interrupted, walking down from the altar, stepping towards the other end of the floating walkway. Spring hovered above it all, smiling down at us in splendor as he spectated the tantrum.

154

Evelynn continued, becoming more and more enraged with misplaced envy, "you have never had to work for *anything*. I have spent years trying to become a capable warrior, worthy of one day taking over the Chateaux for Gaultier when he retires in his old age. But instead of becoming what he wanted, you demonstrate your superiority to me in every way, every day." She barked, her face reddened with spite and displeasure.

"Gaultier only puts me in charge to keep me around; he wants to give it all to *you,* not me." Evelynn continued. She stared into Irene with bloodshot eyes and tear-stained hair sticking to her cheeks as she grieved a crossing that she fabricated out of jealousy. "I don't care how perfect you are- you don't deserve the love we have given you. It should be mine. We should have left you in the rubble of that burning church to starve and die." She finished, laughing in mild hysteria. "At least then I could have had a happy life not living in the shadow of your strength."

"Evelynn what the hell are you talking about?" Irene choked through shock and agony. "You're my sister! I love you! I love our family! We only have each other- we have to trust each other, right?" Irene tried to encourage her, despite the cruel daggers Evelynn's words carved in her back. I remembered back to the timeline before at the Sinclair Estate; the shocking betrayal of Gaultier against her, now mirrored in Evelynn's choice to not only spite her sister, but to forsake entirely in her own rage.

Karine took a deeper stance, "never in all the times Isadora was created have I ever learned truly how

155

it happened." She didn't let go of Irene's arm as she continued, "I honestly never thought that she came willingly to trade her mind for power."

"Evelynn, do you understand what you are sacrificing for this? What are you sacrificing your mind-your soul for?" I called out, holding Irene's other arm that now trembled in my grasp.

"Power." Evelynn responded blatantly, scoffing at the question entirely. "I give up this wasted life of mine, and this god gives me a new chance, enhancing my magic to its true potential and giving me the opportunity to lead the new world." She began laughing more purposefully, "you think I would trade that just to return to a life living in the shadow of my replacement in our family? Appointed by my own father? *My* father?"

Téo held still, almost as if completely holding his breath beside the smiling Alto at the other end of everything happening. Whether he wanted this or not, he believed he owed Evelynn his life. If following her into this was what she wanted, he would sacrifice his heart, mind, and soul, too.

Evelynn walked back up to the altar, laying back down and closing her eyes beneath Spring. The Season looked at us from on high, his smile never fading, "oh, dear, did you think I had stolen her? That this wasn't her simply accepting my offer of pursuing meaningful leadership? While you try to resist this wonderful gift myself and my siblings are providing to stay safe from the Wyvren, Evelynn here is willing to answer the call to lead this haven for the magical world." He tilted his head, his smile churning as his eyes deepened to their

156

aggressive roseate hue, "how noble she is, our new ruler."

Spring raised his hands, willing the magical waters to rise from their resting places nestled in the circumference of the stone Evelynn assuredly rested upon. He opened his mouth, a pale snapdragon falling from it and landing on her chest. It was starting. It was happening. Everything I hoped to undo here was setting itself in motion.

I had to act. Whether or not I lost my life in that moment I had to fight or die trying; the only justification of my borrowed breath placed in Irene's mortal sacrifice to annul the furies of my past. If I died in this life, better myself and these innocent young lives.

I moved faster than I thought I ever could. Every magical circuit, every muscle, every power at my disposal mobilized within me. Almost without realizing that any of the magics in me had fired, a glow of sepia light trailed behind my burning path as my wings launched me with maximum prejudice towards the malevolent father I never asked for.

I heard Karine call out for me to stop, her voice fading in the friction of the burning air surrounding my ears as my wings narrowed to close in on my target. I had seen this before, all too clearly and unfortunately precisely as it was moments before my reckless decision. I was going to die. We all were. I had come so far but in all my years under Spring's will had never been made to show the decision of restraint. This was it.

Before my swords tried to bury themselves in their geometric spiral, bound to attempt to delicately julienne Spring's physically rendered body, I saw a loose collection of buzzing outlines; shapes of familiar bodies, pathways of possibilities reaching outward from Spring, Evelynn's body, my own body.

Time slowed as the key around my neck began to hum- I noticed streams of arms and weapons and swords all piling upon one another. I saw bodies fall, limbs ripping apart. I saw elegant parries and fatal strikes; a symphony of potential swirling around me.

A "Might" is alwasy unfolding, just not on the chapter you're reading.

Every timeline was crashing around me. I could see everything; every moment that doomed and saved us, dancing across the pages of the story we were living. I looked at Spring, his form catching up to the speed I was processing Time against Space while catching on to my access to the perception of the possibilities around us. His Azalea eyes widened with what I could only call delight, his smile now open-mouthed with awe and pleasure.

I followed his movements, anticipating his decisions against my initial vision and the flurries of possibilities echoing on the other sides of Time surrounding us. Just as before, he switched his place with Karine, but this time I knew it was coming. As Karine appeared in Spring's place, I was appearing beside Spring in Irenes; mouth full of a holy fire I immediately unleashed.

I could see it. I could see Spring's Might. Any possible choice he was going to make, I saw the unraveling of his options against the backdrop of Space. I could conceptualize it, follow it, read it. I was keeping up. I had to continue to see anything he Might do. Could Karine do this, too?

Spring fled from me, swirling himself away in his deep indigo robes and propelling himself back towards Evelynn, rendered incomplete in her transformation as the dewy snapdragon pulsed in rhythm with her heart. It was beginning to drink in the waters around it, rooting itself into her sternum. We had to act fast. I had to move faster.

I tapped into the vigor of Autumn's Grace imbedded in my legs, the pain of the Season's touch in my bones splintering my shins bit by bit with each increase in velocity. Spring knew that he had to start trying to become more unpredictable; following the more esoteric pathways of his other instances in attempt of avoiding me. The only way I could dream of keeping up was relying on the stamina he instilled in me, paired with the rage of his sister's gifts tearing through my legs.

Spring sharply turned in the air, diving directly towards Irene on the horseshoe below us. His grasp reached out for her throat as she closed her eyes, preparing for his unforgiving impact. But I saw the inklings of change dissipate from his hands; Irene wasn't his target. Instead of swooping in to save Irene, I displaced myself with Téo; Spring's grasp wrapping around my throat instead of his. It was all a ploy.

159

Everything he did was. I had to stop believing anything he said or did; especially his decisions with the mortality of those I promised to protect.

"You really have come such a long way, starlight," Spring congratulated as his nails grew into claws that dug into the arteries along my neck. "You were designed to evolve, sure; but I never thought you'd come this far. Maybe I should have given you a heart myself all those years ago instead of that pathetic little Lotus you think is strong enough to defeat me."

He smirked, leaning in and kissing my forehead as I was raised off the ground, my burning palms wrapped around his forearm as his grip continued to choke me. "It doesn't matter what you learn, it doesn't matter what you see. It's time to come home, Zorne." He coddled in an imperious voice.

I saw the riddling of potential shimmer across his throat as he condescended me, my vision blurring more and more while I felt the remaining oxygen began to dissipate from my blood. As I began to lose consciousness, Karine's sword screamed with a raging blue hue through Spring's throat, stopping in front of me just before my nose. She spun her blade, decapitating the Season, causing his body to release it's grip on me.

I fell to the ground in time with Spring's head, remembering Zorne's mother Raserei as her head fell beneath the gaze of her possessed daughter. I coughed, rubbing the bleeding wounds of my neck, quickly cauterizing the incisions his razored fingers left on my veins. His sentient cranium rolled to face me as I rose to my knees, finally catching my breath. He winked at me, and suddenly his head disintegrated into a fleeting pale dust that danced away in the tempestuous gusts.

Confused, I looked around frantically as I tried to adjust my eyes to perceive any possibility of his reanimation in another location, but all I could see was his headless body standing there, twitching lightly with no noticeable decisions following it. The visions of what Might happen faded from my view as the bright yellow lights of Grace also faded in from my ankles. It was a short pursuit, sure, but it still demanded a control over Space and a fluent reading of Time. My magical stamina was reaching a new limit after combining all of the new abilities my human vessel could run simultaneously.

Before I could rise to my feet, a gaunt and elegant arm of wood and vines burst from the stump in Spring's head; a small pink flower in it's palm. Outstretched towards the sky, the flower grew and bloomed exponentially, sucking all of the nutrients from the remains of Spring's body as if it were a divine fertilizer for the still-growing blossom.

The petals folded upward, pining with tension until they finally erupted in a glorious bloom. The flower was a massive Orchid, and inside sat a muscular woman, skin white as chalk and hair vibrantly brassy against the fuchsia petals of the bloom. She wore a black dress, barefoot and armed with two swords I knew all too well; the ones I preferred for each of my hands as well.

"Wyvren," I called, rising to meet the lavish entrance before me. "You are nothing but a fragile moment in the thrashings of this great journey of mine,

161

and I shall not be defeated by my past." I bellowed as I teleported immediately to face her within her own chrysalis. "Especially not when my past is as disappointingly weak as you are." I sneered, inches from her lethal gaze.

We stood in silence for a moment- only seconds; our glassy green eyes mingling a quiet storm in the air between our mutual stare. Then in an instant, my wings and halo burned again in great exhaust. The unforgiving heat bellowed from my soles and palms while my swords gathered to meet the great expanse of her precisely articulated blades. Karine dove over Irene, keeping both of them close to the ground as she knew the devastation that was about to ensue.

It was a bizarre experience, to say the least. She was prepared now for what I was, having analyzed my explosive power and memorized my previous attacks from when she ambushed me at Vanna's workshop. It was in her programming. She was designed to know exactly what I was going to do, and when I was going to do it next. Unfortunately for her, I benefited from the same programming.

The fight reached a lethal climax immediately, full throttle for about six minutes; my burning swords meeting her calculated responsive blades, my ignited strikes grazing her keen form as she learned to dodge my burning grasp. I unleashed another breath of fire from my chest only for her to anticipate it with a wind spell, blowing it narrowly by my head and back into the sky.

162

I was faster than her with a Season's Grace in my steps, even with the ever-present repercussions of accessing them so ferociously without reprieve for my legs. Lights flashed as our swords moved in and out of space; finding one another through the various dimensions we battled adjacent to, weaving in and out of planes in hopes of thwarting the trajectory of the other. But we were both too aware of the other's movements now.

I shouldn't have let her escape after learning how I worked. I shouldn't have shown her my whole hand in the beginning if I wasn't sure I could kill her. But, on the other hand, I would never have any hope of killing her at all if I didn't attempt to give everything I had towards her destruction. Her competence was a nuisance, but one I should have expected.

As the cacophony of our blades filled the sky with an orchestra of destruction that echoed through the enchanted city of Hector's design, Karine swooped in and slowed time between the two of us. We stayed there a moment, entangled in the clouds; a Lotus and an Orchid, both fickle flowers fighting for their spot in the sun of a violent Eden.

Karine floated over to me in the great stilling of our fight, tapping me on the shoulder and phasing me into the perspective of her sliver of existence. "Ren, here's your chance- I can't hold her still forever." She kicked off of one of my swords and slowly drifted back down to the horseshoe beneath it all, covering Irene once more. "Tear her apart!" She cried, her voice echoing as time began to start back up again.

163

I seized the opportunity Karine's power granted me. I raised every blade in my arsenal in a concentric strike around her form as her body stuttered in attempts to catch up to the speed of the light around her; her body darkened by the slowing of light that allowed her to pass through time to begin with.

I opened my wings like a mirror, keeping all of the heat of my hands and breath in front of me, unleashing a holy fire into her as my blades sank into her like the jaws of a shark; a great and unyielding maw of metaphysical teeth chewing through the Wyvren's body. Time caught up to her existence again, a muffled scream that ended almost as soon as it began as her blonde hair singed beneath the ferocity of Scimariel's flames. Her devastation was accentuated by a storm of steel dissecting her with the diligence of an efficient predator, ready to devour their favorite parts of their prey.

Her body, riddled with scorched steel, found a way in its Wyvren heart to remain in the air with me, a trembling charred hand reaching out for me. I extended my wings, summoning to my hand my scythe, and sliced her remains vertically from head to pelvis into two clean halves.

With that, the burning Orchid fell from the sky and landed in pieces against the obsidian floor with a disgusting thud. I felt the halo vanish from my neck as the feathers of my wings dissolved into light as well. I was at my limit. My scythe and swords returned to their planar scabbards in neighboring dimensions as I began to fall like a star towards the platform. Karine and Irene lunged towards me, catching me so that I didn't splatter as my past life did before them on the cold stone.

"Ren, you're literally burning up," Karine urged, holding the back of her hand to my head. "You did it, but just barely. You killed the Wyvren." She leaned in to give me a tight hug. "This outcome- this victory; it has never happened before. We're doing it. We're *winning!*" Karine whispered to the two of us.

I could barely feel my legs, the only semblance of knowing they were still attached was the harsh orange light of magical rot that was beginning to crack against my skin and tamper with the health of my bones. Magical rot was curable, but a vigorous tax upon the body. I pushed too hard, too far. While crippled with rot, I was completely defenseless, shivering and burning all at the same time in Karine's arms. As Karine celebrated and coaxed me in my pain, I watched Irene's eyes widen in fear as she looked on behind us.

I turned my head to the side to see Spring standing over Evelynn once again- the ritual continuing as if he had never been interrupted. The snapdragon sank into Evelynn's chest, and it all unfolded before me again, futile to stop it. No matter the victory, no matter the advancement, no matter the tips and tricks of otherworldly forces, he was still always several steps ahead of us.

Evelynn's eyes opened wide as the light of her spirit left through her mouth, lifting itself through the colorful waters she was submerged in. In a crushing tide of voluminous impossibility, all of her magical resources crashed down into her, filling the vessel of her body

165

through her eyes and back through her gaping jaw. This was how he did it; he removed her soul, replacing it with the sentience of her inherited magic. Despite our efforts, Evelynn gave herself to the tidal strike of Isadora; giving into the vanity of her self-proclaimed weakness in the name of a power that quite literally consumed her. It was over.

I reached forward, my legs and body useless to move as Isadora became realized beyond my reach. Karine's eyes glazed over with a numbness, surely having seen this failure before time and time again. I could feel the inefficacy of her esteem leeched by her broken spirit. I grabbed Karine's wrist, weakly reaching to grab Irene's with my other scorched hand, looking at the both of them with a deathly glance.

"We have to run," I choked out of the desert of my throat. "We have to run *now.*"

Karine lifted me into her arms, focusing her gaze at the edge of the levitating platform, a narrow rift opening just beyond us. I still had a hold of Irene's wrist until Karine and I stepped forward. Irene didn't move as my hand left her. I looked over Karine's shoulder to see Irene crying, standing motionless as she watched Spring extend a hand to Isadora, helping her off of the altar on which he just killed Evelynn's soul. Irene couldn't bring herself to look away from the monster that just killed the sister she loved more than anything else in the world.

"Irene, we have to go!" I cried, the fear of her death racing through my mind. Not her; not Irene. She had given so much, fought so hard, sacrificed

166

everything. But above all else, she was here and alive now. I couldn't bear to watch her die again. Not like this. "Irene, please, none of us will survive!"

She snapped out of her dissociation, finally turning to follow and run with us as Spring and Isadora watched on, a trembling Téo frozen in horror at the other end of the horseshoe beside a mystified and delighted Alto. Karine and Irene ran as fast as they could to the escape portal, my nearly useless body dangling in Karine's arms. Just as Karine and I began to enter it, a choked seizing of breath from behind stopped us.

Karine turned, revealing to us the sight of Spring holding her throat from behind, reaching into Irene's chest as if phasing through her being. As his arm receded from her, a luminous silver arm came with his grip, followed by a starlight winged angel. Spring pulled Scimariel from Irene's body.

"I learned from watching your 'alternate' outcomes on the other side of this timeline what caused you to eventually become this happy little ball of sunshine you exist as now," Spring sang, tossing Scimariel across the platform to Isadora's feet. "And wouldn't you believe it- I'm nothing if not consistent! Isn't this little firefly the *perfect* vessel for my Orchid?"

I released myself of Karine's embrace, falling to the ground and screaming to her, "Karine, stop him! Stop him now!" I writhed in pain on the floor as Karine sprang into action, both blades drawn and poised to strike. In a motion of ease, he switched Karine and I,

167

Karine now behind me and my broken body laying beneath him and Irene.

"Without that little angelic failsafe, she will bloom beautifully for me," Spring chimed, reaching the free hand he tossed Scimariel with towards the smoking remains of the Wyvren I just killed, the pulsing cube of its engine rising from its cindered corpse and flying to his hand. "I was ready to upgrade that version anyways- watching you after thriving in Irene and the sheer potential you've unlocked; it's outstanding!" He teased.

I couldn't let him do this, I couldn't let Spring burn out Evelynn and Irene's souls in the same breath. He didn't get to win, not all the way. As Spring motioned to lunge the Wyvren core into Irene's chest, I used every fiber of my being, every cell of my body and fraction of my spirit to cast one last spell. I conjured a sword to my hand, and in a single exhale, switched the Wyvren core with it. The dark device landing in my hand, my war tattered blade landing in Irene's heart.

Scimariel screamed, feeling her charge fatally wounded. Irene's face turned cold with shock, sputtering blood. She looked down at me, at the sword in her chest and the Wyvren core in my grasp, returning her kind eyes back to me and with her dying breath mouthed her final words.

Thank you.

I wailed in agony as Karine collected me from the ground, Spring's face twisted with shock and delight once again as he marveled my decision. I watched Irene's bloody face form her final smile as she closed her eyes, falling to the ground and knowing that despite

168

losing her life, she would rest knowing she was spared the fate of becoming a monster. Scimariel rose to try to charge Spring, Isadora trapping her in a standing vortex of watery enchantments.

The final vision I saw as Karine and I passed through the portal was Spring's pleasured face turning back to the Council horseshoe as Isadora encouraged Téo to join her at the altar, ready to give his feeble body and willing soul to Spring in order to forge Dorian. The misery of failure outbid the pain of my body as I felt my consciousness finally succumb to the overwhelming grief of our outcome.

Everything faded from view as the cold air of a storm pelted my face, my eyes adjusting briefly in their journey to see a bright yellow moon hanging high in the velveteen azure of a twinkling night sky. I heard the mumbled words of Karine and another, frantically taking me to a soft bed of moss where I felt the vague touching of hands across my quickly numbing body. The vision of Irene's bloody smile was the last thing my conscience gifted me as I finally succumbed to the traumatic embrace of my injured body.

Despite it all, despite the efforts we best knew to give, we failed.

We failed.

Authority

My body was useless, crumpled under the stress of burning so hot for so long. I was unconscious but hardly unaware, my eyes only closed because my brain was forcing my limbs to be still and the forefront of my mind to remain as unmoving as possible. My body was forcing me into survival mode, but my consciousness was racing. I was paralyzed by damage but every part of me wanted to go back and find a way to win. Karine had seen this outcome an impossible amount of times, but she tried and tried again for me. I owed these people the same resolve.

I calmed myself, unable to process enough information to fully grieve and physically unable to cry. From wherever I was, I couldn't leave, not in body. But perhaps in mind. I had to find a way through myself to reach the Precipice. I needed Kieran. I needed answers. I needed *something*. Anything to make sense of any of this.

No matter what I seemed to be able to accomplish, no matter how powerful I seemed to become; the culmination of centuries of destruction, imbued with the Grace of an ultimate being, enhanced by the light of an angel and the sacrifice of a holy witch. I was so much good and so much evil, so much power and so much experience. But it was never enough. Spring won every single time. How?

I receded further and further into the recesses of my mind, remembering the nostalgic enclosure of crystal and glass, trapped in the mixture of the sands of that place and Scimariel's vicious fire. I felt the sand in my hair, the ambiguous winds on my face, the coolness of the altar's brisk rock beneath my finger tips. And suddenly I was there, standing on the edge of that mysterious cosmos.

The artificial stars gleamed against the fabricated backdrop of deep space, the gasses and galaxies all the swirling moments of Time, trapped in the light of a frozen world, waiting for the moments of Space to slip up and let those moments become realized in our reality. I took a deep breath, closed my eyes, and followed through with my jump to nowhere, wind rushing through my hair as I all but immediately felt the coolness of marble beneath my ravaged feet.

"I was wondering when you were going to come and join me," Kieran greeted me, sipping his wine as usual, a full glass waiting for me in some kind of hospitable gesture. "If anyone on the planet needs a drink right now, it's certainly you." He finished, motioning towards the wine on the table.

I sat down, lifting the glass to my lips, emptying its contents in practically a single gulp. I set it back down on the table, it instantly refilling before I let go of the stem. I looked down at myself, even my astral body showing the symptoms of my graven state; the orange cracks of magical rot splintering from my ankles in bright lithic seams down my feet and up to my knees, my palms burned and wrecked from an unleash of heat from within they frankly weren't designed to handle, even based in Irene's body. These wounds weren't just skin deep.

"We lost it all," I said, my dry voice withered behind the bite of the wine. "Irene, Evelynn, Téo; Spring has his council, Irene's sacrifice perpetual in seemingly every timeline, my power nothing against his, even with everything I have brought together-"

"You're looking at these situations through a very narrow lens, Wyvren," Kieran interrupted, standing and walking through the magnanimous halls of the Liminal. He raised his arms to the rolling clouds above, releasing nuances and shuttering outlines of swirling dust and particles, all the same groups of people over and over again.

"There are some things that need to happen- that *always* happen. That is something that Karine should realize by now, and something you should accept early." Kieran emphasized. "Irene *always* dies, Evelynn *always* betrays here, Téo *always* follows her; in all of the possibilities of how things Might happen, there are pillars, cornerstones of events that simply must happen because that is how the story ends." He put his hands in his pockets. "People are flawed. *Always.*"

"How exactly should I be looking at these situations then, Kieran?" I asked, my fragile voice raising as loudly as I could muster. "Spring is getting everything he wants again and again, he has to be cut out at the knees somewhere. Where exactly do you suggest that happens?"

172

Kieran turned his head, gently leering over his shoulder as a bright pink iris met my seated posture, "you, my dear, have already interrupted the only thing that has *always* happened to you." He pointed at my free hand, the one I didn't drink the wine from. "You have successfully ended *you*."

I looked down at my hand. I was still holding the bloody and charred cube. It was the size of a fist and shimmering in hues of silver and gold. The Wyvren's core, the same one within me but primitive against my enhancements. The Wyvren from another world, another Time; one that I was able to destroy by my own hands.

"In your original timeline, you are a Lotus blossom," Kieran continued, "in this timeline, the Wyvren is an Orchid. Spring grows flowers, beautiful and miserable in their servitude of him." He walked back to our table, resting his arms against it, "his plan that night was for you to come, for you to kill the Wyvren and show it all of your fancy knew moves so it could eventually learn and master them, and once you killed it, successfully implant it in Irene just like he did with you before. Ren, despite it all, you won that night."

I felt my brow furrow with rage as my face snarled into a hideous confusion of grief and anger, "I won?" I said, still weakly but louder still, "they all DIED, Kieran; every single one of them. None of them survived."

Kieran rolled his bright eyes, sitting down again and rubbing his face with his hands. "Like I said, narrow perspective, tiny lens; you aren't understanding me. Let me say it more plainly: no matter what you do, no

173

matter how or when you do it, their fates are sealed. There is never an outcome where they survive." He said, his monotonous tone drastically contrasting his usual comedic and buoyant timbre.

I dropped my head in silence, wincing at his words and understanding the truth of their finality. I saw it all that night, the Might of every situation dancing around us, informing my decisions at every move. He was right, there was no situation, no decision I could have made that would have lead to us all making it out of there alive.

"You understand she is the one that is trying to inspire this demented sense of duty in you, right?" Kieran stabbed at me, suddenly in a new chair beside me. "I told you not to trust her. The more you listen to her, the more you waste your time ending up either dead or within an inch of your life as you use your power to try to be a human being before you are afforded the privilege."

"What do you mean? Karine loves me, she has only every loved me; over and over and again and again. She has moved heaven and earth to make sure she always finds me, protects me, and-"

"Will you stop thinking about this like a human and start thinking about this like a Season?" Kieran interrupted me again, this time his voice barely emanating from his mouth but more so from the very existence of the Liminal itself. The floor beneath me trembled as his beautiful visage darkened into a sinister gaze, freezing my broken body in my chair.

"You are so much more than human, Wyvren," Kieran spoke again, his face contorted with something that almost looked like grief of his own. "She is trying so hard to atone for her pact with Spring and do the right thing, but it can't be done. Not in the way she thinks it can." He turned his chair, leaning on the table with one arm, propping his head against it.

"Dearest Wyvren, you were created by Spring to destroy the world, but little did he know that you would be his very undoing," Kieran said, whispering as if it were a secret he was trying to convey in a room full of curious ears. "You neutralized four of the strongest Months of the Year, nearly all on your own. You didn't need the support, they were simply there in your way."

He continued, "they were liabilities, restraints on your unbridled power. You could have leveled it all in a moment if you weren't concerned about her, right? One day, when all of this is done, you can go to her, be with her, do whatever you want quite frankly, but right now, you have to focus on the only thing that matters; the *only* thing that has *ever* mattered."

He slammed his hands on the table, knocking over the glasses between us, wine spilling across the table and vanishing before staining the perfectly white floor beneath us, "you have to undo Spring, you're the only one who can do it. The Months are refractions of the light of their being, but you, you're different; you are the only thing in this universe that has ever been forged by the hands of a Season- the most powerful Season at that."

He became almost unhinged as his frantic voice continued, "he cannot die, no matter what you do. You have to become more powerful, more consistent, less human because there isn't time for that right now. The more you cry, the more you give him. The weaker you allow yourself to be, the stronger he gets every moment. Your friends are not your strength, they are your weakness. This is about you, and it has always been about you."

He stood, pacing back and forth, his Spring-like form becoming unstable as his clothes fell into a black coat and his tawny sun-kissed hair turning into a more umber hue. He faced me, his rose colored eyes now burning a bright red, "you have to rip his will from him and claim his mantle. You have to *become* Spring."

I woke up, sitting straight up in a meek bed within a pitched tent, the light of the moon spilling in through the seams of the entrance closure. My breath was shallow and quick as I looked around, my eyes tracing the night-veiled resting place set around me, trying to adjust my vision to my surroundings. And before I could even begin to truly wonder where I was, it all hit me at once: the pain.

I reeled, my spine shooting straight up as I felt the rot eating away at my legs, into my bones and through my nerves. I wretched and vomited, luckily leaning over the side of my bed as my body tried to make sense of the rushing waves of neurotic traumas pulsing with every heartbeat back to my brain.

I heard rustling outside as someone that heard me came to help me struggle through my awakening. To my dazed surprise and faint delight, I saw a familiar face lean in, white scars streaking across his tan skin and bright blonde hair ruffled in the air. August was back, here with me, wherever it is I was.

"Man, you look like hell, Ren." He said, an initial smile running from his face as he watched me shiver and gag, unable to form words as my teeth chattered. The taste of smoke and ash were damp in my mouth; stale somehow. I gestured weakly, pointing outside. I tried with all of my might to ask: *how long have I been unconscious?* August finally understood, nodding and taking my trembling hands,

"You've been unconscious for six days, Ren." August said, gently squeezing my hands. His amber eyes shimmered in the dark, the magic of his Month burning behind his eyes. "Karine brought you here and then came to find me. It was hard for me to agree to return to this place, but when I heard that you were able to kill the Wyvren? Spite Spring in anyway? I knew I had to come." He finished, smirking confidently. "You haven't let go of that thing since you got here."

I looked down to to find my frozen white fingers fixed on the Wyvren core Spring pulled form the Orchid. I tried to bend my fingers away from it on their own, but days of an exhausted and dehydrated body made me resort to prying it from my rigid fingers digit by digit. I heard each joint in my hand crack as I finally dropped the heinous device into my lap, glimmering with light that starkly contrasted the burns and dried blood stains smeared across it.

I stared at it, feeling emptiness against my apparent success against our enemy. I looked up at August, silent tears falling from my eyes and stinging against the silver and gold cube beneath them. I couldn't speak to him, but he knew what I was feeling; the shame and guilt that I couldn't shake. He leaned in, gently cradling my shaking body into an embrace. He stroked my hair, his cool skin and fragrant hair resting against my cheek as I weakly raised an arm to return the hug. With that, I fell back into the unconscious world.

My head fell back as I returned to my dreams, but instead of a soft pillow I felt my head smash against the cold white marble of the administrator's domain. I had never come straight back to this place before; it's almost like I was pulled here. I sat up, looking around for Kieran, remembering his image blurring and shifting from something that looked like a dapper Spring into something very different.

"Administrator," I choked, trying to yell as I weakly rose to my feet, "what am I supposed to do with this? What do I do with the engine?" I could feel my dry throat bleed as my own body stifled my screams.

"Take it into yourself, Wyvren," Kieran appeared behind me, his voice following behind my ear. His phonation was bizarre; incoherent and frictional against itself. There were levels of tones, his voice and a lofty higher pitch humming above every word. "Take it apart; shred it. The closer you can get your vessel closer to taking in Spring's power the better off you'll be. It's the only way you win- the only way you get to have her when it's all over."

178

I turned to lash back at him, but he wasn't there, just a broken table and spilled glass of wine, the scene shuttering like an illusion phasing in and out of creation. I looked up to the clouds, their thick obscuring forms thinning more and more; hardly more than wisps above me now, the ceiling still out of view.

"I can't take that monster into me- I don't *want* to become a Season." I cried, looking around frantically as the room spun around me. I lost my footing as my wounds ate away at my strength and cut me down to my knees. "I am just beginning, you can't ask me to take it all away now. If I'm Spring we can never be together."

"Ren!" Karine's voice stammered, my shaking head in her lap as I opened my eyes once again in the night, her worried face framed lightly with a smile to try to feign her evident concern. "Ren, it's okay. We're safe, I'm here." She spoke fully and calmly, stroking my face as I writhed in my bed. I opened my mouth, still unable to speak. I could feel my hand holding the core again, its dark radiation pulsing against my grasp as I resonated with Kieran's demands to metabolize it. The more I thought about it, they were less demands and more so pleas.

I fought with all my feeble might to keep my eyes open, trying to reach Karine's hand to squeeze. I looked up at her, my eyes stinging as I bit my lip so hard it bleed. My trembling hand stuttered through the air to try to reach her face, but despite my efforts darkness crept into my periphery and my I turned my head as I watched my hand fall to my side.

179

Instead of the softness of Karine's embrace I watched my hand hit the cold white floor again as I laid in Kieran's domain. I felt nauseous, the shifting between here and there against my full control in tandem with the pain pulling my stomach in different directions. I raised my head and looked up, barely able to stand to see the administrator, still cloaked in black and his now brown hair longer than ever. His shoulders oscillating with heavy breath, fists clenched by his sides.

"You aren't understanding me," Kieran's prismatic voice rang in his halls. "This isn't about what you want. Nothing has ever been about what you want. You have spent your entire existence following orders and directives; don't stop now."

I weakly rolled to my side, pulling my body up to rest on all fours, unable to fully raise my head to see him. "Say I agreed to this- say that this is even possible and I am able to house his 'mantle' or whatever you call it. How would I even go about that?"

I could hear his breathing interrupt at my sudden compliance. He was wearing me down and he knew I was not in a position to resist his words too ardently in my condition. "You are his heir, Wyvren," Kieran began quietly. "As I said, the Months are just sterile refractions of the Seasons, but you are made of what he is; you are the only weakness Spring has ever truly allowed himself and I'm not sure he even knows it."

"How do I use his paternity against him?" I replied weakly, my breath labored even more as I rose to my feet again, staring at his heaving back. "I can't keep

180

up with him, will taking the Orchid truly allow me the power to defeat him? And then… absorb him, too?"

I took steps towards Kieran, reaching out to him for him to vanish in a blackened mist that fell like ashes to the contrasting floors. I heard his footsteps retouch the ground as he materialized behind me. He was weakened somehow, I wasn't sure by what but something was causing a depravity to thrive within him; the image he wanted me to see of him corrupted. He was hiding from me.

"I'll hold still so you don't have to work so hard," I finally resolved myself, sitting down on the ground cross-legged away from him. "I want to know how I can beat him, Kieran. If subverting myself from humanity can really end all of this- keep her and everyone else safe- then I'm willing to try." I leaned back on my arms, looking up at the thin layer of clouds above me, "could I go back? Save Irene and Evelynn? Everyone else?"

I felt Kieran lean into something that vibrated through the room like excitement. "With the power of a Season, *the* Season, you'll be able to flip through the pages of these stories however you like. They will be on different planes; different worlds and stories, but you can keep them from ever even experiencing the calamity that is your existence. You can wipe away the Wyvren from history forever."

It was in that moment that I felt more than anxious- I felt fear. "So you're saying that if I do this, to truly make a difference and fix everything, I will throw this identity away? I will throw 'Ren' away and become the new Spring, just in my own image?" I uneasily asked, more in a realization than question.

There was a period of silence between us. In that deep hum of nothingness briefly dancing with the light drafts of the winds above, I knew what i had to do. I stood up, brushing myself off. I turned to face him, and before he was able to fully vanish, I saw a glimpse of "him."

Long brown hair that draped over their shoulders, a narrow face framed with brilliant blue eyes set in a pale face above a narrow neck. They donned a tattered black robe, shredded black leather armor underneath it with tattered leg gear to match. They misted away again before I could truly get a good look at them, but I knew where they would be appearing next.

I turned my head, standing as quickly as I could and taking a large step towards my inverted trajectory, finding myself staring them down in the face. I was inches away from their face, blue eyes staring into mine as I saw scars and wounds across their jaw. The administrator had somehow fooled me. Everyone, everything had somehow fooled me.

I was jarred awake only to see that same face looking down at me that I was just confronting in alarming confusion. If not for the night setting to spite the visions of the white Liminal, I wouldn't know if I was awake or asleep. It was all too obvious- the place, the goals, the knowledge. Even the name.

Karine took my face again, seeing my conscious state as she poured water down my throat in her arms.

"Stay with me, Ren. You've been asleep for too long, we need to get your body healed back up. We can't hide in here forever." She pulled me up to lean my back against her abdomen, my body resisting every inch of movement.

I struggled in place, trying to raise my hands and move my legs, wanting to stand and face her; almost run from and accuse her all at the same time. Did she know? How could she not? She was steps ahead of me, always. Why would the administrator tell me not to trust her if it were true? Why would Kieran ever marvel such a solution for me to follow?

Kieran  Karine.

She didn't even change all of the letters of her name. She just *knew* I wouldn't ever be smart enough to figure out that if she put on the scary face of Spring and shook up a couple of letters. Or at least she thought so. How was she here and there at the same time? Was this a different Karine? Was this really the "check point" of the woman I loved?

"Let... let me go...!" I choked out of my mouth, blood spattering from my lips as I aspirated the rest from my hemorrhaging vocal folds. I rolled off of her, choking and vomiting again, weakly holding myself off the ground and the barf below me. I tried to stand but couldn't, the magical rot in my legs still splintering my stance.

183

"Ren, Ren what's wrong?!" Karine cried desperately, following me to the ground and she gently placed her arms on my shoulders, causing me to wince from her touch. "August, come here, something is wrong!" She cried, tears welling in her eyes. Why would she cry for me? Why would the administrator, the "Year" in disguise be concerned about me? She wanted me to throw my life away so that everything would go back to what it would have been without Spring; without me.

August rushed in through the opening of the tent, his face twisting at the smell of my upheaval and with confusion of my resistance. "Ren, lay down, we can start the process slowly; don't push yourself, you're going to get hurt."

I coughed so hard more blood spewed from my mouth, the thick coagulation further messing the floor. I found a burst of strength in my desperation to project myself past August, bursting outside to find cool damp grass against my cheek, rolling over to see the largest moon I had ever witnessed hanging in the navy night sky. I sharply inhaled at the beautiful sight, almost forgetting the turmoil of my revelation.

I didn't know why I was running. In this state I was as useless against them as I was Spring. I let my body go limp, feeling the blood dry against my cheeks as I resolved myself to stare blankly at the night sky above me. I heard Karine and August come through the tent, their footsteps cautious as they approached me. I could see the two of them come into either sides of my periphery and look down at me, their faces on the left and right of the angelically silver moon above us.

184

They looked at each other in concern, looking back down at me as I felt my strength leave me once again, my mind fading. I didn't want to go back, tears flowing down both sides of my head, adding to the dew of the grass behind me. I didn't want to be thrown back to the Liminal, back to "him." Or "her." Or "them." Or whoever they were. Despite what I had learned I just wanted to be here with Karine.

I felt myself begin to finally fully slip away again, but before I returned to the Liminal a final time that night I used the last of my strength to whisper a phrase to them, their caring faces leaning in closely to listen to me. "Bring core. On chest." I exhaled quietly.

I listened as August reentered the tent, Karine's face stricken with fear and distress. August returned and did as I asked. I felt the weight of the Orchid's heart rest against my chest; it felt like it was almost sinking in on its own. I closed my eyes, intentionally this time so I could gracefully land in the Liminal again on my feet.

"You came back," the administrator's voice whispered quietly, having remained in the form they were in when I left. "Seemingly on purpose. I must say I'm surprised."

I walked over to the table where Kieran was seated, joining them. "I know it's not your real name, but I'm going to continue to believe that the Karine I'm with is different from you somehow." I looked them up and down; their familiar armor above a scarred and immortally youthful face. "What happened to you, Kieran?"

185

"You did," they responded flatly, "you, the Wyvren, Spring; everything. I fell in love with you, you fell in love with me, and the world fell apart. Everything fell apart." She didn't look away from me when she spoke, a completely hollow look on her face as if she had died through those words a thousand times. Just like my Karine, this one had come to this milestone time and time again. I was a due process in their agenda, constantly unfinished.

"If I become Spring, I can finish the story you told me about Karine, right? I can finish *your* story. I can set you free from this eternal life." I rationalized, putting it all together. "You somehow came to become this in your travels; a decision you made, a circumstance you pursued, you became trapped here in the in-between as the Year because you tried to solve this without me. I've never agreed to become Spring, have I?"

A flicker of light appeared behind her empty eyes, a vision of hope in response to my words. "No, you've never agreed. You rarely find me here, actually. I thought that if this time I took on a new persona you would be more likely to comply. Because you were right before. 'Ren' will probably go away if you become Spring." Kieran shed a surprising tear and continued, "I have spent an eternity loving you. It isn't easy for me to ask this of you. But this is bigger than the two of us, don't you see?"

"You're right." I immediately responded. "You're right. This is bigger than me and Karine. I have the opportunity to truly undo every evil. I have the opportunity to become Spring in every instance and undo his deal with you. If I comply, I save the world at the sacrifice of a life I was never meant to have in the first place."

Kieran leaned across the table, reaching for my hands, "I see the Wyvren code sitting on your chest there," they observed. "I can help you take the first step in absorbing that. I can help you integrate it into your code. Once I… became the Year, I learned the language Spring used in your coding."

I reached out and took her hands, "do it. Please."

In a blink I was laying on my back on the table, the completely white room now aggressively familiar. Kieran had modeled this space of the Liminal for me to find after the maintenance room; this entire place was configured for me to agree to be modified, the conditions the same Spring would use to make changes to me, too. It was all too brilliant; evidently years in the making for a "Ren" that would come here and finally say "yes."

She raised her hand, the cube lifting in a slow spiral off of my chest, the Lotus of my heart blossoming in tandem, larger than me and glowing in heavenly golden light. As the petals fell across me and overshadowed my body, I could still see through them as Kieran opened the Orchid core; the same bright blue runes and words spilling out of it as they did from my own.

She reached her other hand to the Lotus and unlocked it, my similar code rising from me like a small cyclone. I watched Kieran work, overlaying similar lines

187

to one another and connecting them, deleting some of the Orchid's information and breaking it apart into usable pieces, not removing any of my code but enhancing it with parts of hers.

As she worked, I felt my breaths get deeper. I could feel the magical rot in my legs begin to recede. As she was installing the other Wyvren into me, it was healing my body. I was taking the Orchid in like food and medicine as it nourished my body, putting me back together but better. Stronger.

After what felt like hours, she finally finished, the Orchid cube completely gone; either dismantled and installed or discarded in bits of scraps that floated up gently to be eaten by the clouds above, lost in the Liminal forever. My Lotus, still vibrant and gold, felt heavier; bulkier and more armored. My petals closed and my blossom retreated back into my chest as I sat up on the table, looking at a dazed Kieran, smiling and dissociated.

"Is that it?" I asked, feeling more than better, but invigorated as well. "I feel incredible, Kieran. You did more than integrate her, you fixed me, too."

Kieran snapped out of their gaze, looking at me with a smile remaining on their face. "Ren, I'm sorry for my harshness." They began, "I'm so, so tired. And every time I watch you come here and fail has made me so bitter." I sat up as they took my hands, putting their forehead against mine and closing their eyes. "Even if 'Ren' goes away and all of this is done, know that there is a whole eternity of our love written into the bones of this place. None of that can ever be taken away."

188

Before I could respond, I felt myself waking up one again, laying in a clean tent in the night still, opening my eyes as an exhausted Karine ran to my side, "Ren, please don't move. We don't know what happened but the other Wyvren's core went into you and-"

I raised a finger to her mouth, interrupting her frantic narration. "I know, Karine. I incorporated it into my code." I sat up, my physical body reflecting the healing done in my astral one by Kieran. "About before… I'm sorry. I woke up, I was confused, I was having visions that didn't make sense. I didn't mean to run from you." I apologized, feeling odd that I knew something Karine didn't.

Karine leaned in and embraced me, squeezing me so tightly in her arms. I leaned back into her, resting my head in the nook of her neck and shoulder. I saw August come to at the edge of the tent, waking abruptly from his sleep as Karine and I stirred in the night.

"It's okay. You've been through a lot." Karine accepted gently, whispering in my ear. "Just because you can take on every enemy on your own doesn't mean you have to. You should have left the Months to us and gotten a head start- you didn't need to exert so much effort defeating them before we went up the Tower to Spring." She squeezed me tighter, "I shouldn't have let you carry so much of the burden."

"Yeah, that's how you end up sleeping for three weeks, dummy." August commented through a yawn, stretching his arms over his head as he settled into consciousness.

189

"I've been like this for three weeks?!' I said, bolting upright from Karine's gentle embrace. "I should have absorbed the Orchid core at least two weeks ago!"

Karine and August quickly glanced at each other before Karine explained to me, "Ren, the core just now finally settled into you. It has been sinking into you since you lost consciousness again after August put it on your chest."

I stood up, a little wobbly from not having moved my muscles in weeks, stepping outside to find the same giant moon and same dewy grass from before. I looked down the meadow to the ridge to find a giant rock face with a reddish green splatter across it, knowing instantly where we had been hiding all this time.

"We're in Midnight," I said to myself, looking around. I turned to find August and Karine coming to join me outside. "Have we been here the whole time?"

"Yes," August said proudly, "you haven't spent nine hundred years here like I have but we have been hiding out here for a couple of weeks."

"Can Spring not find us here?" I asked, fear starting to creep into my voice.

"Not here," Karine said assuredly. "We were able to sneak into this Midnight just before the clock turned. Spring had other things to do, having just created Isadora and needing to create Dorian."

I looked at both of them, more confused than before I asked the question. "*This* Midnight?" I asked further. "How many 'Midnights' are there?"

Karine laughed an innocent chuckle, covering her mouth and trying to straighten up as to not insult my query, "for every midnight lived, one is available to find."

Dawn

I felt heavy, noticing immediately the weight of in my chest of the freshly installed Orchid. The bloom felt foreign and familiar all at the same time as it nestled itself within my heart, now fully integrated and modified to Kieran's specifications in relation to my function. I couldn't shake what she said, thinking over and over again about the Mantle of Spring and the inevitability of my fate. I kept questioning if it was something I could talk to Karine about, but ultimately understood that if she truly saw it as an outcome she wanted to explore, it would have happened by now. She was protecting me from embracing a fate she knew I would receive as a curse.

"We've got to get back to the other side; back to the Chateaux and tell Gaultier and the remaining others what happened." I said, stretching my arms and legs in the grass in attempts to limber my rested body back to a capable flexibility. "If we tell them what happened, is there any way they can help us undo what Spring has done to them?"

"Unfortunately, Spring truly didn't do anything to them that they didn't want to happen," Karine responded, August remaining silent as he swirled the dim bluish green of the grass in his palms. "All he did was answer Evelynn's request for power and Téo's desire to serve her. Even if we could get Gaultier to get through to Evelynn, there is a part of her that believes she is even more useful to him in this way. Spring took what she wanted most and used it to corrupt her spirit for his gain. She's gone, Ren." She finished, watching my dissatisfaction darken my eyes.

I knew she was right. Spring did what he did best: took what was thriving and helped it to thrive. I was beginning to see more and more that despite his aggressive talent for fostering greatness, it was all too often a greatness unwanted. Evelynn was beyond saving, even further it seemed futile to save Irene as well. Everything felt hopeless, futile even. I had a new objective, independent from Karine's grand plan that I wasn't even fully sure of either. How was I supposed to pursue Kieran's objective while keeping my comrades in the dark?

"We've got to start training up." August suddenly broke the silence, standing up and dropping the dimmed hues of night back to the loamy soil beneath us. "Ren, you absorbed the other Wyvren's engine right?" He turned and looked to Karine, the two of them seemingly already knowing where the conversation was headed.

"Yes, it was incorporated into me. I absorbed it with a survival program in my code." I lied, trying to further obscure any contact with the Liminal at all. "It was something I never even knew I could do. Perhaps Spring speculated that I may time travel at some point and other instances of the Wyvren may challenge each other."

Karine reached out a hand towards me, standing up herself and gesturing I rise with them. "We

193

were speculating that may be the case," she began. "We were thinking that perhaps… another Zorne may be locked away in that engine as well." Her face revealed a restless discomfort at the acknowledgement of the potential miserable gnashing beast at the center of my existence.

We all stood in silence as I digested what they could possibly be getting at. The two of them looked at each other, making me feel even further alienated in my absence of consciences through the previous weeks. "You want me to try to draw on the feral power of whatever poor witch was locked away in the Orchid's timeline?" I gestured my hands in exhausted speculation. "I bent Zorne into submission because she meant to make me a beast again. This poor soul hasn't done anything to me-"

"Yet." Karine said coldly, clearly a little bothered by my clear exasperation after weeks of caring for my battered body. "That 'poor soul' hasn't done anything to you yet. But if that Wyvren made it this far, then she will do her best to get to you, just like Zorne tried to." She clenched her fists by her side and met my weighted eyes with a severe glance. "And if I die again in this timeline and you can't save me again, despite everything you've invested in this power you have, the unfortunate weakness of your heart may sway you to seek other sources of power."

"We know that it isn't an easy ask for someone with a conscience," August interacted, his words a welcomed knife through the palpable tension growing between us. I had never been so resistant to Karine's

194

orders before. Could doubling down on the Wyvren's presence within me really already be effecting me in a visible way?

"You're right, I'm sorry." I immediately checked myself, taking into account that giving into the dissonance of this situation, or any for that matter, could further agitate a force within me I didn't take into account when Kieran installed her. At the end of it all, Kieran was still holding more cards than they were willing to show me. It made sense to a certain extent, keeping me a pawn at arms length. Was that all I was here? To Kieran, Karine, Spring? I was built to serve but without my consent am I a willing servant or a mutable slave?

"Ren, are you okay?" Karine asked, relaxing her ferocity and taking a couple steps towards me. Before I even found the words in my mouth to respond, I felt the cold steel of a sword hilt meet my grip at the end of an outstretched arm, pointed at her advance towards me as my vision blurred. It was just for a moment, but somehow, even at the mention of her presence, I felt a loose cage rattle in my chest and my eyes darken in a way they never had before.

August was immediately on me, gripping my wrist and resting a much gentler hand on my armed shoulder. "Ren, calm down. Karine is our friend, remember?" He tried to assure me. I didn't trust him. I felt a creeping anxiety. I felt like I was sinking under water. I lifted my chin as the tension of the imaginary fluid rose to my chin, my lungs gasping for air that was more than available.

Karine tipped my sword down with her hand, my extremities weak and tingling as my body became hyper-oxidized. I stumbled backwards, the weapon dissolving from my grip. I cradled my face in my hands and raggedly breathed through my trembling fingertips, eyes wide with confusion. Was I malfunctioning somehow? I felt like I was fighting for my life as flashes of Irene's death flickered in front of my vision like desperate candlelight.

Karine and August were talking to me, I could hear sounds outside of the crashing oceans in my ears but I couldn't make out any of the words. I had to get out of here. I wasn't ungrateful but everything suddenly became miserably overwhelming; overstimulating. I knew how to escape this place, I had done it before. I knew how to release myself. It would expose me to Spring once again. Was that what I wanted?

I writhed, still unsteady on my feet as every part of my being wanted to run home to my creator. Every fiber of my being craved the crib of stability offered to me in the subordinate embrace of Spring in the maintenance room. The release of emotions, the tender care of someone I made proud, regardless of how perverse and demented. I could feel light enter my hands and a refracting lens began to form around me; the familiar spell of bending the moonlight to sunlight, the spell I used to turn the hands of Time forward and break me and August out of here once upon a time.

But why did I suddenly want to leave so bad?

"It's her, it's already happening." Karine urged, grasping my shoulders and forcing me to my knees with her. We fell to the damp ground together, her hands warm and gentle but calm and steady on my confused body. "Ren, she's waking up as you are. You've got to fight her. Whatever you did to Zorne you have to do to her, too." She urged, trying to coach me through breathing and affirmations as if I were in labor, except instead of bringing something into the world I was trying with all my might to snuff it out.

The refracting lens began to hover above me, the spell taking on an autopilot quality based on my actions before. I leaned back, my hands falling to my sides from my quivering face as my Lotus bloomed from my chest; almost releasing magical pressure from my body as a force dueled with me silently behind my eyes. I felt a sudden rush of pain as my wings burst from my back, from between them a glistening red Orchid bloomed from the center of my spine.

I was frozen, completely breathless as I felt the fabric of my being began to disintegrate from itself. Kieran put this in me to thrive with the Mantle of Spring. Did they fool me? Did they trick me into becoming the vessel for the rebirthing of this monster? My thoughts raced as Karine was pushed away by the force of the bizarre garden that constituted my torso.

Still looking up, I could see the reflection of my body from above, front and back as the flowers swayed in their magical ambience out of me. I felt nauseas when an abrupt pressure hit my back. With striking pain, a slender arm erupted from the Orchid in my back, long and elegant in its extension. With a cutting pain to my torso, I felt a wrenching ache in my sternum as two

197

arms and a head of dark brown hair peel its way out of the Lotus in front of me.

With all of the wringing emaciation of the combative forces rupturing from my body, finally the two forms pulled themselves from me entirely. I choked on the scattered breaths I was taking as the Blooms closed and shrank back into my body. I felt hollow. I felt vacant. My eyes rolled back and for a moment I felt my world spin as my head hit the ground, thankfully the force alone was enough to return to me my vision and consciousness.

I dragged myself across the grass towards Karine, rolling onto my back to try to understand and perceive the abrasive expulsion from the inner expanses of my soul. Before us was Zorne, tall and slender with her thick dark hair chasing down her body, wearing nothing but a tattered and stained white dress. Across from her was the visage of the Orchid Wyvren I killed before we escaped to Midnight; equally tall, but slightly different from her most recent form. Blonde hair cascading in tussled waves billowing over her shoulders, a loose black dress in almost pristine condition covering her body to the knees.

The iteration of my first life as the Wyvren stared down her parallel existence, both of their faces cold and calculated. They began to circle one another, bare feet christening the grass with an esoteric poison that hissed and rendered the very soil to ashes in the path of their destruction. Zorne raised her hand and called a sword I felt leave my arsenal. She had access to my powers not

198

independently from mine in this form, but in tandem to them. Goody.

Much to my surprise, the blonde antithesis motioned not swords, but spears to her disposal; all in the same circling geometric reactions my blades were akin to. I distinctly remember crossing swords with her, perhaps she diversified her weapons over time. Could it be that she developed a preference of one over the other on her own without developing humanity the way I did? Was that something Spring would truly allow her to do?

"I knew that one day I would be released from my prison," Zorne said, still carefully treading her steps in the dewy grass between them. "I never thought it would so directly come from something like this."

I finished dragging my shaking body to Karine and August, my refraction spell still lifting higher in the air above the five of us. The Orchid grasped a spear in one hand and called a sword to the other; the both of them poising their levitating weapons behind them in the striking pose of a scorpion.

"And never did I think that I would need such liberation." The blonde Wyvren responded. "I was simply trying to escape that mortal flesh over there." She snidely commented, gesturing her head over towards me. "Trust me, releasing you was never a part of my agenda. But what a happy accident that there was more than one person to share in my miserable fate."

It was indeed the other "Zorne;" the original life sacrificed from the Orchid's timeline. Instead of sharing

199

her identity, Spring had come upon another talent in her youth to embed this Wyvren. She was capable of speech, showing us that this was not the fully evolved Wyvren that I destroyed, but the initially talented lifetime imbued with the Wyvren's powers. Where there was once one atrocity in this world with only myself, now here in this timeline were three.

The two Wyvrens slowed their steps, and before they mutually completed what appeared to be their final turn they were almost completely gone from sight; centuries of rage and entrapment exploding through their motions. Even with my keen eyes for combat I could only watch the collision of their weapons; glimpses of sparks and the flashing lights of spells beginning and resolving. Ultimately they were a perfect match of carnage for one another.

"Karine, what's happening," August said, Karine readying a magical barrier around us as she helped me to my feet. "Who are those people? Can we leave them here?"

After catching my breath, I realized that I didn't feel weaker. Sure, there was a trauma of Zorne being ripped from my code and my body; exacerbated by this mysterious blonde woman's mutual unexpected exodus. But there was a levity in my chest. I felt lighter, some how even more flexible. It was light a metaphysical and literal weight lifted off of my chest.

Before Karine could speculate I explained Zorne and her existence as my beginning lifetime and Spring's initial sin against my mortality, and that she was doing battle with the Orchid's first lifetime. "I wonder if it is somehow a natural conflict happening in front of us," I began to speculate as well. "Something of two apex predators finding one another and instinctually doing battle in hopes to claim territory."

"What territory would they be claiming in this place?" Karine said, summoning a thick protective barrier as the whirlwind of violence scarred and scorched the lands in front of us.

I stood up, phasing myself through her protective barrier and invoking the burning heat in my chest; spreading my wings and igniting my palms and feet. I turned to look at Karine's face as it faded to a calm and confident understand of my resolve.

"Me." I said turning back to face the ancient evils before me. "The territory they're fighting over is me."

My halo illuminated in divine circumference around my throat. I could feel my skin rise in temperature as my runes emanated a gentle glow and steamed the air around me. Zorne was using all of my swords, but perhaps it was time that I left those old weapons to her and her past anyways. After all, they belonged to her people to begin with.

I raise my head towards the floating lens above, still holding its position in the air above the battlefield from my failed manic escape attempt. I called it down to me, the gentle ring of light wafting back towards my grasp. I transmuted it's purpose; keeping the purpose of light manipulation but changing from refracting light to honing it.

201

I bent the ring onto itself to form a semicircle, winging each of the tips and spinning a thin string of light from my forging hands. After gently stringing my creation together, I had forged a great bow to respond to my luminous angelic magic; one step further from the resources Spring stole from others and gifted to me in some perverse parental care.

I was not here to entertain the mettle or resolve of souls beyond the point of salvation on their own. These women, these poor, talented, destroyed women; they were fighting to take control of me as a vessel to continue Spring's work in some narcissistic attempt towards independence in their destructive choices. They couldn't even see that they were fighting, even now, for his gain.

I took a deep breath and closed my eyes, exhaling a cloud of steam as I crouched into a lower stance and readied my wings for take off. They were moving fast, but they were each the prototypes of destruction. For better or for worse, I was the current model. I was faster than them. I was stronger than them. I sensed their impossibly fast movements and anticipated their next landing points. With another deep breath, I launched forward into the uncertain cataclysm of their battle.

It was like stepping into a sandstorm. There was so much magical residue from spells being interrupted over and over again by mirroring almost perfect understandings of each other's move set. They were a perfect counter for each other, leaning not on their own understandings but the mindless repetition of the code left in them by the ghosts of their engines my body now sustained. My endless thanks to Irene for giving me a heart and mind to think for myself.

I stood in their midst, their focus on each other's destruction so fixated they never began to notice the burning starlight that stepped into the fight. I took a moment and watched them above me from the ground below, a small fire starting beneath me as my potential energy ached to leap into their commiseration. They were interlocked with one another just a few feet above me; faces laced with conniving pleasure.

Instead of disgust or fear, all I could feel for these mutual forces of nature was pity. It was watching two lions in captivity fight for the steak thrown to them by a zookeeper; once kings of their domain now reduced to spectacle for the cruel man that fed them.

I let my wings release their aching tension and ripped sharply and vertically into their gridlock, knocking them backwards from each other with my burning inertia. They both snapped out of their polluted pleasures and aimed their rage towards me in calculated tandem.

"This isn't a fight for you, monster." Zorne roared at me. "You could never understand the sorrows we're discussing- the lives that we are mourning with our blades."

A barrage of spears narrowed towards me from behind; I turned and weaved my way through them with graceful ease and anticipation. The other Wyvren spoke, "you are the summation of cruelty and evil. You are the devil that took our lives, whether on this plane or the

203

next you are what ended my life as Victoria and started it for your own carnage." She readied another onslaught of spears with the raise of her short sword. "You made me kill my family; you made me end my people."

Victoria launched another set of spears towards me, Zorne following suit with swords I actively chose to retire to her. I followed the Might that trailed around them, passively dancing through them in a calm disregard. They were both blinded by the birthing lights of their Blooms forced in them by Spring; even now not understanding that it was he who took their lives and that I was just as much a victim as they were.

"I want to help you," I said to both of them, each of them beginning to erupt in dissonance towards my statement. "But I know that neither of you can ever receive the peace I have for you." I raised my celestial bow and aimed it at Victoria. "I won't even pretend to know the struggles both of you faced in the captivity of the dark machine that kept me and my kind alive, but you are the very beasts you fed for all these centuries. If you can not accept that, then I will resolve your fates for you."

With that final threat and resolve, they were both on me from either side, practically white in the eyes with rage and armed to the teeth with their weaponry tearing through the space between us. I bent my light bow into two short swords and deflected their blows, concentrating the enchanted density of my transmuted light blades into tangible weapons.

They orbited me like Mercury and Venus, both enduring the intensity my Sun as I dried the moisture from their cracking lips and heated their steel with my magnanimous heat. I could smell their skin burning with each strike against my materialized blades, my flapping wings gusting bursts of heat and disrupting the courses of their projectiles.

The battle carried on in abstractions as I could barely begin to consciously keep up with the initial workings of spatial magics the three of us began to introduce. We constantly swapped places with all of the flying swords and spears, dancing through the shimmering pockets of the spatial recesses Midnight had to offer in its limited existence; clashing blades and deflecting hits. Had it been one on one, I was confident that I could defeat either Zorne of Victoria, but with their combined efforts turned towards my destruction, I simply added a third party to their stalemate. They were very destructive in their unbridled rage.

Suddenly in the heat of the enduring battle I felt an abrupt shift in my intertia, followed by what seemed to be a rapid acceleration but instead was a return to temporal continuation. My adversaries slowed around me and I glanced down to see Karine, dual time swords wielded and her Clock Key resonating in activation. She grinned at me and gave me an affirming wink; I was foolish to think that there was anything I could do alone, or rather *should* do alone. I didn't have to bear this weight by myself, not when I had her on my side.

In the dulled activation of their passing light, Zorne and Victoria failed to fully realize their slowing to near complete stillness as I mapped out my strike pattern. I flew even higher than they we were positioned in the sky and reassembled my bow, the string whispering back into existence in the pinch of my fingers. I drew the string back until the notch point touched my halo, fueling into my weapon a spiraled arrow of light that rested against the luminous arrow rest and released the shimmering projectile, becoming slow as it left my grasp and entering the radius of Karine's temporal trap.

I darted around, racing through the air and repeating this process with haste and careful aim, lining up an onslaught of arrows from as many directions as possible, letting them fly into the thick slowing storm that was gradually beginning to return to natural temporal progression. I was impressed at how long Karine was able to keep the two enraged Wyvren's ensnared in her chronological stillness. I was always so impressed with her, forgetting that she was not just a cunning inspiration but also a formidable warrior.

As soon as I lined the sky with as many arrows as their were visible stars in Midnight's limited sky, I swooped down to the ground, landing beside Karine as she stood in front of a still-warded August within her barrier. With a snap of her fingers and a look of beaming pride, she smiled her knowing smile at me and released her spell. The destruction was unreal.

The air burned with flashing lights and smelled of spent oxygen; the blitzing storm of angelic projectiles riveting through the air with precision and maximum prejudice in their impressive speed. As the lights clashed and stellar explosions resolved, we watched without blinking the silhouettes of witches burning in the

206

night sky. When the twilight of our battle resolved, our eyes followed our prey as they fell from the sky, hitting the ground and dusting into near charcoal on impact.

"Are they dead?!" August asked loudly and abruptly. "What the hell just happened?" He speculated, outside of the time magic Karine activated to ensure our success.

"I'm not sure," I said, beginning to walk towards them, the light of my bow fading away as it dissipated from my hands. "We have to make sure." Karine joined me as we walked towards the cindered souls that emerged from me just moments ago, stunted in the first chance of freedoms they enjoyed in eons. I felt guilty, but not guilty enough to let them destroy me; much less treat my body as a prized vessel they felt owed to have.

I came upon them, their bodies badly burned and hair singed into uneven lengths. Victoria's eyes flashed open as she gasped for air, rolling over and struggling to stand from her crippled position.

"You will not take my power and leave me here to die, monster." Victoria choked out of her burnt throat. "You took everything from me… All I wanted was the chance to live." She continued to spatter smoke and blood amongst her words as the arm she struggled to lift herself with snapped off as an ashen husk. In all of the outcomes I could have predicted, her next action surprised me more than any other could.

In her fury and defeat, she began to cry. I couldn't tell if it was from her wounded pride or her failure. All the same, I never thought I would see the day that the beast of malice forced to carry the mantle of my creation, feeding on the souls and running the code of the Wyvren engine would shed tears.

"I will fix it." I said gingerly as I knelt beside her broken body. "One day, I will make all of this right; not just for you, but for her, too." I said, gesturing towards the still burning Zorne. "I promise."

"I don't want your promises, you miserable bitch," Victoria said, transmuting a spear suddenly from the ground between us, the tip heading towards my face. I moved my head slightly to the right, feeling the draft of the the weapon's speed gently wave through my hair. I reached down to her and grabbed her throat, igniting my palms again and burning through her already marred flesh.

"You don't know it yet, but Spring is the enemy here." I strengthened my grip, Victoria's eyes widening as I began to melt through her arteries and into her esophagus. "You don't know it yet, but there is a way that you get to live again. And I am going to make sure that none of these evils on your soul ever come to pass."

Her eyes rolled back into her head as I felt my my fingers meet my palm, effectively burning through her throat her and incinerating her spine. Victoria's head rolled off of her shoulders and I remained kneeled beside her, lowering my head and taking a breath of something that tasted like regret but was more akin to remorse. Karine walked towards me, placing a hand on my shoulder that caused my wings to lower into a more relaxed fold. I raised my head and looked at her, sharing in the gaze of her empathy.

Karine looked down at me with a loving smile, trying to unpack the welling tears that were beginning to teem from behind my eyes. "Let's get out of here." She said, helping me to my feet.

I looked behind me on the ground at the still smoking body of Zorne, "what about her? We can't just leave her-"

Before I finished Karine took her longer blade and ran it through the sleeping throat of my first lifetime, severing it without even so much as a flinch from the fallen sorceress. "She is dead." Karine said, wincing and shuttering as she pulled the blade from the ground. "I'm sorry, I know that was less than graceful…"

I turned her around, her swords dissipating as I wrapped my arms around her and grasped her head in my hands and raised her mouth to mine, kissing her with the heat of my sunlight still on my lips. Her abrupt surprise relaxed as she returned the embrace, carefully placing her arms around me and in between the wings on my back. We pulled apart and looked into each other's eyes.

"I'm sorry I'm so complicated," I said, the tears from Victoria and now this apology running together into my words. "I have so much turmoil inside of me and I never mean for any of it to spill out onto you. I love you, Karine. I love you so much." I started crying even harder, dropping my head and closing my eyes. "Please don't ever leave me."

Karine hushed me gently, keeping one arm around me and lifting my chin with the other, despite her being shorter than me. She wiped the tears away from my cheeks, "Ren, the only thing you've ever done to wrong me is to try to fight your battles alone. You can ask for my help and still be the hero of your story." She pulled me close, resting her head on my shoulder. "Lean on me. You don't have to win every battle alone. Not anymore."

We stood in our silent embrace for a while, before August eventually interrupted, "… I don't mean to break up this tender moment with my third wheel suggestions, but now that Ren is clearly up and running, can we actually get out of here? Please?" He clownishly suggested, relying on his humor to try to weasel into the conversation no one was having.

We both turned to look at him, my face immediately rushing into a light pink as I came into the realization that we did in fact have an audience. The three of us broke into laughter. Sincere, heart felt, cackling laughter. I can't really remember if it was hysteria or just actual tension release.

"Sure, August. I know this place can be a bit… triggering for you." I teased. Karine chuckled at my jab at August's immortal torture in response to his eye roll towards my comment. I summoned my bow, fashioned from the lens that was intended to refract the light of this world, and drew another arrow, this one not meant to concentrate light, but to prismatically change and accelerate it as originally intended.

I let my arrow fly, straight into the moon in the illusionary sky. After it lost structure and became a loose light spell once again, it took only moments to reach the moon, touching down on it and erupting into a burning

210

and magnificent star. The light of the artificial sun refracted the atmosphere into a bright and fiery orange, blurring out the stars as my arrow bent the moments of Midnight into Dawn, breaking the plane down and opening a rift around us. Together, the three of us leapt into the rips that would take us back to the world we knew beyond the tethers of frozen seconds within this endless night.

Vilomah

We stepped through the nooks and crannies threshed through the Midnight dimension and out of the artificial dawn. Looking around, we found ourselves not quite where any of us thought we would end up. I'm not sure I had any true expectations, but the unfortunate sight before me filled me with a mourning grief. In this life I had never chosen to have, I found myself spending far too much of it witnessing the horrors of an unrelenting Spring, thriving in the cruel Eden of his creations around us.

We traversed the lined cobblestones of a familiar village; the stones beneath our feet the only thing truly remaining intact. We walked through various burning structures, still fresh with the enchanted fires that lapped at their walls and fueled the esoteric smokes that rose from them.

The village was the one just before one might make their way to the Chateaux, a peaceful place with simple people, leading simple lives in a simple way. Once pleasant and bright, now completely crushed under the thumb of an oppressive force, the only things left alive being the bright pink azaleas that lined the sidewalks of the now deceased town.

"Vanna…!" Karine gasped more than she spoke, shaking herself from the daze of the unexpected destruction of our accidental destination. She shook her head back and forth, composing herself and rubbing her face for a moment. Even in her sudden grief, Karine was able to seize her emotions and choose control of herself.

"Where is August?" I said, turning myself around fully for the first time. "Did he not come with us?" I was not as in control of myself as Karine was; I began to feel panic settle itself in beside the creeping dread of Vanna's fate. "We have to find him."

Karine stood still for a moment, turning slower than a grinding stone to face me, her pale gaze meeting mine. "If August isn't here, then he didn't make it through with us. I'm… I'm not sure what that could mean other than he was taken again." Her graven face hollowed even further. "The two I've never truly been able to liberate from the fate of severed life completely: Irene and August."

There was the slightest crack in the fortress of her collected demeanor as her lip trembled ever so slightly. She closed her eyes and turned away from me again. I wasn't sure what to do. I walked over to her and put my arm around her waist, rotating to face her and curtained her long dark hair away from her face.

"We can change all of this," I told her, my voice a hoarse whisper as my magic resolved back to my normal form. She seemed so helpless I felt I had to tell her. "I know a way that we can undo everything. I know how we can save Irene and August; how we can set ourselves free and-"

"No." Karine said without raising her head. "I already know what you are going to say. I don't know

213

who Kieran is but I've talked to them, too." She closed her eyes and gnashed her teeth together, speaking through them in frustration. "I won't let you sacrifice yourself to *become* what I've worked so hard to save you from." She finally opened her eyes and looked at me, her normally docile and kind blue eyes colder than the harshest winter, "I will spend the rest of my life making sure that you never have to give into your abuser."

I didn't have the heart to tell her that certain things were already in motion; Kieran already recoded parts of me to be able to house the Mantle of Spring. After some time to truly think about it, that must have been the reason that Zorne and Victoria were ejected from me once regaining consciousness. My code was making room for Spring.

"Alright, I won't pursue it," I blatantly lied to the only person who ever loved me. "Let's survey this place and try to find out what happened to it. There could be survivors."

Karine walked passed me, her gaze following suit as she stormed through the village. She wasn't dumb, Karine was easily the smartest woman I had ever known. She knew what my true intentions were, and now felt the cruel weight of a potential future that she might have to endure yet again. The terrifying inkling of a time when Karine may finally give up on her journey to save me from Spring crept through the dark corridors of my worst fears.

We turned every stone, extinguished every fire, gusted away all of the smoke. Finally we came upon the gentle auburn shell that was Vanna's workshop; cracked in half and almost completely empty in its decimation. Karine and I looked at one another, the dissonance from our conversation fading away in a mutual graciousness that the other was alive.

We stepped through the threshold, once a heavy wooden door now just a frame and scorched collection of baseboards. It was a horrible display; priceless laces and fabrics burnt and charred, antique displays busted against the ground, dresses and tailored suits ripped to pieces. Karine began to look for evidence of what may have caused the destruction in the first place while I descended deeper into the ruins of our friend's former abode.

"This place was enchanted- protected for generations by an ancient ward. What could have been strong enough to simply ravage through it with such ease?" Karine pondered aloud, hardly within reach of my hearing as I crouched through the hanging innards of the apartment I once held refuge within. I silently continued, passing the broken table where we once learned about each other, walking through the halls of generosity that once housed me and others that shared my goal of justice for this world. It was all gone. Destroyed.

I made my way finally to the guest room at the end of the hall where I stayed my single night with the young artisanal hostess. Somehow this was the least impacted region of the building, perhaps being on the other side of the Main Street and away from the initial carnage. I sat down on the bed, eventually laying down fully and placed a hand on my abdomen and another across my forehead. I felt tired. There was no reprieve. Even in destroying the Wyvren of this timeline there was still only destruction across the world. It felt hopeless to continue.

I rolled over and found myself gazing into the bright pink flowers that found a way to survive in all of this. Surely it was Spring, surely this was his calling card. Karine and I both knew it but what was further confusing was possible motive. He held all of the cards: he had the Auspice, he had the Seasons, he had the Months; what could possibly be gained by destroying this place? Was it really that important to hurt our hearts? To ravage our minds?

I watched the dust of the bedroom shift and sway in the gentle passing of sunshine that danced through the window, the only calm and forgiving part of the unrelenting devastation this place had seen. My eyes followed the dust and slowly I realized that there was a pattern in the particles that wafted through the air. I sat up, fixing my gaze towards towards them as I followed them around the room; outlining the movements of a conflict from a time passed, mingling with the possibilities of a violent future. It wasn't dust at all, but all the Might remaining from a time before and the potential of the future that Might unfold.

I rolled over, still watching the delicate swarms of Might from the bed as they practically vaulted across the guest room. I watched two loose figures crash into wardrobes, bust open walls and door frames, and most

importantly I watched someone get impaled by
something of a long and precise weapon. It was a spear.

There was a thunderous sound of impact
outside. I turned to watch as the glass of the window
splintered and rained across me. I sprang from the bed,
catching a spear expertly vaulted into Vanna's guest
room. I activated the burning Grace in my legs and feet
to keep the glass from slicing into them, only to raise my
head to meet a pair of frozen green eyes an inch from
my face. The Might of the room sparkled and spun in
erratic hordes, like birds throwing themselves into the
magnetic patterns of their migrations. Not again.

Before I could muster a single spell in my
defense, a sword ran through me, precisely running
through my diaphragm and severing my spine. I felt
my the feeling in my legs leave me, the Grace's power
resolving from me and feeling blood rise through my
throat.

No, not again. I had seen this before, this the third time.

I felt the blade in my torso stop in place as I
took a moment to focus and gather my self; the Grace
in my legs burned and began to resonate with a burning
against my chest. The Clock Key. I opened my eyes and
found the room completely still before me, my wound
fatal and irreparable without Spring and his
maintenance room. But I looked at the unyielding
ringlets before me that somehow framed a living version
of Victoria's head. Around her flaxen hair, I began to see
the wisps of what could be start to form.

I watched her movements, her potential decisions and reactions, almost as if they were moving backwards and forwards simultaneously in their atomic integrity. I was already wounded, so there was nothing more I could do to stop this attack. But what I could curate was a uniquely effective response. I shifted my focus to my own arms and legs, looking down at my maimed body and finding all of the possibilities of my potential.

There was an upward kick through the pain, shattering her jaw. There was the formation of light daggers in each hand that would slash across her chest and later form a bow, launching a burning star at her once she was away form me. There was a punch in the nose. The options became limitless, dancing in the silica that shown in the sun around us. It looked just like the falling sands of the Precipice.

Victoria started to move again, slowly but surely jolting forward as my weak dominion over the already accidental activation of the Clock Key began to diminish. I couldn't decide on what would be the most effective, so I took a chance and did the only thing that I thought would truly be the most capable response: I followed all of the outcomes.

Once my mind was made up it was almost like the Clock Key heard me and began to execute my command. In an impossibility of strikes, it almost seemed like I had more arms and legs than I truly did. In pursuing every attack, in choosing every outcome, every piece of me from every timeline existing beside the one I

218

was living crashed into the Wyvren in a cosmic onslaught of unpredictability.

Victoria stared at me, wide eyed and bleeding once again, as she did just moments before we even arrived to the ravaged town. But instead of sputtering and dying before me, she dissipated into strange ashes; black particles that looked similar to the Might around us but almost as if spent somehow; as if the potential of that moment was exhausted completely. An outcome burned out and no longer available.

Karine rushed into the room at the commotion, my bleeding body turning to face her. Before the conviction of pain truly set into the broken cells of my body, the wound dissipated as well, fleeing me in turns of ashen dust. My body was whole, intact, and healthy. I felt my vitality return to a point of completion, just as it was before I entered the room and encountered the battered memory of this place.

"What the hell was that?" I asked, rubbing my abdomen in disbelief as it healed, the odd circumstances of temporal dust swirling away from me. "I saw her, I saw Victoria; it was just like my first morning here before I came back to the Chateaux to find you." I felt anxiety clutch at my throat as Karine remained averted from my gaze, deep in contemplation and rationale. "Karine, what the hell just happened to me?"

Karine jerked to a startle at the sound of her name as if coming up for air from beneath a pool of water. "It was just as I observed…" She speculated, still not fully giving me her attention. Finally she looked at me, gesturing to the dancing Might at the corner of a beaten wardrobe. "Here, look," she said, gesturing to what I saw as a simple piece of battered wood. "The moments; they aren't resolving."

I looked outside to find that she was right; it wasn't just the memories of Victoria scarred into this place, but the events of the town were lapsing over themselves in their destruction. The buildings would be burning, completely crumbled and scorched to the very bones of the structures and then for just a brief moment they would seemingly glitch back into being upright and intact. Even as I looked out the window, I watched the cracks of it shattering begin to form and reform.

"Why is this happening?" I asked, looking around and following anymore potentially dangerous events that could surprise us. "It's like the time of this place is malfunctioning. The moments are all sitting on top of each other; like the light isn't passing across Space like it should be."

"You're right," Karine agreed, raising a hand to her chin in speculation. "Whatever broke this town and attacked this place whittled it down to the very fundamental fabrics that constituted it at all." She finally looked at me, returning from the swirling oasis of her brilliant mind. "Spring beat this place so hard that it is barely incorporated into existence anymore."

There was something else, almost more pressing that was bothering me than the sheer disrepair the village was in. "Where are all the bodies?" I asked, confused and gesturing around. "Surely there were casualties and I doubt that Spring was courteous

220

enough to sweep up behind himself after the massacre."

Karine and I thought for a moment before our faces shared a graven expression of realization. The only thing that was left untouched, the only signs of life at all in the whole place were the new azalea bushes that lined the streets; alive, thriving, healthy.

"You don't think…" I began to speculate.

"I do, actually." Karine interrupted immediately. "He didn't kill them. He repurposed them. That was his message here." She began to sway as a wave of shock washed over her, bracing herself against the wall. "Together the two of us can control Space and Time, but we can't simply shift reality from the higher dimension like he can. At any moment, without us ever even realizing, he could simply turn us into a flower if he wanted. With complete ease."

Karine eventually leaned her back into the wall. "I thought that if we worked together we could eventually counter him but this is beyond reason." She turned and looked at me with broken blue eyes and choked, "Ren, I don't think we can beat him."

It was the first time, including watching her die, I'd ever seen Karine have real fear in her eyes. I walked over to her, "Karine, you have to come with me to the Liminal. Come at least talk to Kieran with me. They may have more answers than what they have already shared with me."

Karine shook her head and winced her eyes shut at the thought. "Ren, I know that is me in there. I know that 'Kieran' is what I will eventually become if we

221

can't conquer Spring. I don't want to be trapped in that place, suffering in an immortality I never asked for in the 'between' of all realities. I don't want to face myself in there and look into the eyes of my inevitability."

My face had surprise written all over it as Karine smirked, composing herself and wiping her face briefly. "As soon as I knew that you had gone to where you were, I knew that 'they' told you about my past. I know that you know who I really am. There was no way that Kieran wouldn't try to bait you with more information than you had."

She stood up from her lean against the wall as I felt the guilt of my omission stir into a lump in my chest. "I was eventually going to tell you everything, once it was all over." Karine continued, twisting her Clock Key necklace in her fingers. "One we defeated Spring I was going to ask you to help me find a way to either finally die or ask you to find a way to stay alive with me forever."

She pulled out her swords and turned towards the hallway, looking over her shoulder back at me. "I'm not mad at you, Ren. I just need you to learn to truly trust me. And only me. I am the only force in the world that you can truly trust, and I don't say that with vanity in my heart. This is too dangerous. The first and only thing I have ever asked of you, back in that dusty apartment a couple of realms back, was to trust me. Please, find a place for me in your human heart and outside of your burning engine. I'm of much more use to you there."

I followed her in silence as we left the workshop and returned to the ominously quiet village, building itself up and tearing itself back down in subtle inconsistencies; quivering in and out of the little tether to Time it had left. We decided to head to the Chateaux, if anyone was left alive or unchanged, they would probably be taking refuge there. We made our way back to the Main Street lined with haunting blossoms and traversed our way out of the interrupted town.

The Might around us settled down as we made our way further towards the forest around the city. It seemed denser; fuller with greenery and luscious foliage I didn't remember. The woods were wilder than they were before, not in a magical sort of way but it was almost like they were… older. The previously tranquil woods were now dense and dark, harder to traverse. There was no longer a clear and welcoming path to our destination.

We brandished our weapons; a sword in each of our hands as we cut down the brush and vines around us. Karine was behind me, cutting extraneous brush away from the width of our path as I carved ahead. While I continued to slash the ambiguous greenery before us, I turned my head back to speak, "I can barely see anything, are we sure the Chateaux is this way?" I asked, my breath somehow losing steadiness against the constant swinging of swords into ambivalent topiary.

"This has to be the way; I can see the traces of my steps in Time trickling down this pathway. However, I've never known it to be this obscured." Karine responded through her own slashes. "It seems we were just here a couple of weeks ago... I thought I returned us to the proper timeline but everything seems so wrong." She continued shredding our surroundings to create more breadth for my reach, "we were only away from this timeline for a couple of weeks while you recovered in Midnight, maybe I should take us further back..."

Karine was interrupted by a razor thin blade ripping through the canopy above us. She dove forward into me, seeing the attack first and tackling us both to the ground as the impossibly thick forest above us was leveled almost instantly. I did my best to quickly stagger to my feet; the sudden influx of light from the afternoon sun now beating into my eyes and forest floor disoriented me in its sudden shining presence.

I felt another shift in the air. Without the cover of the deep forest I was able to sense the oncoming attacks much more clearly. As the breeze of our unseen assailant's steps diverted through the remaining meadow around us, I turned to catch the wrist of the incredibly nimble warrior targeting us. I twisted their arm and pinned them to the ground; grappling my legs over their arm and grabbing a fistful of thick brown hair in my remaining hand as Karine poised a sword at our attacker's head.

"It seems you both really are as capable as I was told about," a delicate feminine voice resounded from beneath the veil of hair I clutched in my grasp. She she relinquished her razor thin, needle-like blade from her grip behind her back and tapped the mossy ground her face was planted against with an open hand. "I give

224

up, I surrender. I didn't see who you were. I wouldn't have tried to fight you at all given that I knew I was trying to take out the Wyvren and her human escort."

I kicked the gaunt weapon away and released the young woman's wrist, leaping back to create distance between myself and the potential of a continued threat. Karine stayed on her, steadily raising her blade as the woman's chin lifted with her gait from the ground. The agile warrior didn't stand very high from the ground, her slender body accentuated by her thick shoulder length hair. She raised her callused hands above her head in surrender as Karine's face illuminated with something akin to relief but steeped in the titillation of shock that widened her eyes.

"Vanna…?" Karine managed to utter as the nimble swordsman turned to look at me, fully revealing her formerly kind and enthusiastic face. Her right eye furrowed with a cunning rage, one that was fueled by righteousness in her resolve while her left was now gone; in its place a broad and complexly stitched eyepatch that encompassed most of that side of her face. From her jaw line to the edge of the covering fabric a deep and ferocious scar left by horrors of a past I never knew we left to come back to.

With a twitch of her raised right hand I noticed a thin translucent thread tug from her learned grip, swiftly returning her thin weapon to her hand and she deepened her stance towards me. The weapon was hardly a sword, but more of a rapier sharpened so finely that it was now more of a needle; the thin thread around her fingers even slipped through an eye at the base of the ornately wrapped handle. Even now in this strange place she found a way to remain a seamstress in some way.

"I let you into my home!" She said, lunging towards me with a precise jab. "I gave you refuge, fed you, even clothed you!" She continued as I began to tenderly dodge her acrobatic onslaught. She was accurate and precise, impressively quick even. But she was still small and without much strength, the only threat she posed to Karine and I her delicate skills and now-spent element of surprise.

"Vanna, yes, yes you did do all of those things for me," I responded, dancing around the finely sharpened weapon in her vice. "I came here to help fight the Wyvren-"

I could see Vanna's ear twitch at the word, "*you* are the Wyvren; you lied to us and deceived the only protectors we had!" Her strikes became more rhythmic, more precise and deadly as her erratic vengeance began to fuel the adrenaline raging through her response. "You gained our trust and then lead them to *slaughter.*" She said, nearly grazing my cheek in her tenacity.

"Vanna, please, tell us what happened- we haven't killed anyone," Karine began to tenderly pursue Vanna's merciless advance towards me. "Please, tell us and we can help you. You don't have to fight us."

Vanna turned on a dime and poised her needle inches from Karine's eye, stilling the three of us into an abrupt silence. "Not another word from you, dog." She spat at Karine, "my mother trusted you, even raised me to trust you. I never suspected a thing because my mother was all I had, but you've been playing this game for years, *lifetimes*. Not just with me, but with all of us." She smiled as the hysteria began to mingle with her anger. "You laid the bait; you trained all of us to follow you right into the mouth of the beast!" She finished, keeping her narrow blade on Karine and turning a flickering amber eye towards me; tears beginning to well as trauma danced behind it.

"After you killed Irene and Evelynn, the Auspice had no choice but to occupy this place and follow the trail of the Wyvren. They interrogated everyone. Imprisoned those ignorant, saying it was in the spirit of their lack of 'compliance' in their search. And then *you* came back here, whirling swords dancing around your dark black fur as you tore through everyone; Auspice and innocent alike." She cackled. "I can still see those green eyes staring me down just before your claws shredded my home and took my eye from me."

I quickly shared a fearful glance over Vanna's shoulder with Karine. How was I here? Was there *another* Wyvren? "Vanna, I think there has been a misunderstanding," I began, now calmly raising my hands to either side of my head to yield. "You're right, I haven't been completely honest with you. I *was* the Wyvren, but with Karine's help I was able to persevere from Spring's control-"

"You tell nothing but *lies!*" Vanna interrupted again finally turning her blade from Karine's eye and back towards my throat. Even in my circumstance I felt relief knowing that Karine was at least temporarily out of immediate harm. "If it wasn't for Spring, none of us would be alive. He nearly killed you- he battled you until the both of you were within an inch of your life; until your fled him in your cowardice." She accused, confusion further riddling my face. I knew that Spring was here, but how was he illustrating such a manipulative tale to win Vanna over? Why would he even bother to want to win her over in the first place?

"Vanna, what about the Azaleas?" Karine mentioned, trying to calmly gain any control over the situation, "Spring turned all of the people in that town into those flowers."

Vanna lunged away from between the two of us, facing us both now and fleeting her eye back and forth to keep us within her view, "of course he did. We didn't have the time or resources for a mass grave before everyone started to rot, so Spring used his great magics to memorialize those lost at the hands of the beast into an eternal garden."

I was so confused. Spring was actively illustrating himself as a hero once again. He didn't need to put on such an elaborate performance. "Vanna, you saw the Auspice, the Council. You said they were here?" I asked, hands still raised.

"Yes, they were all here; they forced their authority on me and made me house their during their inquisition here while they searched for you." She said, keeping her needle pointed towards me.

"The brutish one Dorian, and the leader of the Council, Isadora?" I gestured, waving my hands slightly as I spoke in more comfort as Vanna entertained the

228

dialogue. "That was Téo and Evelynn. You're right, Irene lost her life in that battle with Spring, but he turned our other two remaining friends into the Auspice leadership, along with two other innocent people who became Hector and Alto." I finally lowered my hands and felt frustration strike my face. "Spring is manipulating you. Karine and I have been gone for the last two or three weeks elsewhere trying to recover from that very fight."

"Weeks?" Vanna said, lowering her sword. "Weeks. You despicable bitch you took them from us six years ago." She bellowed, her chestnut eye darkening with an anger so deep that even I felt threatened by her intensity. "It all fell apart. When the Auspice came to occupy us in their search for you, Gaultier heard the news that his daughter's died and he hung himself in the Chateaux. With only Sabine and Sara remaining they approached me and asked for my help, which I gave as much as I could until the Council took them away. The only way I knew to make sure they stayed safe was to join them and become one of their warriors."

"Spring can't be your hero, Vanna," Karine said flatly and quietly. "Spring and the other Seasons *created* the Council. How can you say that they came to occupy your town and then thank him for joining them?"

Vanna stood quietly as her jaw visibly dropped in disbelief, "you really do take me for a fool don't you? You always have, even now trying to exploit an innocence that was devoured years ago in the maw of the monster you've aligned yourself with. The Council was formed to hunt down the Wyvren, and when it finally came to attack, they failed to kill it. In Spring's

229

diving mercy he couldn't bear to see the final defense of the magical world fall and so he descended from his heavenly throne to do battle with the beast himself."

She stared me down and finished, "but you didn't have the strength or courage to finish what you started, so you ran away to the human you've brainwashed into taking care of you." Vanna turned her attention to Karine, "That's right, Spring told me all about you, too. He took me in after he agreed to lead the Council. He trained me. He gave me magic and power unlike any the Chateaux or the rest of the world had ever seen so that one day I might find you again and kill you."

A bright yellow light began to glow from behind Vanna's eyepatch, rippling in golden radiance with oppressive force and brightness. As the light touched Vanna's needle, it began to resonate with a deep and ferocious light that matched Vanna's aura. There was a sound; a faint and gentle ringing as the light kissed her armament that continued to hum from the blade.

"Spring entrusted his light to me, his Grace," she announced as the humming grew louder. "A weapon of truth, blessed with unalloyed accuracy and prejudice towards evil. The light that will kill you, Wyvren." She finished with the resolution of a prayer. With a powerful lunge, she thrust the needle towards us; a mighty and blinding light burning the air as something like lightning crackled towards us.

Act VI

Vanitas

I was certain we were going to be met by Vanna's cruel edge, Spring's corrupted light pulsing through it. But I was wrong; before we met the impalement of the seamstress's thrust I tasted the bitter dust of ethereal earth as my body and face skidded across the familiar sandy plane of the Precipice. It was as if I was thrown from a horse, the inertia tossing me aside like a plaything as I watched Karine in my periphery roll ahead of me, falling from the edge of the upper plateau and heading straight for the Liminal.

Time was, and still is, a tricky thing for me to perceive and handle. As I chased after my companion in my unwilling tumble I eventually felt my body crash into the cold and unwavering Marble of Kieran's domain, only to struggle to my feet and find Karine and her future; both bloody with dual swords intertwined. I reached for my weapons, truly for the first time in this realm only to feel them rumble beyond my reach, locked out of this plane. Surely at the design of Kieran once they understood how Spring's magic functioned after assuming the title of "Year."

I had no choice. I ran towards both of them relying on my strength alone and tore between them, catching either of their blades in my forging palms in resistance to their dismemberment from my arms.

231

"Stop!" I yelled, clutching the weapons of the woman I loved in one hand and her unforgiving choices in the other. "Stop, we have to talk. Kieran, why did you bring us here? Karine, we have to listen to what they have to say; they saved our life, surely for a reason."

Karine retracted her blade and wove an intricate advance towards Kieran around my body, "Ren, we can *NOT* trust a word this monster says. They are one of *them.*" She emphasized, leaping into a calypso across my back to add more momentum to her strike. "She has already gotten to you… changed you. I knew it was her that must have said something to you back in Midnight. But she is more selfish than Spring, and just as conniving." She finished with a decisive strike down into Kieran, forcing them to cross their blades in a shivering attempt to deflect her merciless blow.

Kieran raised their hands and emanated a thunderous force from the cloudy skies above, forging a powerful spell that ripped Karine's blades from her hands and blew all three of us apart form each other, creating space between us that I was happy to welcome.

"Kieran, how did Spring get to Vanna? Why even target her at all? What does he gain from polluting her mind?" I viciously inquired, my hands outreached towards the two of them in anticipation of unpredictable advances.

Kieran's weapons dissipated as they wiped the hair from their aged and scarred face as Karine remained ready for combat. "Polluting Vanna is the last defense of the allies either of you have in regards to the

232

choices you've made; the people you've aligned with are all now either dead or working for the enemy." Kieran bluntly responded.

"Tell me the truth, Kieran," I continued to press, "I need to know why the two of you hate each other; are you not one of Karine's futures? The result of one of her timelines?"

Karine tensed herself into a structure more rigid than stone as she somehow rooted deeper into the glistening marble beneath us. Kieran looked at her, grinning a brittle smile that echoed the knowing lips I loved so dearly, "I'm not one of Karine's outcomes. I am *all* of Karine's outcomes."

"That's not true!" Karine screamed, immediately breaking from her statuesque posture and lunging forward again. Before she could reach her target in Kieran's throat, I caught her blades with my burning hands again; the sheer force of her strike sinking my feet into shattering floor beneath me. I looked into the eyes of someone I thought I knew only to see the glacial stare of a ferocious mind; unrecognizably reflecting my visage back to me.

"She has spent her lifetimes; every single one of them trying to find a way to not become me," Kieran continued, summoning a chair with a sarcastic gesture as their brittle smile remained on their face. "For thousands of years of enduring your destruction, she always comes back here, to me, with you, and makes her choice. Would you like to know the fate of your lover, Wyvren?"

233

Karine's oppressive force continued to sink into my hands, "don't listen to this monster; especially don't answer to 'Wyvren' when it snarls anything at you." She persisted, trying to persuade me while still unyielding her blades from my hands.

Kieran raised both of their hands in their seated position and in the air between them gathered three lights; a bright pink light, a cold blue light, and a warm golden light. "It took me eons to become what I am; to finally make the decisions in the appropriate order, for the appropriate reasons," Kieran began to explain.

I managed to conduct enough heat into Karine's blades to such a point she had to relinquish them to me. I stabbed them into the ground on either side of me and watched her crystalline composure begin to erode against Kieran's words. I didn't want to hurt her, but I had to understand the bigger picture. Kieran knew how both of our stories ended and was becoming less and less cryptic about it each time we spoke. If there were answers to gather here, I had to retrieve them.

A cube appeared in the bright pink light that gently floated between Kieran's hands. A Clock Key manifested in the chilling blue light on the far side of it. Lastly, in the golden light between them a ring of light shimmered into existence. Kieran lifted them into a circular formation above him, rotating them in on a horizontal plane that orbited his head.

"Each of the Seasons can be reduced to three simple components; two more simple than the last, but the third fundamentally attainable and understandable." Kieran began to explain with a voice bustling with

234

eagerness while watching Karine's displeasure smear over her face. They gestured the pink light surrounding the cube to the forefront of his orbiting artifacts.

"First, there is Space," Kieran explained, gesturing to the luminous fuchsia cube. "It is in the Wyvren he shed his capacity for Space; a gift to his disastrous monster." He rotated once more counterclockwise, bringing the blue light of the Clock Key forward. "Secondly, there is Time; his tribute to the dying prodigy of my past." With another whimsical gesture, he presented the golden ring of light. "Lastly, there is Grace. Grace is the abstract, truly higher dimensional material the Seasons' possess; his gift to the forgotten seamstress."

I stood there, dazed as I felt the feeling leave my head and dizziness disrupt my senses. "So, Spring divided himself into three pieces?" I asked, confusion and subtle panic filling my mind and chest. "How did he do that? If that is what a Season is made of, how does he still exist?"

In a fugue state of dismay, Karine's body gave up the will to stand as she fell to her knees, clearly aware of the answer I was going to hear from Kieran next. With a now cruel smile and dimly lit ruby eyes, Kieran happily obliged me with my answer. "You are all living components of Spring. So long as you, Karine, and now Vanna are alive, Spring will also endure and survive. The three of you are the source of his power."

I suddenly felt the crushing weight that brought Karine to her knees as I stammered a response, my engine churning irregular heart rhythms through my

235

body. "So… the only way to *kill* Spring completely is to kill the three of us? Why would he make himself so vulnerable? Why would he expose his powers and gifts to us? Didn't that practically make him killable?"

Kieran rolled his eyes and stood up, the artifacts and chair dissipating as they folded their hands behind their back. "Of course this makes him vulnerable. But he sees everything; every timeline, every outcome, every scenario. He can practically see everything that was and will be simultaneously. He knew that eventually there would be a Karine that would try to save the Wyvren, and that the two of you would seek allies in Vanna and the rest of the Chateaux."

Karine remained silent, I couldn't tell if she was ashamed of her secrets or simply ashamed to be a part of all of this in general. I wasn't satisfied, "so he did all of this as a back up? We are currently in his 'Plan B' scenario where Karine and I rebel against him so he turns the world against us?" I stopped, suddenly allowing my brain to catch up to the conversation. I could practically feel the information settle into place, as such was apparently evident while Kieran's eyes almost turned to the hue of blood with pleasure watching me piece it together.

"That's why Karine had me go through the previous timeline as the Left Hand of Dorian. She knew that Autumn would give me her Grace as a weapon to use." I turned to Karine as my eyes continued to widen with disbelief, "she knew she would die at the end of that scenario; she probably has a thousand times… that's why she gave me her Clock Key." I turned and

236

looked at Kieran again, about to burst with laughter at my despair. "I already have the cube, but Scimariel altered it. I had to have one in its original configuration to have a congruent component to each…"

I felt myself taking involuntary steps backwards, trying to instinctually retreat from what my body was recognizing as a very real threat, not just in Kieran, but in Karine, too. "Those artifacts you just showed me… they weren't projections, were they?" If there was a wall in that place I could have backed into I surely would have hit it in my yielding. "You have a Wyvren core, the Clock Key Spring gave you, and one of the Season's lights of Grace, don't you?"

I was beginning to have a full blown panic attack. "That's how you became the Year- you combined those components and took up the Mantle of Spring, using that superior position in their hierarchy to slay the other Seasons in your timeline and consume their powers as well." I looked at Karine, her face crumpled with ugly tears as she began to weep into her hands on the ground. "You told me to become Spring so I could become the Year instead of you. Karine was right; everything you said was to manipulate me."

Kieran clapped sarcastically, "wow, you really are somehow much smarter than any of the other Wyvrens I've encountered through my glorious escapades. Each and every time you blindly did what I said until you finally got to Vanna, but every time you failed to kill her. You couldn't. Your humanity had developed far too thoroughly and you didn't have the heart to go through with it."

Kieran glanced a cunning grin of satisfaction towards Karine, "but this time, my past had the foresight to plan ahead and let you not only receive Grace from the Seasons, but be *gifted* it! Bravo, Karine, bravo!"

Karine lunged forward and reclaimed both of her swords from the ground, aiming them both at Kieran's throat with a speed so blinding I was unable to even perceive her initial approach. Kieran's form phased into particles and appeared behind her, indignantly kicking her in the back and into the ground.

Karine turned to look up at Kieran, "I didn't take the steps I did to sacrifice Ren. I don't know the future you know, and I don't belong to the choices you made." She sneered, spitting at them.

Kieran rolled his eyes again, summoning their own Clock Key above their head to recall their two blades once more. Since seeing them when first arriving, they were now much more worn and even visibly denser; the energy they emitted practically dripping from them as they entered Kieran's hands and pointed towards Karine.

"I am quite literally the culmination of your choices." Kieran said, suddenly warmer and consoling as if cooing a toddler. "I have inherited the will of the Seasons. *All* of the Seasons." Kieran stepped back and gestured outwardly with their swords, slowly spinning as they presented the surroundings to us. "This place is the beginning. This place will likely one day also be the end. The Liminal is the tarnished remains of the beginning of creation, only accessible by the first altar humanity ever constructed."

Kieran looked over his shoulder at us with a grin before fully turning towards us once again, each sword pointed towards one of us, "this place is where heaven meets hell, where the first breath was drawn and the last breath with breathe. This is Eden." Kieran winked at Karine, "and no matter how many times you try, no matter how righteous you think you might be, you will always bring your sweet Wyvren back to me."

Kieran directed his glance towards me, "I already told you once, starlight; the only way to defeat Spring is to become him. I just took a couple extra steps while I was ahead." With swift molecular movement, Kieran dissipated his form into a cloud of atoms and reformed with both blades at Karine's throat.

"You have two choices now, Wyvren," Kieran stated in ultimatum. "You currently have all the tools you need to overcome Spring; the Orchid's engine, my Clock Key from another timeline, and Grace. You can either conquer Spring and sacrifice this elective life you were never even truly meant to have, saving your darling Karine from the fate of becoming me, or…"

Kieran tightened their blades, beginning to slice into the soft flesh around Karine's throat, "I kill her. Here and now. And you are left with nothing; Vanna hunting you and Spring inevitably repossessing you as his property." His eyes were truly like Spring's; reactive to his feelings, practically black with intention. "So, what will it be, songbird?"

I froze. I didn't know what to believe or what to say. I reached for the first rational thought that came to mind in that impossible situation. "You can't kill Karine,"

239

I began, my voice dry and crackling with hesitation and a misplaced train of thought. "Spring made her immortal, even without intentional time travel buffs and magics. She'll just reappear at a check point; you're bluffing."

Without a word of response Kieran sank their shorter sword into Karine's shoulder, enticing a blood curdling scream from her throat. "Are you really still so much of a monster to believe that she is safe in this situation?" Kieran teased, sinking the clock-faced weapon another inch into Karine's collar bone. "Surely you understand how long I've been here, how long I've wanted this, how long I have been trapped in this place to endure this fate."

Karine's tear stained face lifted to meet mine, her eyes back to their kind and loving glow. "Ren, there is another way, you don't have to meet these demands." She winced as Kieran tightened their grip around her, bringing the larger blade closer to Karine's throat and beginning to sink into it.

I was paralyzed with indecision. I watched Karine die once before and knew what it was like to be completely lost without her. I was helpless to save her then and I was helpless to help her in Kieran's clutches, too. I was supposed to be the most powerful being in the world; the most dangerous and most volatile force in existence and at every turn I found myself completely defeated. I was out of my league. I was truly beginning to believe that I was better off as the servant I was supposed to be rather than the person I had become. I clearly didn't have the capacity to do the good I wanted to on my own.

"Tick tock, Wyvren," Kieran badgered, closing even closer and closer around Karine like a sentient vice. "What will it be?"

Almost on perfect cue to Kieran's conniving tease, I watched the mysterious yet familiar scatterings of Might start to buzz around the three of us. I watched as the alternate timelines of our tandem decisions unfold around us; staggered and somehow simultaneous. I felt my own Clock Key begin to hum and burn against my chest, wrapped around my neck with the same yellow ribbon Karine gave me in another Time that felt so innocent and distant from this moment.

Every gathering of Might around the three of us outlined either Karine's death or my compliance one way or another. I had no real choice between the two options than to lose either Karine or myself. One way or another, Kieran would either forge a new Spring in me or the current one would simply remain, awaiting a time with Karine would somehow gather the resources to unwillingly ensnare him.

However, there was a third, very fine outline that traveled gently from my heart to Kieran's head; the possibility no more than an ant trail in the vast sea of Time around us. I wasn't sure where those actions would take me, but they were the only potential outcome where both Karine and I would make it out of there both alive and ourselves. With the same faith I leapt from the Precipice to the Liminal, I reached out and grasped that trail of Time between us, and in a cosmic snap, everything around me went completely dark.

Kieran, Karine, the marble, the clouds; all of it was gone. The only trace of the Liminal Eden that remained was my panic and confusion, the adrenaline pumping sensation back into my chilled, numbed body. Everything was dark, my eyes struggled to adjust as the faint outlines of metal bars began to come into view. I couldn't feel any ground beneath me as I turned, looking for anything else in the darkness until my eyes returned to the faint metal in the dark, now fully realized as a familiar cage. It was a copy of the same prison within my own Wyvren engine where Zorne and Scimariel were held captive within me.

Just like before, a small fire was lit within the enclosure. As my eyes finally fully allowed the view in the darkness to be revealed, I saw a figure seated by the meek blaze, back facing me in a lounged position as the fire flickered around their silhouette. I reached forward and touched the cage, and even that gentle sound was enough to startle the person locked inside.

"Oh, dear," I heard a familiar nectarine voice chide in response to my advance. "It's been so quiet in here for so long that your little chirp startled me!" The man's tall figure cast a formidable shadow as he stood. "Forgive me, I would have cleaned up the place had I been expecting visitors."

My breath stopped and my eyes narrowed, desperately trying to make out any other outline and trying to reimagine the familiar voice into any other set of sounds. "How... where are we? How are you here?" I

242

whispered, my quiet voice somehow dramatically loud against the hushed sounds of the fire; a gentle pile of cinders cackling at my dismay and confusion.

Spring turned to face me, his wafting steps gliding just as gracefully in his captivity as they ever did. He leaned close to the tight bars my fingers intertwined with and breathed his cinnamon sugar words into my face, "that Faust girl of yours is much smarter than I ever gave her credit for," he snickered. "I originally thought that one day I could bend her to become the Wyvren I always wanted. Unfortunately I made the decision to settle with Zorne; that choice haunts me to this day as I waste away by this fire."

Kieran's words echoed in my mind; back when they were Karine, they were able to assimilate Time, Space, and Grace. "This cage… this is all the parts you left with us through the years." I realized. "Right now, we're inside the Wyvren engine that Kieran holds. They never became Spring…"

"Karine used her cunning strategies to manipulate an iteration of you eons ago to control Space in tandem with the Time I gave her, and combined with her understanding of Might, she found the opportune moment to rip 'your' heart out and snatch Winter's Grace right out of her soul." He laughed, flipping his dirty blonde hair over his shoulder and cutting his azalea eyes at me. "I must say, it was quite impressive."

"So right now, we're inside Kieran's stolen Wyvren engine? What's happening in the outside world? What's happening right now?" I frantically asked,

243

watching Spring's loving smile spread over his pearlescent white teeth.

"Do you think I know anything outside of this darkness? Anything besides this comedically small fire I installed here as a taunt to those special spirits I knew your engine would wait to digest or slowly feed upon over time? No, starlight; I have no idea what's going on outside." The Season cadenced.

Spring brought his lips closer to the edge of the cage once again, "but I can guarantee you that if your Karine is out there with the beast I know? She won't last much longer. This isn't the first 'Karine' that they've slaughtered since my tenure here. I don't know much about the outside world but I do get to savor every kill, even from here."

"I followed the Might here," I defended, trying to justify more to myself than to him that there was a chance that Karine was still alive. "Of all of the scenarios, of all of the outcomes, I was able to come here and get to you because I followed the Might. This was the only chance that either of us survived."

Spring's eyes brightened and his brow lifted, an inquisitive expression scattering across his face in both contemplation and delight. "You're able to see Might, darling Wyvren?" He asked with wondrous interrogation. "You were designed to only exist in Space, even if you came into contact with the Clock Key… curious indeed."

"Listen to me," I urged, trying to maintain my creator's lofty attention. "I think we both have something the other wants here."

244

Spring's eyes deepened with speculation, "and what exactly might that be, beastie?"

I closed my eyes and chose my following words as carefully as I could, trying my best to consider the potential passage of Time in the outside world around us. "I can't defeat Kieran, not so long as they exist as the 'Year,'" I explained, more than obviously. "But if I can dismantle their power, their status; I might be able get Karine and I out of here."

Spring grinned an inhumanly wide smile, "are you implying that you are going to let m out of here?" He cackled hysterically for more than a moment, savoring the possibility that I would willingly release him back into the world.

"Yes." I responded flatly. "Getting you out of here is the only chance of both of us leaving alive. Furthermore, Kieran explained that you can't die so long as the two of us and the holder of your Grace survive." I raised my chin confidently at him. "I followed the Might that kept us alive. I know you can't kill us, even if you wanted to. It isn't a potential outcome."

"Well look who has it all figured out," Spring condescended. "If you're so sure, then absolutely. Release me. Watch what I can do with these thousands of years reverberating in my bones. If you're so sure you can survive me, let me out."

I grinned, my viridescent eyes locking with the garden of his rose petal irises. "Stand back, and watch me do what you haven't been able to for a miserable eternity."

245

I raised my hands to the bars of the cage. Metaphysically, at least from the outside, it was just a simple cage. All it needed was a simple magic. I reached into myself and activated the familiar burning of Irene's forge again, poetically using it to dismantle a part of a Wyvren engine, even if from another time. Something told me that even in all of these scenarios, after all this time, that this core was once embedded in her chest at one point as well. The poor witch was always destined to be my prey. I hoped one day that I would be able to liberate her of that.

As soon as the bars melted through in my grasp, even just the two of them I was holding, there was a fluorescent pink explosion, illuminating the darkness and blinding me. I felt a thrusting force pushing me back until I felt myself hit and slide across the marble floor of Kieran's Eden. I stood, clumsily but quickly, wiping my eyes and steadying myself until I was able to clearly see not just the three of us, but now four. Myself, Karine, Kieran, and the steaming fresh form of Spring, stretching like a cat in the bright white light beneath the clouds above.

Karine looked at me, her eyes initially wide with horror. I responded to her fear with stillness and confidence, a broad grin of assurance across my face turning her dismay to confusion. The two of us turned our attention to Kieran and Spring, both now seemingly oblivious to our presence as they stared each other down.

Kieran's swords visibility withered in size, now disconnected from the Mantle of Spring. It seemed that even with all three pieces that could harness his power, one didn't simply inherit the Mantle of Spring by becoming him, but trapped his existence within the prison that was the Wyvren engine and manipulated his power. While Kieran still held dominion over Space, Time, and Grace, the mastery of the three in tandem abandoned them as Spring was freed from their soul.

"I still hold the abilities of the Seasons that I slaughtered with your power," Kieran sneered at Spring, willing a colorful array of magics in several hues, darkening the clouds above us. "I have all of the resources you do, only with the heat of your siblings to increase my power behind every blow. You can't defeat me alone."

Spring scoffed and crossed his arms, "even if you were right, darling Faust, I'm fairly certain there are two young ladies here that would happily help me tear you limb from limb."

Before Spring could even finish his taunting words, Karine and I were on either side of Kieran while they remained facing Spring. Unable to summon my own swords, I tapped into the power of the Clock Key in my possession and summoned the temporal scythe I forged with the "other" Karine's blades from before, Karine summoning her own swords in tandem. We both struck opposite sides, anticipating Kieran's escape upward where Spring was waiting for them, open hand forward as Kieran jumped straight into his grasp.

"Well, well, well," Spring chuckled as he hovered in the air above us, his grip on Kieran's throat turning their face a choking blue. "I don't suppose you expected this to happen in your perfect little world, up here on your perfect little throne, torturing my perfect little pawns, did you?"

With seemingly no effort at all Spring tossed Kieran with such a force that the impact their body made on the marble left a shallow crater. The Season tilted their head in delight to find that his prey was still breathing, floating to the ground gently as he landed with one foot on Kieran's throat. They tried to dissipate, turn into their fluid molecular dust form and whist themselves away, but Spring had a firm grasp on every atom in their body. Kieran wasn't going anywhere.

With a lift of their hand, Kieran summoned the three colorful artifacts around Spring, "I trapped you once, I will seal you again!" Kieran spat from beneath Spring's foot. They clenched their fist and the three items began to spin around Spring, gaining momentum as the gold, blue, and pink began to smear together in the air to form a multi-chromatic cage. With a smirk and a snap of his fingers, just as the cage fully realized itself, Spring switched his placement in Space with Kieran's, locking him within his own trap.

"You don't actually think I would be dumb enough to let you do that now that I've discovered that I even *have* a weakness, do you?" Spring scoffed as Kieran's face collapsed with shock and fear, grasping at the bars of the cage as the light left it and it formed into a tight metal enclosure. As the final glimmers of color faded from the cold iron, a meek fire ignited in the center of the cage, as it apparently always did.

248

"No, no you can't-" Kieran began to plea before Spring snapped his fingers, condensing the enclosure to the size of a coin; smashing Kieran's body out of existence as the matter that once composed them scattered into rogue particles across the room. Completely gone.

Spring dusted his hands off with a couple claps and then turned his deadening eyes towards us, satisfaction never leaving his face. "Now, what to do with the two of you?"

"Nothing at all, administrator." I responded, crossing my arms and widening my stance. "I don't think you'll be doing anything with us."

Karine's head spun almost completely around her neck as she turned to face me, her eyes wide with understanding and mouth twitching with shock. Spring scoffed, "administrator? I don't quite believe I understand what you're implying here."

"This place, this domain, was made from the bits of you, the Spring that lead us to the conclusion of this timeline. This place is the beginning and the end. The Eden of Time and Space at the beginning and end of a complete ring of existence. This was the end of Time and Space, constructed with the remaining Grace of a world devoid of the Seasons."

Spring squinted his eyes and turned his head skeptically, "there is no world without Seasons, darling. That is impossible. We are a part of absolution in the world."

I smiled, feeling my eyes darken with malice as his always did. "You said it yourself; you had one

249

weakness. You, the Spring of this timeline, the Season before me now, unknowingly distributed your powers across separate wielders of magic, only for a 'Karine' to gather them in singularity and become the Year and assuming the identity 'Kieran.'"

Spring began to piece together what I was saying as the words fell from my lips and rippled through the room, forming tidal waves in his often smooth composure. I continued, "those resources were in Kieran's possession, and all of the Grace that was left in this timeline, within this Liminal world, was always in Kieran's possession." as I spoke, the ground began to crack and the clouds above began to dissipate.

I sneered the words through my teeth, "as long as Kieran was alive, you were able to tether to those powers. While you learned not to let yourself be trapped by your own magic, what you failed to understand is that you are powerless without it." I reached out and summoned the coin-sized remains of Kieran, "in here lies your Grace, the Grace of your siblings, and the broken remains of your navigation tools through Time and Space; the Clock Key and the Wyvren engine."

Spring, now frantic, began to gesture wildly; desperately trying to activate any of his powers as horror almost dripped from his futile hands. "No… this isn't possible. This can't be true- I am more than a god; I am a facet of reality! I can't be stripped of my power! It is impossible!"

"Correct," Karine, interjected, finally finding the words to participate. "You can't be stripped of them… but you yourself have the power to destroy them." She looked at the coin in my hands, "you destroyed your only chance at ever truly leaving this place. You destroyed your own freedom, tricked by your own pride. As far as your existence goes on this timeline, you have nullified yourself." She smiled her knowing smile, "you are nothing."

I activated my power over Space from within my chest, while Karine activated her influence over Time. Together, as the world around us fell apart, Spring began to run at us in his futile desperation and the two of us, hand in hand, slipped through the rift we mutually created and escaped the crumbling world, sealing the portal from the other side as we watched a version of Spring dissolve into the shattering world of the dimension in between them all as he died a mortal death. Lost forever.

As we finished sealing our escape route, Karine turned to me and embraced me, fully and tightly. I could smell the blood of her deep wounds fill the air around us. I embraced her briefly before pulling back, "Karine, we have to take care of your wounds." Without a response, Karine leaned in and grabbed my face, kissing me for the first time in what felt like centuries. My words left me as fatigue washed over both of us, and we chose to instead talk without our words, and rather discuss our relief with our bodies.

We leaned on each other, keeping the other standing, and just held one another in a silent comfort until we both realized where we were. With no real destination in mind other than "out," it seems we both took ourselves to the one place we found comfort

251

together. I made my way to the dusty window sill, her hand in mine, and looked out over the refugee town the Auspice built, sunlight filtering in through the inconsistent glass.

"When are we?" I asked Karine, her head leaned against my shoulder as her hand remained in mine.

"We are when we were when Vanna attacked us," she stated softly, her other hand cradling her wound. "No more running. Not anymore. If there is one thing facing Kieran taught me is that running through decisions and redo's over and over again will eventually lead me to a fate I don't want."

She turned and leaned against the window sill to my left, facing me and gently caressing my face, "I don't know if there is a reality where we can save the Chateaux; I don't know if there will ever be a way that we save Irene. But what I do know is that I just watched a version of Spring die, and despite my hate for that cruel fate of mine, Kieran showed us the steps for how to possibly defeat Spring in this reality, too."

I lifted my hand to meet hers on my face, pulling it to my lips to kiss it, "yes… we watched Spring die. And we know how to do it again. But first… let's clean you up. Everything has been happening so fast. I just want to take some time and be here with you." I squeezed her hand in mine. "Is that alright?"

Karine weakly leaned forward into my sternum and wrapped her arms around me. "That sounds nice." She said, whispering as she practically fell asleep standing in my arms. "That sounds… really nice."

252

Machiavellian

My eyes were still closed but I could feel the welcoming greeting of another day caress my cheek as the morning sun tiptoed through the meager window of the first place I ever really learned to call home. We were back in Karine's apartment; the one within the magical village run by the Auspice, hidden in plain sight in this enchanted safe house. Reluctantly opening my eyes, I rolled over to find Karine sitting at he edge of the bed wearing one of the modest nightgowns she kept in her dimensional suitcase. She was still. Quiet.

I sat up, silently and calmly, crawling over to her and tossing her long dark hair over her shoulder, revealing the seared remains of the wound I burned closed across her other shoulder and collar bone from Kieran's heavy threat in the Liminal. She barely retreated from my touch as I gently grazed the charred flesh. With her powers depleted from fatigue and shock and my inability to perform healing magic, the best I could do to sterilize and stop the bleeding was to cauterize the wound.

"It really didn't hurt very badly at all," Karine's voice finally scampered from her quiet mouth. "You did a good job, only burning the wound and all. The bone will take time to heal, but you saved me from infection and blood loss. Thank you." She took my wandering hand and pressed my palm to the burn with more pressure, taking a deep exhale in attempts to show me that our choice was necessary and life preserving.

I felt every ripple of burnt flesh on her shoulder press into the crevices of my weathered palms, forgetting for a moment that they matched perfectly because it was in fact the forging grip of my hand that caused it. I shook off the clinging remnants of guilt and finally responded to her. "I knew you were tough enough to handle it. You might be the brains here but I've never doubted for a moment your fortitude."

"Me? The brains?" Karine scoffed, slowly turning her torso to face me and crossing one leg onto the bed. "You managed to not only defeat Kieran while I was paralyzed with fear and guilt, but used our ultimate foe to do it; alternate timeline or not." She boasted, even blushing a bit as she praised me.

For a moment we were just as we were the night before, right after I cleaned and closed her wound. Tired and quiet, but calm and satisfied. The silent sunshine spilled across the floor like a clumsy glass of water, reaching to the doorway to the stairwell that would lead us back to our whirlwind of fate below, but just before it, in that simple wooden box with shabby wooden rafters, I felt whole. Complete.

"We could stay here forever." I stated plainly, much louder than I intended. "Away, just the two of us. Surely with the culmination of my powers I could live almost as long as you." I took her hand, laying my head down in her lap for a moment as my conscious mind began to wade into a make belief world of serenity.

254

I sighed into her thigh, "we could just rest, finally rest. Be together, without fear or doubt. We could eat bread, every day. I *love* bread." I continued, rooting my head against her. "I'm sorry I've been less than trustworthy to you." I said. "Back then even, in the Chateaux before we watched Irene die again. The night before... I told her everything."

I felt Karine's body tense for a moment, a subtle rhythmic shift in her breath followed before returning to the normal subtle cadence of her stasis. "I know you did," Karine whispered. "I had honestly forgotten about it; I didn't think of it twice after I realized that she was somehow much more prepared for our battle and all the more ready to martyr herself for our freedom." She glanced down at me, the knowing smile I loved so much on her face as her messy hair draped into a sun-kissed frame around it in the morning light. "Thank you for confessing your dishonesty, Ren. It means a lot to know that you still love me enough to confide in me."

I jolted upward, my long tussled hair streaming behind me as my face contorted to concern. "Karine, nothing about Kieran is or ever will be you. Of course I 'still love you,' how could you think otherwise?"

I leaned my forehead against hers and closed my eyes, exercising the fledgling empathy beginning to prosper in my heart, "Kieran was your Zorne, your Wyvren. Just like Isadora is Evelynn's, Dorian is Téo's... I'm beginning to learn that we all have a bit of a beast within us. But you taught me that it is what we choose to do with who we are that is more important than who

255

we were, and will help to forge us into who we become."

Karine's face flushed with hot tears of redress as she chuckled to herself, wiping her eyes as soon as they wetted, "see? You're becoming quite the poet, darling. Each and every day I get to watch you grow more and more into the person I thought I knew once upon a time. But now, here you are, more yourself now than ever." She cradled my face with her hands and kissed me, her eyes teeming with war torn nostalgia, "Somehow, I feel like even after all this time, I'm just now beginning to know what it means to fall in love with you."

We leaned against each other again; both in exhaustion and resistance to relenting ourselves back to the duties we had proclaimed for ourselves. Above all else, knowing the inevitability of the ones we cared about, it was time to move forward, truly. We couldn't save everyone, at least not so long as Spring was in control of the universe. Those moments together in that morning creeping into the Autumn were some of the final true moments of peace I would know ever again. So long as I spent it with her, I knew that it was a treasure worth saving.

After another nap and a full hardy meal of sourdough and some of Karine's miraculous vegetable soup, we strapped ourselves into the armor a Vanna we once knew and loved tirelessly fabricated for us. I felt the pressure of guilt with every strap of my greaves and gauntlets, so meticulously and thoughtfully constructed just for me and how my angelic form would react to it.

256

"I didn't think Vanna could use magic…" I more muttered out loud to myself while lost in thought than specifically to Karine. "She was just an artisan, an ally… How did any of those things befall her?"

Karine, fully sleeved and garbed in her long dark coat and obscuring armor placed a hand on my bare shoulder between the sleeveless top and leather bolero situated above my tricep covering gauntlets. "Vanna has always had the potential, her mother was a member of the Chateaux years before either of us even came into the picture of their lives," she justified. "Unfortunately, a combination of trauma, desperation, and an opportunity from Spring was all she needed to become what she is now."

I thought for a moment, "I know we agreed to not try to save Irene, Evelynn, and the others for now while Spring is in control. I know that. And I agree with you. But is there any way, any chance of liberating Vanna?" I felt the tension of anxiety knot in my throat. "Do you think there is any hope of her to come back to us? To trust us?"

Karine sighed and smiled; it was so nice having her back to her composed self, accepting my knowledge of situations and letting go of the control she held onto on her own for so long. "I highly doubt it. I know your heart is in the right place, but like you said, we agreed: we have to defeat Spring and save ourselves before we can begin saving anyone else."

I closed my eyes and relaxed my brow, physically shaking the thought from my head. "Yes, yes. You're right. We can't help others if we can't even help

257

ourselves." I wrestled with the impatience in my heart as I struggled with the morality of selfishness. I knew that she was right, that we were right. But it still felt so painful to survive knowing that those we knew did not.

We stood at the threshold of the only calm place in our lives. The small unfinished attic apartment Karine chose however many years ago to exist as the eye of the storm of our story was an incredibly difficult place to depart. As the eulogy of our rest tapered, Karine reached for the handle and turned the door knob. She pulled the door towards us to reveal the dark and musty storefront that laid at the bottom of the noisy stairs between us and the street front below.

I took a quick breath as if I was about to jump into a frozen lake, and with one step forward I could instantly feel a tug at my ankle. I looked at Karine and without meeting my gaze she affirmed my suspicions with a quick nod. They were waiting for us. Someone was ready for us to reveal ourselves, and that gentle sensation was their spell over the entire town finally reacting to our presence like a trip wire.

"Vanna," I whispered to myself, shaking off the feeling of the thread around my ankle and traversing the stairs with more speed, Karine closely behind. "She's tracking us. How did she find us so quickly?"

Karine shushed me with a finger and illuminated her eyes with her violet telepathy spell, *she can probably track us by the armor and outfits we are wearing, having made them herself. I think the Grace Spring gave to her manifested fully with threads and garments in tandem with that needle-like blade she has. We have to be careful, don't let on that we know she can follow us with these clothes, we might be able to draw her away from the Auspice if she pursues us alone.*

I nodded, carefully and quietly maneuvering through the old relics of the cobwebbed storefront before arriving at the antique glass panes of the display settings facing the cobblestoned road. I looked around, frantically trying to find someone or something suspicious, but other than the faint presence of Vanna's threads, nothing seemed to be a threat.

We slowly stepped outside, inconspicuous in the the casual crowds of witches and their families walking up and down the streets in the various garments and armaments of their own. As we walked, I pulled my hair up into the high ponytail Karine showed me and secured it with the fresh yellow ribbon Vanna gifted me during our first meeting. As I tied the ribbon, I felt another tug, but this time from around my hair.

Karine's telepathy spell was still in effect, so I responded mentally, *Karine, I think something more might be going on here. I just noticed Vanna's presence again but this time from another point on my body. If she was just tracking us, then why would her spell activate again?*

Karine kept a steady pace, walking just ahead of me until we were out of the bulk of the crowds. The town's Main Street let out in two directions; the Auspice Obsidian Tower behind us at the North side of the street, and the forest that contained a hidden gateway the Auspice used to traverse between the corporeal world and this hidden one beyond the veil. As we got closer to the forest, I began to feel more than just the presence of a tracking spell, but eyes on my back; eyes that I couldn't see or detect physically.

Karine, I tried to think, louder somehow without the volume of my breath, *Karine I know you are trying to get us away from the open and civilians, but I think we might be walking into a trap.* She remained silent, her legs steadily keeping pace and head straight forward. She reached behind me to grab my hand and pull me along faster.

Upon finally reaching the end of the road and the majority of homes and businesses behind us, I finally spoke aloud, "Karine, listen to me, I know we aren't supposed to be talking right now but I think this is a bad idea!" I pulled her around by the hand she embraced me with so she faced me; the sight of her face arresting my breath in my chest.

Karine's armor had always been a full body garment, covering everything but her hands and face. In this instance, the cloth and leather from her breast plate and pieces from her cloak snaked around her neck, obscuring themselves behind her long dark hair and covering her mouth. A piece of metal at the end of the fabric made from part of her armor peeked out over her ears and met in the middle, covering the center of her forehead and being the reason my telepathic responses never reached her.

It was just like August on the other side of this very forest; arrested by March's patchwork magic. I should have assumed that under Spring's tutelage that March would have been a key teacher in Vanna's

260

magical corruption. The very outfit Vanna made, even before her indoctrination into the powers of magic, reacted to the tenacity of her craft that she shared with her past self, arresting Karine. After brief assessment and revelation, I frantically began to strip my clothes and armor from myself, Vanna having made my own armor as well.

It was too late. Each strap and every layer of thoughtfully woven material would return to me almost in perfect retrograde as I peeled them from my body. I invoked my Grace and ignited the angelic fire within me to try to gain the speed to evade their tethering back to my form, but as I darted around the canopy of the trees I was outrun by my own bound silhouette, determined to capture me in its embrace.

As each piece of my armor refitted itself to me, the kind and thoughtful Vanna's inspiration to make the armor resistant to heat and fire magic as to not burn away from me was now an unwelcome curse. No matter how hard I tried to burn the bespoken layers around me, they did not incinerate. As quickly as I was beginning to think, the bolero around my neck and chest gathered itself around my face and nostrils, cutting off air from my lungs.

I was never particularly feminine at any point of my existence, so as my vision blurred and Karine eventually lost consciousness near me, I couldn't help but think to myself the irony of falling prey to some kind of malevolent fashion. Despite the humorous thought in my perilous situation, I felt my knees hit the ground as the remaining oxygen in my bloodstream failed to

261

maintain my constitution while everything turned black around me. We'd certainly been had; a trap years in the making as Vanna awaited those six years for us to return to this timeline from our escape into the Liminal. Just a night ago for us, a series of annual traumas for her.

I remembered being just conscious enough to resist dreaming as I felt myself lifted up like a child; strong and formidable hands cradling me as if I were nothing but a wounded bird. My ears were ringing, still unable to fully function as the fabric released itself from my face. Even with oxygen, my body was struggling to register and reallocate resources to my senses. There were mumblings, several voices both high and low. There was an argument, there didn't seem to be a resolution.

I eventually opened my eyes to find myself still in the prison of Vanna's armor around my body; not different in shape but much more terrifying to know that it could constrict my breathing at any moment. I was alone in the Auspice Tower, laying in a bed in the infirmary hall. I could barely remember the details from my time after being treated here, surviving my brawl with Dorian after the Left Hand test. It seemed so unassuming, especially with my face free. It looked like I was just laying in a hospital bed.

"You're finally awake." I heard an inherently gentle voice say to my left, just outside of my view as the bolero of my armor kept my neck and head straight forward. With a few more footsteps Vanna's face came into view above my frozen head, her remaining fiery brown eye peering down her nose at me as I laid at her mercy. She was clad in the red uniform of the commanding Left Hand, star shaped emblem on her chest.

"Vanna, we were going to try to find you. We don't expect you to come with us, but I just need you to listen to me-" my statement was immediately interrupted by a stinging and stabbing pain. I felt the wetness of blood start to form around my abdomen as I tried to understand what injured me. "Did you just… stab me?"

Vanna raised her grip to reveal a handful of sewing needles, all glowing faintly with a pale yellow light as they were imbued with Spring's Grace. "I've got plenty of weapons and plenty of time," Vanna boasted, posing another needle between her thumb and middle finger before tactfully flicking it straight into my jugular vein; blood starting to flow from the narrow impalement with each heartbeat.

"I'm going to torture you, Wyvren," Vanna said with a terrifying calmness. "I'm going to make you pay for your sins before I figure out how to rip your core out and present it to Spring. With your pieces, he said he can take me back to a time where we can save the lives you've taken; not just from me, but from everyone you've ever robbed of happiness since the beginning of your creation."

Vanna flicked three more needles into my arms and throat in her methodically demented acupuncture. "Once we reset everything, he's going to change your engine and turn it into something he can install in me,

263

allowing me to protect the ones I care about and never watch any of my friends die ever again." She raised a glowing yellow hand above me, resonating an agonizing frequency through the needles where they stuck in me and sending incredible pain through my body between the points.

She precisely delivered more and more needles into my body. "Please, stop!" I winced, trembling in pain as my body remained fully unmoving in the prison of my armor. "Spring is deceiving you; the Wyvren engine can only be the Wyvren engine- he's trying to use you to take me apart because he knows I know how to fight him now." Vanna clenched a fist over me, sending more thunderous shockwaves of affliction through my bones. I coughed blood as I felt the needles sink further into my throat and arteries.

I had a choice here. "He is trying to undo the beginning of my lineage as the Wyvren; without me, Karine will never rebel against him and I will never meet Irene." My torturer's grip tightened further as her own nails dug into her palm, drawing blood that dripped down on my face as the suffering continued to tear through me.

I was running out of meaningful options. "With me and Karine out of the way, he will make you the obedient monster he requires." The loyal new Left Hand to Spring raised her other hand, arming her needle sword in hand. The blade shared the shimmering pastel light that was still reverberating through my body. "Vanna, he learned from his mistakes with us. He is going to have what he needs in you so long as you continue to lean into your misplaced vengeance."

Vanna poised her sword beneath my throat in the notch of my clavicle, sinking it in just enough to break the skin. "Why should I believe anything you said to me after you lied to me? After you manipulated me and the noble protectors of our humble way of life?" Her warm brown eye shifted from its umber hue to the bright golden light still emanating from her needles. "I trusted you. I won't be made a fool of again. I've lost too much."

"I still wear your ribbon," I choked out, the constant dynamic and pulsing ache almost pushing my flesh out of my skin. "I care about you. Time doesn't always work the way we want it to, but we came back for you Vanna. *I* came back for you." I watched her eyes look up into my hair and saw her expression shift to glimmering nostalgia. I watched her not only glimpse the favor in reality, but could also watch her mind remember giving me the daffodil dress she loved so dearly. "It is precious to me. I'm sorry we were late. But we can fix it. We can change this story if we work together." Desperation superseded the agony on my face, "please."

I began honing my spatial power. This was my last chance. Even though Vanna had restricted my angelic powers and physical movements, her restricting armor only accounted for the powers she truly understood. In the dimension just beyond the one she tortured me in, I aimed twelve swords around her in a delicate pattern of deadly geometry. I didn't want her to die. I didn't want to kill her. But all I could hear in my head as I laid there at her believed mercy was Karine telling me that we have to save ourselves. We have to. Without us, he wins; the world unravels in the perverse grip of his cunning hands.

Vanna stopped. Her gaze shifted from me as she lost her focus in a series of thoughts. I was getting through to her, I could feel it. I tried again, "you know, deep in your heart, years before we failed to come back to you in time, that we wanted to save not just you, but the world. You ran after us, you bid us farewell. I know in the heart that I am still learning to use that we meant something to you once upon a time. I know that isn't an excuse for leaving you behind, whether we meant to or not." I felt a tear fall down the side of my face. "Vanna, I am so, so sorry."

Vanna's face contorted from nostalgia to sadness as tears began to reciprocate in her eye. She looked down at me and her sword, unclenching her gripped spell hand and wiping her face with the inside of her elbow. "Wyvren… Ren… What…" I watched the yellow light fade from her eye as she seemed entered a new lucid state. "Ren, Ren I'm so sorry. I never wanted to hurt anybody. I never wanted to her you," she trembled as the words left her, almost convulsing as the sudden rush of sentience returned to her. Was she brainwashed completely?

"Vanna, you don't have to apologize to me," I said, smiling at her. "Karine and I, we messed up. We should have been more careful, more intentional. But we are newly navigating this whole thing, too. I won't

266

exploit you for you newfound powers, but your magic could really help us stand up to the tyranny in this world."

I took a deep breath and focused my eyes with ardency. "But I would never expect that of you. There is somewhere we can take you. You'll be safe there. You can run a safe house for others like you did for me, like you did for so many others. You can sew and stitch and mend and create all you want, and I will do my best to make sure the tragedy that befell your workshop never happens again."

"I could… let this all go," Vanna whimpered, "Ren, I don't know what's wrong with me. I can barely remember anything. It's like the last couple of years have just been a haze." Good, good. This was good. I didn't have to kill her. She pulled the needles out of me with quick and precise movements, minimizing the pain as much as possible. "I know where they're keeping Karine, give me a minute to release the spell I have on your armor and we can go to her."

Vanna put her sword away in a sheath on her hip and positioned her palms over my body. Almost instantly, I felt the stitches begin to unfasten in their tightness and return to a fitted position rather than a strangling one. Piece by piece, gauntlets to grieves, I could feel the sections release and the tingling feeling of blood rushing back to my limbs overwhelmed my nerves. She took a satisfactory breath and looked down at me, "okay, once you're loose enough we can get…" her voice trailed off and her eye glazed over with a ghastly yellow mist. Dammit.

267

I watched the phantom grip of a hazy collar fasten around Vanna's throat as she returned to her conniving comatose state. Before I could get up, she immediately closed her palms over me again and nearly rung my limbs dry of their blood as my armor constricted again. From the blurred obscurity of an illusionary spell, March stepped forward from behind her, right hand out and gesturing towards her throat. He was dressed in the uniform of the Lead Right Hand.

I should have predicted that she was controlled once I saw her Left Hand uniform. Left Hands could think for themselves, but when unable to perform the mission the Auspice wanted completely, the Right Hand could temporarily exert control and influence over their Left Hand with a rush of purpose, endorphins, and chemicals to the brain and mind. Before I could try to break her free of influence again, a flurry of needles from her pockets levitated over me in flaxen light and rained down into me, immediately pumping cruelty back into my body.

"You almost lost sight of the life we have given you, Vanna," March's sultry voice whispered into her ear from over her shoulder, his dark curly hair bouncing off his gait. "Remember, they are master manipulators. Lean not on your own understanding; in all your ways acknowledge Spring and allow him to direct your path."

"Of course, teacher," Vanna's hypnotized voice responded, devoid of any semblance of autonomy while freshly under the influence of her Right Hand's collar. I was so close. But this was it. I was going to be deactivated. Killed. They were going to dispatch me and strip me down to parts to defile Vanna further, turning her into the ideally obedient Wyvren without the evolutionary flaw of freewill. I thought back to Irene's smiling bloody face as I saved her from the fate of becoming my kind and repositioned my swords back to their obscured positions, now twenty-four in two pairs of twelve; half for March, and half for Vanna.

"I'm so sorry we did this to you," I shivered from my lips as I suffered in her spell. "I hope that one day, I can build a world where you can forgive me." I triggered the onslaught of steel, my blades efficiently and swiftly phasing through their dimensional sheaths; each swirling in a rippling "S" shaped swing. I closed my eyes as their bodies were dismantled in the unsuspecting carnage, feeling Vanna's blood splash over me as one of her arms bounced off my torso.

The tensions of my armor finally fully resolved and the needles implanted across me dulled from their glow and fell out of my flesh. I opened my eyes, finding myself completely soaked through in the blood of another friend that never needed to die. I swung my liberated legs over the side of the bed and saw March's twitching, still-living body try to slide together in a desperate attempt to quickly reform. I snapped my fingers and with the fire of my palms fully ignited his remains. It wasn't a permanent solution, but ashes would reincorporate slower than pieces.

I rose to my feet with a sloshing sound as my sopping wet clothes left a conspicuous trail of crimson evidence behind me. My dazed steps quickly increased in pace to a full on sprint as I tore through the enchanted halls of the Auspice Tower. I occasionally glanced at the forming geometric shapes dancing in the lights of the ceiling as they turned their ambient attention towards my progress. I had to find Karine fast, the Tower knew that I was free and was going to do everything it could to alert Isadora, the rest of the Council, and most importantly the very much alive Spring still thriving on this timeline.

I felt heavy with the weight of Vanna's blood as it began to dry in my hair, the smell of iron and oxidized platelets wafting from the nape of my neck to the bottoms of my feet. Finally I turned a corner in the seemingly endless corridors to find Karine crucified against an X-shaped structure that hung just off the ground bolted to the wall. Beneath her was the petite and formidable figure that was October, to her left the viciously contrasting shape of Dorian.

Without turning to face me, October addressed me with a demanding avarice in my dismay. "Well it seems the monster has finally reared its ugly head to us." She chuckled, casually flicking a malicious hailstorm spell off her wrist at Karine, attacking an already frost bitten set of limbs as she barely hung onto consciousness. Karine looked up at me, her still and bloody mouth framed with pleading eyes.

I felt a quiet rage stir within me; something familiar to my time as the killer they still believed me to be. As October finally turned towards me, her snickering face immediately shifted to horror and disgust. "Oh my," she addressed, nausea dripping from her words as she covered her mouth with a gag. "I knew you were a

270

merciless killer but did you simply *shred* my subordinate?"

Dorian turned suddenly as well, understanding that his Left and Right Hands were the ones directly responsible for watching me. In contrast to October's disgust, a paternal sorrow washed through Dorian's eyes as the fate of his soldiers dripped from my fingertips and ran down my throat. Without a word he activated his gauntlets, emanating with the Grace of the Season that gave them to him. As his mighty transmutations of strength began to activate and augment his power, the rumbling storm of rage began to overflow from me. I felt something I never truly tasted before begin to nestle within my heart.

Hate.

October raised her hands, her disgusting pride sneering from ear to ear as cruelty swelled in her heart with the same joy of watching a child's first steps. The anticipation of my destruction was the closest thing to a familial emotion in her body. Dorian's bright green light ripped through his armaments as he began to rush me like a bull horns first. But the Clock Key around my neck hummed its simple song as I watched the two of them flicker into slow motion before me, everything that Might happen dancing off of their bodies in intricate swarms of possibility.

But in that moment, I didn't care about tact. I didn't care about almost anything. Spring kept dealing impossibilities to me that kept me in the realm of doing

271

his evil, no matter how much I resisted. Irene and Vanna both died by my hand in this iteration, not his.

I didn't have to hide who I was on this side or reality as Téo's magic-possessed body charged me or Autumn's prodigy daughter threatened me and my lover's life. I was built to kill; no matter how many times I tried to escape the innate programming of where I came from, the violence of my breath was one of the only certainties I clutched in my handful of truths. I narrowed my eyes and ignored the strategy of possibility before me, giving into the hunger for carnage begging for blood at the bottom of my hungry stomach.

Time began to move forward again and as October and Dorian's forms began to recenter and their pace return to the rate of frequency I existed on, I didn't even raise my hands to cast the spell. I didn't speak. I didn't blink. I reached down into the darkness I knew bore me and activated a gravity spell so green, so steeped with density and concentration it was barely light.

The gravity around the two Auspice agents charging me became almost wet with concentration; viscous with my rage and tangible with fatal intent. Silently, before the two trained warriors took another step, I watched them be crushed so quickly, so violently, they liquified before either of them could understand that they not only died, but were atomically stripped from this world. Dorian certainly, but not even October's mind remained to reform herself in her stature as a Month. They were simply gone; the only thing remaining a shallow crater of my wrath between Karine and I.

272

I stood still, barely breathing as I tried my best to search for the humanity, the kindness that Irene had died to give me and Karine so lovingly fostered into a beating heart. But all I felt was anger. Sadness. Guilt. Hate. I didn't want all of these people to die, but I didn't know what else to do. Karine coughed weakly, snapping me out of my dense meditation and jerking my dilated eyes to her weak, fading ones.

I inhaled sharply, feeling oxygen rush back into my lungs and reinvigorate my mind. I sprinted towards her, leaping over the crater I'd recently impacted and unfastened Karine from the odd crucifix she was fastened to; making sure to gently melt away any remaining ice with my forge palms. I delivered her to the ground beneath her restraints and comforted her until she was able to speak again.

Before Karine chose any words to share with me, she reached up to my face with two fingers and wiped some drying blood from my cheek. She rubbed it between her fingers and looked back up at me with tired eyes, clearing her throat to weakly ask what she already knew. "Vanna? Is this Vanna?"

The hate in my heart broke against the crashing waves of guilt weighing my spirit as my face bent into the ugliest tears my face could wring from my body. I held her in my arms, leaning my face into her sternum and I wept loudly and wildly as the rush of my hideous decisions replayed in my consciousness. Karine weakly raised her hand to my head and comforted me in her battered state.

273

"You did what you had to do," Karine whispered to me. "I know you didn't make that decision lightly." She always knew what to say to me. I slowly pulled my head away from her, my nose running now with my tears as I tried to blubber any words at all to justify the choice I made, not just in killing Vanna but in mercilessly annihilating my other opponents. There was no honor in what I did. Only destruction.

"We'll fix this one day. Remember that." Karine consoled me further, sitting up and beginning to exercise healing spells across her wounds. "But right now, we have to get out of here and regroup. Our objective was to try to find Vanna... that didn't work out how we wanted." She smiled her knowing smile at me and continued to walk me through my agony. "One thing at a time. Let's get out of here, okay?"

"And how exactly do you plan to justify leaving here after destroying four members of the Auspice?" A strong feminine voice echoed from the end of the hallway, the geometry in the soft lights gathering above her cloaked figure and retelling the horrors they witnessed beneath their glow. "You can not simply escape the consequences of your actions. You will stay here and pay the price for your gluttonous evils, Wyvren."

The woman stepped forward, shedding her hood and revealing her face. "As the leader of the Auspice Council, I will administer punishment justly and fully with maximum prejudice." Isadora barked; I hadn't seen her since the timeline that was years ago from this one when Evelynn willingly gave herself to become her.

274

"Give yourself willingly." Isadora commanded, the very walls of the Tower bowing into something like a kneel. "I won't be the one to kill you; I know Spring wants to be the one to steal the light from your eyes."

Pride

I looked down at Karine who was thankfully beginning to make a full recovery, using my grip to help her rise to her feet. I felt the stark hollow feeling of destruction begin to ache in my chest again as Isadora walked down the hallway; stalking footsteps echoing as the heels of her militant boots struck the smooth cold floor beneath us. We had not left our small sanctuary for more than a couple of hours and yet both of our lives had been in peril every moment of our venture.

"Isadora," I growled, my voice brutally low and unfamiliar to my ears. "You do not want to fight us. You do not want to fight *me*." I lowered my stance and reached both hands outward to summon two of my heaviest and cruelest swords. "Should you continue your advance, you will not survive me. I guarantee your demise." I angled one sword offensively before me, the other ready at my side for any potential surprises.

"Oh, you seem awfully confident," Isadora said, lifting an elegant hand above her head. The walls shifted from their bowed position and back to a taller and more rigid structure. "But I believe that I may have a little more power to me than you might believe I do." Karine rose and summoned her own weapons, preparing herself for what we were both certain was going to be challenging. The last thing we were going to do was underestimate the innate power of the woman Spring hand selected to run his magical government.

Isadora halted her advance just a handful of steps before us, smiling with her chin held high in her finely pressed black uniform. "Please, it is an awful chore to keep this attire in up to standards. And now that you've mercilessly slaughtered my seamstress it seems that it will be even more difficult to maintain." I felt my heart accelerate as she continued to antagonize me. "You can't win, not in here. You certainly have a chance outside of my walls, but in here, they are just that. *Mine.*"

With Isadora's hissing resolution the floor between Karine and I split. Karine was forced back to the wall against her former crucifix and I found the floor beneath my feet sliding me straight towards Isadora. I manifested a sword behind her and threw the one one in my left hand into the wall beside Karine, thinking as fast as I could. I displaced myself with the sword beside Karine and grabbed her hand, then switched our position with the sword behind Isadora. My make shift form of teleportation could only continue to work where I had my pieces where I needed them in Space.

Without any further discussion, we both charged Isadora's flank with swords dripping in various potential magics as they awaited our intent. Without turning to face us, Isadora raised both her hands to an ictus in front of her, and began to weave a series of communicative gestures in front of her. Without any color signaling or magical aura presenting around her, the walls began to move and shift in chromatic spirals.

The geometric symbols in the ceilings were now creeping across the walls and floors, all luminous with

277

the shimmering colors of the Seasons. Karine and I followed them as best we could, trying to make sense of or dissect what could be happening. As I turned to follow a particularly enigmatic shape, I felt something around my ankles; I looked down to see the lights from the floor circling up my legs like a whirlpool, pulling me down into the riptide of the floor.

I struggled against the current and looked around for Isadora, but more shockingly I found the corridor was no longer a simple hallway, but a complex series of platforms and staircases; all impossibly connected and oscillating in the lights of the potential geometries that raced through the architecture around us. Isadora was standing on the highest platform from us, waving her hands in pleasant calmness as she orchestrated the Tower around us.

"As I said, you are probably quite formidable outside of these walls," Isadora cooed in a condescending and noble tone. "But these walls exist directly in tandem with my magic. The Tower is a part of me, and I a part of it. The light that runs through the halls of this place mirrors the blood that runs through my veins, and the shapes that dance across you and my various constructs are my creation magic; awaiting to be birthed into whatever I need them to be."

This was the full potential of Evelynn's magic, realized through the manifestation of Isadora. Instead of controlling only fluids and waters, Evelynn's magic fully self-actualized its potential and imparted aquatic qualities into other things; light, stone, magic itself. Evelynn was fixated on the subject of her magic, not her

278

magic itself. That's why Spring needed her, that's why Spring created Isadora. With this kind of power, the Auspice Tower would be the ultimate fortress of defense between the Seasons and anyone that opposed them.

I looked at Karine, her assured face confident with understanding as she nimbly skipped through the changing structures while they were solid. She looked at me with her violet eyes and thought to me, *use the Clock Key. Predict what the shapes will be. Find your footing and get out of that damn puddle!*

I stopped struggling, sinking more and more as I centered myself around pumping magic into the temporal artifact around my neck. I opened my eyes and saw the already changing room and the stuttering shifts of where the shapes Might go. There was a solidified chunk of floor in front of me that the light of the hall eddied around; I reached outward and grabbed it, slowly pulling myself out of the whirlpool.

Isadora rolled her eyes with disgust, a stately smile never truly leaving her lips as she gestured towards me, liquifying my tether and sending me in a rush down the hallway and up the wall with a reverse waterfall of colorful lights. As I have always been assured, Time has always been my most difficult venture; even with the Clock Key activated it was difficult for me to meaningfully maneuver through the desired outcomes before me.

As I struggled against the crashing lights, I looked to Karine who was effortlessly weaving through the constructs and actually reached Isadora. The smile left the Auspice queen's face as she lowered into a defensive position, raising various pillars in each color from the platform she was on. In her distraction, the waterfall that was attending to me lost power and I was able to roll out of it, falling from the ceiling and landing on the shifting floor beneath me.

I responded to Karine's thoughts as she began to advance further, closing in on Isadora with each passing strike. *It seems as she allocates resources to other parts of the Tower, she loses focus on maintaining ongoing spells*, I projected to her.

Heard. Karine responded briefly, her focus clearly on closing more distance between her and Isadora. I looked around and followed the trail of potential that would lead me to them. If she was able to function best long distance with a focus on overwhelming individuals with oppressive force, I had to find a way to distract her. Karine was going to be able to more efficiently deliver damage in a fight like this. More importantly, she would be able to exercise restraint. I didn't want to kill anyone else today.

If the Tower was a direct reflection of Isadora, then the Tower was my strategy. Karine was struggling to land an attack on Isadora with the constant obstacles and constructs, even with her Time magic; it seemed that not only the quality but the nature of light itself was at Isadora's command in this place, impacting the effects of Space and Time collectively across them.

I turned my attention from trying to catch up to Karine in my stumbling attempts to participate on her temporal level. Instead I faced the shifting walls and staircases around me. I charged as much heat into my palms as possible and slammed the burning forges into the floor; the light bubbling and steaming as if I were quenching a blade. I heard a shriek come from above me and saw the walls stutter in their movements.

Whatever you just did, do it AGAIN, Karine thought to me, confidence and momentum in her thoughts as she seemed to gain an advantage in that moment. I reached into myself, focusing all of my magic on activating the modified Wyvren engine within me, and felt the crackling of fire and lighting roar from my chest and out of my eyes and mouth, showering me with light and divine strength.

My halo burned into existence in a cyclical glimmer around my throat, ankles, and wrists. Furious burning wings erupted from my back and the weight of Scimariel's burden sank into my constitution, made flesh by Irene's sacrifice. I raised my burning hands above me and summoned all fifty-two of my swords, all in a spiraling helix around me that reached from where I stood to ending wall of the shifting light room around me.

I flapped my wings and forced a burst of propulsive fire from the soles of my feet, launching me through the metal tunnel of my arsenal and igniting each blade with the whitest and hottest fire I could produce. I landed in a crouched position on the wall at the end of my spiral, my searing hands and feet boiling the hydrous luminance beneath me. I raised my head to look through the spiraling paths of burning metal and willed them outward in every direction; taking a path of

281

cursive movements that would only spell the dismantling of this place.

It was unlike anything I had ever seen. The sporadic and unyielding cacophony of enchanted blades ripping through the flesh and bone of the organic Tower's lights drew out radiant vapors, refracting even more brilliant hues in the remaining lights around them. My weapons moved as one body, one organism lashing out against the belly of this place, desperate to chew through it and survive.

The shifting of the walls began to cease as the destruction began to outweigh the structural integrity; where there were once layers of enigmatic brickwork were beginning to expose darkness where the light had simply evaporated. I beckoned my swords around me and in a burning seed of life, I launched myself towards the platform Karine and Isadora fought upon. The destruction was feeding into a pleasure center in my programming and was no longer inhibited by what little restraint I was working with.

In a burst of light I skid across the platform behind Isadora, locking wide eyes with Karine as we shared a nod of duty. If we could stop Isadora, we could being to dismantle the Auspice and its influence at large. Isadora was out of breath, but still gracefully maneuvering through Karine's attacks and dealing blows of damage to her with various strikes from the constructs around her. All things considered, Isadora was winning; she was fatigued but had not yet endured a single blow.

I charged her, my speed parting the viscous platform of light with a shimmering golden wake behind me. Isadora looked over her shoulder at me; eyes wide with anticipation and as she turned fully towards me, I was surprised to see an excited grin across her face as I approached. I pivoted defensively, and thank everything good that I did. As I rolled in evasive maneuvers away from her with a strong gust from my wings, the lustrous liquid that composed the platform beneath me sliced upward in a blade so fine and sharp my keen eyes could barely perceive it.

I repositioned my approach and landed back in on the platform, my feet boiling the magic beneath me. Isadora winced but maintained her confidence somehow, even as Karine approached her again from behind. Isadora didn't turn, but motioned the razor sharp wall that almost sliced cleanly through me into a wire, and rotated it in a furiously rapid spin that covered the diameter of the platform. I watched the deadly stream cut over my head as I slid into a deep crouch and narrowed my wings behind me, but Karine was still in full swing of her swords behind her. There was no way she would evade it in time.

I knew that Karine couldn't really die. I knew that she would simply reappear at the check point she had last made; probably where I found her again years ago on this timeline at the Chateaux with all of the others. That seemed to make the most sense. However, not only did I want her to have to suffer the pain of being ripped apart by Isadora's enchantment, even more selfishly I didn't want to navigate the rest of this

283

journey alone. Without Kieran and the Liminal realm, I wasn't sure how to use the Clock Key to go back and meet her. I had no chance of finding her again on my own.

I watched the golden expanse narrow further as it approached her face and made a choice. I activated my spatial magic again, and in a blink Karine was slashing the air where I was just planted, and Isadora's razor wire was within inches of my face. Knowing that it was coming and seeing where it was coming from, I had a statistically better chance of evading the blow in a way that I could survive. But that decision certainly did not come without sacrifice.

Isadora's face beamed with surprise and she made a decision I was too short sighted and too naive in my cognition to predict. She still had the rest of our entire surroundings at her disposal. From below, she raised another guillotine expanse as she had before, and I was caught in the path of her perpendicular strike. I bent my body, launching myself into a backflip away from the vertical advance and into the path of the horizontal one. I felt the surprisingly chilling water rip through my left wing, tearing it from my back as I watched it be ripped apart at the contact of her structures.

The Wyvren code had no real reactions to pain on its own, as I was never designed to be injured. But in the insanely painful wound of dismemberment I felt my periphery turn white as vengeful retaliation beamed towards my attacker began to sear through my vision. I called my fleet of swords to me and directed them from the havoc they ensued below us into the singularity that would find their target in Isadora's head.

"Did that hurt, monster?" Isadora chuckled as the meteor shower of my steel came upon her in a dazzling orbit. Her eyes widened as the smile left her face for the first time in our battle. She raised as much of her resources around her into a barrier, trying to almost sink completely into the floor below her as the my fully wrath came down upon her. I burned my angelic fire deeper within me, my halos invigorating more heat as they fashioned a new wing for me out of their holy fire.

I felt exhaustion hit me. The weight of carrying the Mantle of an angel in combination with manipulating all of my swords was expending a lot of energy in my mortal body. Furthermore, enduring a dismembering blow that forced my angelic form to restructure demanded even more power from me. I couldn't keep up like this much longer. I looked over at Karine, thankfully fine, as she ran over to me.

"You really sacrificed a wing for your immortal girlfriend?" Karine scolded with words that I couldn't take seriously. "You could have been completely killed! You can't sacrifice yourself for me- you have to be completely reincarnated, I can literally just-"

"Did you just say I was your girlfriend?" I asked, my already literally glowing face blushing with the thought that Karine really wanted a relationship with me when all this was over; well, I guess in hindsight wanted one with me even then.

Karine stared at me dumbfounded, a goofy grin spreading on her face as she laughed loudly in my face, "of course, you're my girlfriend, Ren. We love each other? We live together? We kiss from time to time?" She rolled her eyes and continued to briefly cackle at my expense, "anyways, that is *not* what we should be worried about right now!" She finished with discipline in her tone. She was right, of course she was right, but the simple thought of something happy in my life took precedence over the pain and exhaustion in my bones. I felt invigorated. I felt ready to fight. I felt loved.

We turned to face what would have been Isadora's tomb built by my blades, but the both of us knew better. There was no way that the Auspice queen and commander-in-chief would be decimated by a couple dozen blades enchanted to the brim with a divine inferno. It would be too easy. I readied the lambent arc spell I created in Midnight and fashioned it into a bow once again while Karine remained at attention with her own blades.

To our expectation, the mausoleum of swords began to rumble, the nectarous waters beneath us reverberating with booming ripples and waves. Out of the crevices of my swords began to rise remains; literal bits and pieces, limbs and parts of Isadora, all lifted by the golden illuminated waters and dancing with geometric constructs. Above where she was struck down, she began to reform crudely into the outline and shape of her corporeal form until the usable parts finally aligned into their proper place, the completely destroyed parts now comprised of her magical waters.

286

"You didn't think you could actually kill me with weapons you found hundreds of years ago, did you?" Isadora's voice echoed, now not from a moving mouth but from the Tower all around us. "I am the Tower, and the Tower is me. There is no way for you to win while you are within my domain."

Neither Karine nor I fully realized just how integrated Isadora was with the Tower. She was more than in command of it; she had actually become it entirely. I commanded my swords to recede from where they impaled the queen's remains, revealing a crimson smear in the waters below where the bits of her that couldn't be reformed by her magic drifted. She was insanely powerful on her own; it made me begin to wonder why Spring needed the rest of the Auspice at all when he had so much power through her alone.

"We have to engage with the entire structure as whole," Karine said, breaking me out of my awe at Isadora's power. "If she is truly all of this place, she is focusing her consciousness into this domain we are in. We have to stop attacking 'her' because there is no 'her,' only 'here,'" she concluded. She was right. We both immediately turned from the floating body that was the facade of Isadora and made our way back down to the levels below.

"Just because you understand my power doesn't mean you are able to overcome it." Isadora chided from her avatar above. "You still can't outlast me in my own space."

"Yeah, okay," I said, fed up with her confidence, "just because you believe Spring made you the most powerful being doesn't mean you truly inherited the horrors of his power." I patronized. As we fell to the lower levels, I was sure to reignite my swords and spiral them down around me, gradually increasing speed, power, and even more heat as centripetal force incurred in my descent.

"You could never enjoy the graces of the Seasons or their powers," Isadora responded in her superior tone. "A monster like you is beneath such perfect creation."

Karine rolled her eyes, enchanting her blades with destructive spells and sending out shockwaves with continuous strikes in her circumference. "You all are literally the most pliable, submissive, and malleable minds I have ever had to deal with in my entire existence!" She screamed up at Isadora. "Spring is the problem! He has always been the problem! He literally *killed who you used to be* to remove the obstacle of Evelynn's mind to create you! The unbridled manifestation of her potential! Does that sound like a 'graceful and perfect' being to you?!"

I turned to look at Karine's fuming expression as we continued to fall. I couldn't help but take a moment and smile at her as she disregarded the sheer peril of our situation to take an opportunity to criticize our foe. She really was the most magnificent woman I'd ever met. I turned my attention from her and faced the rapidly approaching series of platforms beneath us, directing my swords in their blurring spiral into that of a single point, aiming a drill from the maelstrom of heat their heat.

288

We tore through the layers beneath us, gaining more and more distance between Isadora and ourselves. I looked over at Karine as we tore through more and more of the Tower, "what's the plan? Do we bust our way out of this place or do we try to completely tear it apart?" We landed briefly on an especially thick platform as Karine took a moment to ponder a response, massive pieces of the higher levels crashing down around us.

"We tear this place apart," she finally said, looking at me with a determined and almost playful excitement. "We have spent so much time trying to be careful, trying to preserve as much as we can. But what's been done to Evelynn on this timeline can't be undone, and I have no use for the pretentious bitch that is running this place." She walked over to me and grabbed my face, pulling hers to mine as we shared a kiss, surrounded by the burning lights of my swords and the wailing lights of the Tower's destruction. "Are you good with that?" She asked.

I felt my cheeks flush with affection and enthusiasm. This beautiful woman was asking me to release the inhibitions of my humanity and give into the destructive wants of my inner demons. I had never been more in love with her. "Back me up, Karine. I'm going to invoke as much of my power from as many sources as possible. I'm going to be an arrow of destruction and you are going to have to be the one that aims me."

I carefully handed her my bow, restraining the light as best I could so human hands could handle it better. All the while, the walls were beginning to sharpen as they caught up with our coordinates during our strategic sidebar. "Are you ready?" I asked, beginning to call in my swords and all of the inertia they incurred on their descent with us. "It won't be long until I'm critical."

Karine took the bow in her hands, forming her own enforcing magics around it and reinforcing braces around her arms to be able to withstand the recoil. "Yes. I'm ready. Top or bottom?" She asked, deadlocked in the eyes. I tilted my head in stunned confusion with wide eyes as my fiery wings began to engulf me in nearly blinding white light. Karine giggled, "I mean, do you want me to aim for the top of the tower or the base of it?"

I chuckled, my laughter hot and smoking against my burning breath as my skin began to form small cracks of magical rot in the crucible of stress I was cooking myself within. "Bottom," I said, winking at her as my form heightened into a white burning narrow bird with a long narrow tail and tightened wings, my actually body holding the form together from within the breast of the manifested phoenix. Karine rested the bottom tip great long bow against the ground next to me, its size increasing proportionally to mine as she aligned the tail of the infernal avian against the enchanted bowstring and drew it back.

The walls began to erratically form into sharpened spears, manifesting out of the illuminated geometries, trying to pierce Karine in a lattice of malicious extensions. Using her perception of Might, she navigated the predictive blows and dancing through them, my presence in her grasp beginning to singe

290

away the sleeves of her coat and facets of her armor. The avatar of Isadora began to understand our strategy from the several layers of Tower above us and started a rapid descent towards us. As she approached, Karine drew the bow and let me fly; a screaming eagle of fire tearing through the remaining lower platforms and crashing through the foyer and platform below.

The foundation of the Tower went several stories deeper than I originally thought as I continued to chew and demolish the structure. When I finally hit the earth beneath it all, all of my fire extinguished itself. My halos left, my wings retracted, the light left my extremities and I fell to my knees in weakness. I hoped with all that I was that we made the right decision in our attack. I was completely out of power. I looked down at my body, pleasantly surprised to find the bright orange cracks of magical rot not nearly as plentiful as I had feared during my fiery transformation.

I wiggled my fingers and toes. Good, I could still feel everything. I warily rose to my feet and looked up through the now gaping center of the Tower; hollowed out and scorched like a massive chimney. I felt something wet hit my face; looking down and touching it to further examine it within my fingertips I found it was the glimmering light of the Tower's power.

Slowly, more and more drops of the shimmering waters rained down upon me in my crater; gently and unthreatening, completely devoid of intent. I reached and was able to summon a sword; using it to dig into the earth around me and climb out of the crater as the liquid light started to fill the expanse. I surfaced in what

291

was once the brilliant and illuminated foyer of the Auspice Tower, now without a lift platform as it lay in pieces around my point of impact and completely devoid of any light or shapes whatsoever.

The rain eventually ended, completely filling the the crater and stopping just over my ankles in the great foyer. Lastly, a ragged form slammed into the viscous pool of light around me. I stepped closer to see the dismembered remains of Isadora, the remaining half of her face bearing a lifeless eye as she began to sink; her corpse not fully formed enough to float as the magical waters around her began to fill her chest cavity, taking her deep into the crater below.

"Karine!" I yelled, my throat hoarse with dehydration from the intense heat I produced. "Karine where are you?" I coughed, my voice unable to carry further. I took a knee, dizziness beginning to take hold of me with that final bit of exertion. The room began to fade around me but I slapped myself in the face, resisting the call of my subconscious begging me to let my body begin the healing process. Outside of the physical traumas, operating at that level of temperature and magical density was more than dangerous and often deadly.

"Don't fall asleep on me now, Ren," Karine's soothing voice soothed as she skipped down the rubble of the layers above, slowing her speed with her Clock Key to prevent any deadly falls. "We've still got work to do."

I looked up at her, still taking a knee, and laughed harder than I had laughed a day in my waking life. I was so relieved to see her, not only well but teasing me after such an intense battle. The last time we were here together Irene was killed, the time before that Karine was. While rare, we took a moment in the deadly midst of enemy territory to share the sanctuary we had both known in our sleepy apartment in the wreckages of our victory.

She finished her wafting descent, landing in front of me and beginning her regiment of advanced healing spells that shimmered in hues of blue and green. "We've got to get you fixed up; we've got to get out of here and try to find a way to take on the rest of the Council now that Isadora is defeated."

As her spells put me back together, I raised a serious glance at her, "I don't think we should retreat, Karine." I whispered quietly through my charred teeth. "I don't think now is the time we run. We defeated their leader, Spring's anointed mortal in this world." Her spells reached my throat as moisture returned to my tongue, clearing my words further. "We can do this. We can fight."

Karine kept steady with my glance, continuing her healing spells and taking note that I was right. The Auspice queen was defeated. The Tower was in shambles and would only continue to fall apart without her. October, March, Vanna, and Dorian were all defeated, easily at that. As she finished her revitalizing magics, she responded, cooly and calmly, "alright. Let's win today."

Prejudice

The Tower was much more difficult to traverse without the help of Isadora's magic holding it together. After the impact of our collective strike to foundation of the obsidian structure, there was nothing that allowed us to make sense of the levels above. We both looked up through the collapsing shell of the once magnificent Auspice, knowing that should we choose to stay on this timeline, it was going to take a lot of explaining and damage control to the citizens of the refugee town they organized in hopes of rescuing them from my very presence. Another problem for another day.

"Once we reach the top of this place, you know we are going to have to deal with more than just Spring, right?" I motioned, looking at Karine with concern as we stood abreast, still awing the eviscerated structure.

Karine took my hand and looked to me, "without worrying about anyone to protect, we have a real chance. We start by saving this world, no matter what. Then we can do our best to put the others back together." She turned into me, wrapping her arms around me and pressing her head to my chest. "No matter what, we are going to get through this. Don't focus on protecting me, I'll reappear somewhere in Time and I'll know where you are. We just have to make sure you survive this."

She cradled my face with both hands and looked deeply into my eyes with, the severity of her glance darkening her ocean eyes. "The Seasons are going to do everything in their power to stop us at the top of this Tower, but remember their strengths, and that the sum of the other three Seasons are equivocal to Spring's power."

I nodded, unblinking as I recited their powers, "Summer takes and thrives, Autumn wanes and withers, Winter decays and buries. Spring creates; more power, more events, more tragedies. He is the beginning of their cycle; the initiator of generations."

Karine kissed me on the cheek. We stood in a brief silence much like the one we shared in the artificial peace hanging within the threshold of our doorway. Exhausted but magically revitalized by Karine's esoteric healing spells, I reignited Scimariel's fire within me and called upon Autumn's Grace that coursed through my body. Once both power sources circulated to the Wyvren engine, my wings sprung from my back and strength filled my limbs as my halos returned.

I scooped Karine up into my arms and looked into the abyss of wreckage above us as though staring into the blackest night with no stars and widened my wingspan. With an igniting push from my feet and a soaring flex from my pinions, we burned through the expanse in a shimmering vertical pillar, straight to the top of the Tower's remains.

We passed through the various halls, now shed of their divine blessings and worldly incorporation. Each remaining magical corridor no longer lead to an enchanted place of value to the Auspice, but instead laid as an empty hanger, devoid of anything at all. As we

295

reached the higher levels above our fight with Isadora, we found that they were beginning to fully disintegrate; the steady waters of light that constituted each remaining floor now a luminary cascade down through the shell below.

We landed at the top, and with little surprise found July, September, and December standing between us and the doorway to the platform that would call the Seasons to us. I landed on the opposite edge of where the platform once hovered; the circumference of the great loft being plenty wide enough for navigating around the empty chamber we arrived through.

Karine heaved an exasperated groan, "please, this gets so much easier if the three of you would just move." She brandished each of her blades once more, both of them humming with a harsh purple and black hue. "We have defeated your your most competent warriors, their superiors, and your leader. If you choose to face us, none of you will survive." Karine turned and looked at me, a vicious confidence in her eyes. "Don't hold back." She commanded me. I felt a chill shiver down my spine.

"We will not yield our ground…" July began to command, her blonde igniting and her whip forming in her left hand. As she began to address us, I had already closed the distance between us, cleanly slicing her left arm off and holding it in by hand behind her just as her whip manifested into existence. She screamed in pain, clutching the bloody shoulder her arm recently hung from and took a knee. I clenched the limb in my hand and rendered it to ashes in my grasp.

296

September fell to his knees, raising his hands in attempt to slam them into ground and summon his great obscuring forest spell around us. Before he had a chance to even call the green magics to his palms I stole them, leaving only bloody wrists above him. His already meek face twitched with fear and devastation as the magic that was once guided to his hands fell down his forearms alongside his ichor. He slowly turned his head to find me behind him, swords in hand as I the last thing his eyes would see were my blades slicing straight through them. I was on fire; alive with the carnage of our victory.

December froze, not in her flurries of magic, but in fear that any movement should it insight the maelstrom of my violence. July stumbled to her feet and tried to charge me with the sheer fury of her Summer flames, only to be met by my much hotter hand grasped around her face. She burned with the heat of a desert, I burned with the magnificence of a star. In her scorching heat my fire crept through her blaze, burning through her cheek bones as my grasp met itself, the top of her head toppling from my grasp as the fiery Month fell still, cold for the first time in her life.

Karine appeared behind December, swords poised into shears around her neck. "As I said, should you be foolish enough to face us, none of you will survive." December's pale stature remained unmoving at the mercy of the temporal warrior, dark black hair gently wafting from the great winds whipping outside of the door that was our goal behind her. "I know your kind will simply reform eventually, but if you make another move, I will personally ensure that it will be the cruelest death you have ever known in your eternal life."

December raised her hands, not to cast a spell but to surrender, knowing that she had lost and that the final vanguard of the Auspice had been conquered. She looked to me and asked in a bright soprano voice, "may I advise you, Wyvren?"

I turned to her, my eyes a glaring blaze of green in the midst of my crackling white visage. "What do you have to say to us, December?" I responded in a voice that I only recognized as the beast I unleashed against October and Dorian hours ago.

"You have defeated most of us, but not all of us," December advised in a surprisingly steady voice. "Beyond that door will not be another group of my brothers and sisters to overcome, but a foe that you should be wary to face." She looked up, her face upside down speaking to Karine as she laid in the mercy of her fatal vice-grip. "While you killed our leader and warrior, there remains the cunning minds of those you are bound to underestimate."

I looked at Karine, wary and alert of December's final warning to us. Karine looked down to December, "thank you for your advice, Month. I will not take your life with my swords." She said, retracting her blades from December's throat. Before the wintry Month could rise to her feet, Karine whipped her body around into a roundhouse kick, sending the shocked adversary falling down the empty shaft of the Tower. "… but I'm certainly not going to let your survive to kill us later." She turned her bright eyes back to me. "Are you ready?" She winked.

The heat of my magics coursing through me simultaneously pressed a smoky heat on my vocal folds; I simply nodded in response as my long hair began to catch fire in an infernal mane to catch up with the rest of my physical form. I felt hot, but not overwhelmed. I wasn't breaking down from the magic like I was when I had to be recuperated in Midnight for weeks. The Wyvren was digesting the powers I gained. I was evolving again.

I turned towards the door, the sheer heat off of my body turning a miserable gust with my head that tore through the doorway, breaking the entrance from the threshold before us as the cold air of elevation blustered through the loft level around us. Before us the intricate grid of levitating platforms manifested into their positions for us to traverse. Together we made our way outside, Karine carefully walking across the steps as my wings clung to my anti-gravity; a dim red beginning to emanate from my feathers as they allowed me to weightlessly glide forward.

"For someone so seemingly righteous in their cause, the two of you seem to be committed to an oppressive level of destruction against us." A calm and juvenile voice rang through the air, vibrating even my teeth with volume and resonance. It was loud, but it was beautiful. As the elegant sound echoed through the air around us, it reverberated through the horseshoe that was the Council's meeting place, physically presenting sound waves that seemed to assimilate together. The form was one I had seen rarely among the ones familiar to me in this place.

The small collection of sounds crashed together like church bells, the altar they resonated above acted as a conductive steeple to its command. The sound remained intense, but somehow bearable, pleasant even. I could feel a calming glee tremor through the hate in my heart. My magical form spread a peculiar smile as a drunken feeling of pleasure crashed through my veins. Was I getting tired?

I could feel my magic start to unfocus as my feet touched the ground, I looked over to Karine who seemed even more effected by the compelling harmonies ringing through the atmosphere around us. The light frequencies of my halos started to hiss and sputter, losing structural integrity as I felt my teeth begin to resonate with the peculiar song shaking through the platform.

The sweet melody started to sing vowels and consonance together; a sweet harmony weaving together sweet words in voices I knew. "Ren, Ren it's okay, you can relax now. There is no danger here." Irene's soothing voice rang though my ears. I snapped my head around, suddenly more alert when I heard the sound of her call. I smiled, joy rising in my heart and tears welling in my eyes as they turned to steam against the raging heat of my cheeks.

"You're safe now," Irene's voice continued to coo. "You've fought so hard for so long. Just rest now. Once we leave here we can go back to Vanna's and maybe she can stitch a new dress for you to wear." *That sounds so nice* I thought to myself. *Let's go, let's go see Vanna.* I felt the ache of sleep begin to tug at my eyelids as my fire dimmed more and more.

Suddenly I felt a raging discomfort, followed by a strange heat in my abdomen. I looked down and in the haze of my sleepy vision I saw a young man stabbing my stomach with a narrow dagger. *Ouch* I thought to myself. *I'm in danger. I have to fight. Where is Karine?* My anesthetized mind stumbled through the words like rummaging through a book, looking for what I was trying to say.

"No, it's okay," Irene said to me again. "Karine is safe; *you* are safe. Hector is only cutting the sickness out of you. Once he pulls all of that red out of you, you'll feel the relief I felt when you left me to die in Spring's arms." I felt my eyes bulge, drunk with confusion as Irene's voice became as poignant as the knife in my stomach. I watched Hector pull his weapon back out of me and plunge it in to my ribs; slipping between my intercostals and rupturing my lungs.

"Yes," Irene's voice sharpened further, "you killed me. You lead me here to die. Your lies fed Evelynn to the beast of this place. You killed Téo just moments ago in slaughtering Dorian. You liquified Vanna moments before that." The disembodied voice that so recently enchanted me with comfort began to sting my ears. "It's almost like you never intended to try to save any of us at all. You really *are* a monster, Wyvren." My nose started to bleed as the soft sounds grew louder and higher in frequency. "And to think I ever gave you a name."

301

I looked down again, grabbing Hector's forearm and snapping the young man's limb, pulling it further and messily stringing the visceral sinew that held it together from the upper part of his arm until it fully tore off. Crazed by the enamoring danger of sounds around me, I screamed and slammed my hands against my head, a compact sound spell in each of my palms. When the impact and magic hit my ears, my eardrums ruptured completely; more blood spewing from my nose and now trickling form both of my ears.

Everything was quiet; the music, the stinging sounds, Irene's cruel taunting- everything. The faint ringing of tinnitus set in as the drunken feeling was replaced by subtle vertigo as my balance was disrupted with the damage to my ears. I slapped my face, stoking further the fire that began to dim within me in the idle temptations. I focused my eyes to find Hector wounded, gathering the remains of his arm and running to the altar where the sound resonated from. The loose collection of sound waves was an auditory illusion. On top of the altar stood Alto, a gentle smile on his face as his eyes glazed over; light and music resonating from his open mouth and causing the acoustic illusions that tormented me.

I looked to Karine, already prepared as she wove a wind spell around her to disrupt the clarity of Alto's hypnotic noises. She activated her violet eyes and thought towards me, *Alto's song is only supposed to impact fully human life forms; I didn't realize that you would be so vulnerable to it, I should have better prepared us for this potential encounter.* She thought

302

apologetically. *I've never seen Alto forced to use his magic so crudely- I have never gotten this far before. If we can defeat them, we have removed all of Spring's defenses, and we can trap him in Kieran's cage spell.*

I nodded affirmatively, turning to watch Hector hold the remains of his arm in his living hand; his magic slowly dismantling what made up the limb and reprogramming it to assemble back to his body in a series of flashing cubes and sparks. Hector was the manifestation of Constantine's magic; they were able to duplicate objects for various lengths of time. This demonstration articulated to me that Hector, using the full potential of that magic, was able to both build and rebuild copies of objects in either order, fully commanding the molecular make-up of every object. Even organic, it seemed.

My hearing was disrupted but not fully gone; the ringing and damage stood enough in the way of Alto's magic but I was still vulnerable to it. I advanced, swiftly and strategically forward in a low flight pattern towards the two young witches. I summoned my fleet of swords, narrowing them around me to create a more concise strike around my silhouette. With an effortless gesture, Hector activated his flickering cubic manifestation spell. For every incoming sword in my arsenal, Hector had fashioned one to meet its blow with his own; he perfectly mirrored my attack with a series of exact copies.

I landed on my feet and began to operate my blades in tactical procedure; dueling in and around the new artifacts only to find that they mimicked my movements. They weren't only exact copies, but truly mirrored objects that countered my arsenal. Distracted my the brilliant counter, Alto narrowed a group of his oscillating sound waves towards me, striking the ground in front of me to reveal that Hector had somehow rode in on them like a wave. He lunged forward with his dagger and I dodged around him, grabbing his arm and tearing it off again.

Before he was able to synthesize a new one, I burned the limb to the bone in front of his face. Discouraged, he retreated again across one of Alto's allied sound waves and back to the altar. My experiment showed that he was only able to heal if there were still remains to copy and reincorporate; without something to copy, he could not reform dismembered limbs. I could work with that.

Reaching out towards me with his remaining hand, Hector gestured a clutching motion at me. I felt a tug at my chest and looked down, realizing just how injured I was. In the haze of Alto's song, I hadn't realized that the tear in my stomach was much higher, reaching into my solar plexus, and his second strike had carved a profusely bleeding hole in my ribs. Hector was reaching for the Wyvren core.

They were a formidable combo that I never imagined would put up such a fight in their seemingly peaceful roles. Hector had already copied my swords; he was trying to now recreate a copy of my engine to build a new Wyvren around it to fight us for them. They were trying to revive the Orchid. I did my best to exert an energy field around me, charging the air between us

304

with an obscuring aura in attempt to disrupt Hector's spell. I looked to my right and saw Karine glancing around the room, following the sound waves and observing them. Surely she knew the danger I was in; what was she doing?

Karine enchanted her blades with a bright yellow spell and raised them over her head. She stood still, closed her eyes, and focused. Alto's song danced around her, now able to reach her after she shifted her own disruptive wind spell. As I watched the affects of the drunken siren song swirl into her ears, she slashed downwards, somehow cutting the sound waves and stabbing into them as if they were physical tendrils.

Much like Hector, she shared the yellow spell to her boots and stepped onto the symphonic onslaught. The magical sound bounced around the room but always came back to Alto; Karine was counting on that. As she surfed across his Aria, the current of his spell eventually brought her straight to him, where she delivered a concise blow into the acoustic gathering that constituted Alto's body. Even in my deafness I could feel the silence choke through the battlefield; the angelic sound of his voice finally stopped.

Hector turned, devastated and angry to face Karine and willed the copies of my swords to fly towards her. She shielded herself as best she could with a series of magic and parries, but there were too many of them. I displaced myself with one of my nearby blades to cover more ground, my swords gathering around me in hot pursuit. As my blades collided with the remaining threats that sought to shred Karine, I formed my light arc spell again to summon my bow to me. But of course it was a ploy; I reacted too quickly and would certainly pay the price for it.

Back within closer proximity to Hector and focused on protecting Karine, my disruptive incantation was interrupted, allowing him get back in range to perform his copying magic. The Wyvren core was Spring's creation; something of a higher dimensional technology. Could he really pull off making a copy of it?

In the flurry of swords, I felt myself losing my footing. I hadn't lost this much blood in a while and I was starting to feel the dire effects of my wounds. I took my bow and an arrow of light from the celestial bowstring formed to my fingertips. I steadied myself, carefully aiming the projectile towards Hector and his steady grip reaching back towards me. Even while controlling the armada of weapons, the formation of an intricate cube began to sputter and spin beyond his grip. As it did, a peculiar pink light ignited in his irises.

It was a shimmering semblance of not just Spring's Grace, but something more. Spring had collected each of the people to appoint to his Council because he knew he could tap further into their powers and allow them to reach their full potential in the sacrifice of their minds and souls. ~~Evelynn's~~ magic to fill the Tower with life, ~~Téo's~~ magic to lead the great power of his commanding government, ~~Kyrie's~~ magic to bewitch and bewilder anyone who would not accept their order, and ~~Constantine's~~ to not just build this city, but was also the ultimate failsafe to restart his Wyvren project this entire time.

306

I poured as much fury, power, and angelic light as I could muster in my condition into my crackling arrow and let it fly, aiming not just for Hector but through the forming heart of my replacement in his hand. If he was successful, he would not just create another Wyvren, but one as advanced as I'd become. Zorne and Victoria were easy enough to dispatch because I had more skills and power; should Hector give Spring a perfect match to my magic and skill set now, we couldn't begin to stand a chance against them.

My arrow whistled towards him, the booming slams of thunder ripping through the air around it as it reached Hector and his Wyvren copy. In a burst of light and fire, Karine and I were blown back to the edge of the platform, the general collective of swords belonging to both me and Hectors scattering across the ground and sliding off into the clouds below. As the dust settled, I tried my best to adjust my eyes, to what was happening.

Suddenly I felt hands on my head and I turned in surprise; it was Karine, placing healing hands over my ears in hopes to restore as much hearing as she could. Healing magic did its best to heal wounds, but could only do so much to restore senses. After that, she quickly went to work on my rigorously damaged torso.

"Are- y-u —right?" Karine tried to ask me as the ringing began to subside from my ears. She snapped on either side of my head, trying to get the magic to respond more quickly in my eardrums. "R-n, ar- yo- al-ight?"

307

I rolled over onto my back to allow Karine to better access my wounds. "Yes, I think so. Hector, he was trying to create a copy of not just my weapons, but of me, too." I tried to urge, the formation of words causing unwelcome pressure to my lacerated diaphragm. "I think I hit it, but the explosion obscured my certainty."

Karine was a brilliantly talented healer, practically tickling my muscles back into place and revitalizing my organs as best as she could. I hadn't expended nearly as much magical energy as I had in our battle with Isadora, but with wounds that severe I only had so much vitality left in my mortal body before healing magic would simply stop putting it back together. I was back together, halos and wings fully burning, but I could only endure so many more blows before I would die.

"I think I saw the arrow make contact," Karine said, "the energy from your attack crashed against the delicate formation of the cube. That has to be the only explanation."

"Is that really your most informed conclusion?" A sweet voice slithered through the ashes and dust from the impact. Within the settling smoke a pair of azalea eyes burned, fuchsia light glittering around them. With a concise wave, the obscuring particles in the air dissipated, revealing a horrific sight I couldn't have fully predicted.

Hector's body was split from his head to his waist, and out of it Spring's form began to sprout, cradling the fledgling Wyvren engine in his hands as it continued to assimilate. "You didn't think for a second I would actually let this perfect response to your unique and untamed evolution pass me by, did you?" Spring asked me.

"What… did you do?" I asked, my face contorted with shock and disgust. "Hector… his body is…"

"As soon as I saw the two of you absolutely *decimate* the defenses I placed here in my happy little sanctuary, I knew that I had to take drastic measures," Spring began to explain. Placing both of his hands on either side of Hector's withering husk, he allowed the cube to float in front of his face as he pulled himself out of the corpse, stepping naked out of the vessel and summoning a series of ornamental purple and golden cloaks around his body.

Spring paced leisurely, the cube beginning to revolve in a steady stride as it increased in size and complexity. "So, I began to feed myself into Hector's body by way of the Grace I gave him, infesting him like a parasite and waited." He folded his hands behind his back casually and looked up in disappointment. "I gave him the opportunity to accomplish the task himself, but once I saw him about to miserably fail I fully realized myself inside of him. The sheer presence of my sudden arrival tore through the Space around him; that's what caused your little explosion."

We were stunned. I looked at Karine, and she shared a look of concern with me. Instead of responding to Spring's explanations, she changed her expression from worried to motivated, truly or not I couldn't tell.

"Are you ready?" She asked me, helping me back to my feet again. "We're going to have to be perfect from here on out."

I looked at Spring, patiently waiting for us to gather ourselves with a patronizing smile. I turned to Karine, sharing in her intensity. "Let's kill him." I responded, coldly and firmly. We summoned our weapons back to us and faced the blithe enemy we shared.

With a calm smirk and an empathetic stare, Spring whispered with force strong enough to rush the gusts back to the platform around us, "come to me, my little songbirds. Struggle against me; perhaps if you survive you may learn something."

Adamas

My burning chest was still; lightning crackling between my clenched teeth as the star fire raged through my veins. My eyes were steady on Spring, his posture as still as a cypress as my the recreation of my existence hovered above his head. I dared not to take my sights off of him, feeling Karine's readied presence to my right as she shared a thought with me.

You go for Spring, I'll focus on destroying the Wyvren core, Karine's violet telepathy echoed through my head. I opened my mouth and took a deep breath, smoke and steam rushing from my lips as my skin rippled with blazing white fire upon my steady exhale. Without taking my eyes form him, Spring was suddenly gone before us; engine still rotating and turning into formation where he previously stood.

"Trying to divide and conquer? That seems a bit confident of the two of you, doesn't it?" Spring's voice wafted between us from behind. Without turning to see him, I burst forward with Grace and fire from my soles and made distance between us. I knew he was there, it was a waste of time to confirm the obvious. Karine surely did the same, I could only hope she was fast enough to truly break away in time. She was right; I *had* to survive, lest I potentially lose my humanity in the next Wyvren reincarnation.

During my launch, I pivoted midair and shifted into a full Wyvren skillset. These angelic powers were mighty additions to my stamina, but in force alone; I needed to fight Spring in the same language he spoke to truly keep up with him. I leaned into the dimensional magics of the Space around us and clutched the Clock Key around my neck. In activating them together, I attempted to predict a lay out of both what Spring Might do, as well as exercise consistent dominion over the Space around us. I could feel the overwhelming presence of Spring push back against me as I tried to level our playing field. I immediately felt heavy, dropping more than a foot in the air.

Spring grinned at me as I turned to fully face him, brilliant pink magic dripping down his body in phosphorescent mists. As his magic hit the ground, gardens of flowers burst into existence, spreading mosses and meadows as well beneath their colorful expanses. Without any gesture, the Space around me constricted as he arrested my relation to gravity. I activated my crimson anti-gravity, but it wasn't strong enough. With a flick of his eyes the ground beneath me compressed with the green concentration of pressure, exponentially increasing my gravity and slamming me into the platform.

A crater formed around me as I felt myself sink deeper and deeper into the obsidian material; the black glass cracking and splintering around my body as I resisted with all of my power to rise to my feet. I sifted though every power source at my disposal; Scimariel's light, Irene's fire, the Wyvren's anti-gravity, and the sheer strength of my magical durability. He was too powerful.

I was collapsed, completely trying to lift myself with both my arms and legs as I felt my wings pull down further. I looked up and tried to focus my vision, watching Karine mercilessly dance with Spring in graceful battle. I hadn't been on the receiving end of a gravity spell this strong; as I watched their movements, I noticed how slow they seemed from my perception as the Time around me dilated in the concentration of gravity.

I saw every movement. I also wondered how Karine was so fast for a human witch, even with her astute understanding of magic. She worked seamlessly with her Clock Key, every moment she almost endured a hit from Spring's magic or fist she blipped herself out of this timeline, stepping through a parallel existence and dodging his attacks. I watched Spring's eyes follow her, but even in his dimensional prowess he was unable to effectively stop her ahead of time, unable to predict where or when she was going to phase through.

Spring clapped his hands together in front of his face as if to pray, his bright azalea glow expanding from his eyes and reforming the neon mist around his body. "You're always so clever, young Faust," he teased in his honeysuckle voice. "You've always found a way to stay just far ahead enough to survive. You truly are the strongest witch this world has ever known."

Karine didn't respond, instead reweaving herself higher and higher in the air; freezing Time again and again and projecting herself into a more formidable altitude. "I don't need your praise, Season," Karine finally hissed, arching both swords around her as she began to spin downward towards him, activating another yellow spell and crackling with lighting and velocity.

Karine's inertia was so concentrated she bolted straight towards him, striking the ground in a divine rotation and digging both swords through his body. She tore through him, landing just feet behind him with both swords impaled in the ground. It wasn't a fatal blow, but it was enough to distract his power allocation from concentrating on the crushing gravity around me. His oppressive spell dispersed, bouncing me off the ground as it resolved. I felt my ribs crack and my left femur splinter in the releasing impact; air rushing back into my lungs as the reformed from near collapse.

My wings lifted, heat burning through my flight feathers as I wasted no time. I gathered my swords about me and dispersed them in a chaotic circumference around the altar platform. I fired myself towards Spring and as he turned towards me, his misty form was putting itself back together from Karine's attack. He smiled at me and raised a hand, prepared to launch another gravitational trap as the cruel green magic collected in his hand.

I was ready this time; as Spring launched his attack I displaced with one of the reimagining swords behind him, third back from the closest that landed there. He turned to me again, now completely reformed with a look of pleasure on his face as his eyebrows lifted with delight and surprise. I grabbed the two sword from the ground in front of me and spiraled towards him again, trying to mimic Karine's strategy of gathering as much momentum in a concentrated moment as possible.

Before Spring was able to fully react, Karine remained just a stone's throw from him from her previous attack, recharging her velocity spell. She zipped towards Spring in a vibrant line of burning amber as her two blades met mine; two in his chest running through where his heart should be and the other clanging together through his throat as his head soared through the air.

Karine and I looked at each other, ferocity and destruction dilating our pupils as we mustered all of our force and continued to tear apart the remains of his body. Every strike, more pink mist drifted from his wounds instead of blood or carnage. Even without his head his body was doing its best to stay incorporated to itself. In a fit of what felt like impatience, the mist retreated to the body and converted to Spring's sickening brightness, exploding outward and pushing us away.

We immediately landed and held our ground; both of us interlocking arms and driving our four swords through the floor to keep us nearby. We couldn't afford to let him keep distance between the two of us. Even still in our ardency, Spring's body made its way to his head and gingerly placed it back on the stub of his neck.

"I designed the Wyvren, I should expect my creation to be the most capable adversary here," Spring chided. "But still, even now, you are simply the best Karine." He began to step forward, reaching towards us and ripping Karine's blades from her hands. "I wonder," he seemed to consider, maneuvering Karine's weapons in his grip, "were you destined to be the best *because* you are Karine Faust, or are you who you are because you *are* the best?"

I felt Karine's resolve flicker for the first time since our fight with Kieran; Spring clearly struck a nerve somehow with that and I wasn't sure why. "You're spitting nonsense, Spring," I preemptively responded, breaking through whatever trance he was trying to bewitch Karine with. Both sides were stalling; Karine and I waiting for the opportune moment to trap Spring, and Spring waiting for my twin in the forming Wyvren engine to be born.

He has your swords, I thought to Karine, mimicking her violet eye spell for the first time, almost surprising myself. *That is Time. We don't need to destroy that Wyvren core; we need to use it.*

Spring continued his approach, tilting his head with the interest of a scientist as he observed his experiment's behavior. "I saw the flicker of your mind spell, Wyvren," he acknowledged. "But… curiously enough, I couldn't hear a thing."

Karine switched her eyes at me, reflecting her understanding. I released my grip on the hilts of my weapons, allowing Karine to take them in her hand. She was especially vulnerable now; relinquishing her assets of Time to Spring in hopes that the cage would find its way to him. I reached deep into myself and remembered who I was before; a learning machine of destruction and evolution. I was relying so strongly on just the Wyvren's latent abilities and the new skills I had been granted by the circumstances of this lifetime. I had so much more to fight with.

I formed an umbra, a projection of magical manifestation, and fashioned its likeness to mine. The collection of burning and angelic energy hummed and sparked in the formation of my likeness, but hollow like armor. I turned to Karine and cloaked her in its power. Surprise and hesitance struck her expression at the abrupt granting of power, but she relented in understanding of her vulnerability. Just like that, I temporarily granted Karine a copy of Scimariel's wrath.

"Now you're using that sweet little brain of yours," Spring condescended, launching towards us with Karine's blades. Karine flew straight up into the air, burning with speed and power to avoid the attack and begin to navigate how to pilot the sudden gift of power. I displaced with one of the swords in his hands; Karine's short blade resting where I stood before as my hand clasped his in my sudden grip. I looked at him and smiled, activating my own gravity spell around us.

Within the domain of my own magic, the crushing gravity was much more forgiving to my form as his hand crumbled in mine, smashing his body into the ground as he had mine just before. Spring raised his head to gleam a contorted smile that bent before my enchantment, using his anti-gravity to lift Karine's long sword towards me. Without hesitation, I tethered to the Space around Karine's short sword I previously displaced with, launching it through his face and splitting his head vertically with the impact. Even in his certain immortality, it interrupted his red spell of resistance.

It wasn't enough, and I was very aware of the futility of these decisions. I couldn't waste time, I just had to make sure he wasn't in a position to escape or fully understand what was happening; otherwise he could certainly find a way to counter the trap. I was sure of it. I pulled from on and beyond the platform all of my swords and Hector's doubles; tearing Spring's crumbled hand from him as I retreated from the gravity trap he was in and allowing the full might of over one hundred blades to tear through him. I threw his hand into the pile and converted the gravity magic to holy fire, incinerating him for good measure.

In the brief moment of reprieve, I looked at Karine who was still high above, ready to enact the caging spell. She knew she had to be the one to do it for a couple of reasons: firstly I was powerful enough to keep up with Spring in a truly combative way, and secondly, Spring could find a way to tap into my engine at any point as a trump card and stop me from completing the cage. It wasn't a certainty, but the possibility of his influence over me was something that haunted us at every turn.

I looked to the fledgling Wyvren core, almost fully formed. I looked at the pile of ashes that was Spring, already beginning to emit pink mists of reformation around the two swords of Time nestled in them. I burned Autumn's Grace as brightly as I could within the pyre of my body. As soon as my dark twin was born, that was our moment, our opportunity. We didn't have a lot of time, but we needed her power before she became fully realized.

Karine wove a spell she seemed to memorize perfectly from Kieran in the Liminal; tugging at the Grace running through me, activating the brilliant blue of her blades, and tapping into the sickening fuchsia light of the forming Wyvren cube. Between the three sources, the triangular prison began to form at the median distance between our points. With a decisive "click" from the Wyvren cube, the spell was complete.

To my horror, Spring's mist shed away completely, exchanging its haze for a completely reformed body. I tried to react, but my movements began to jostle and disrupt the forming cage; I thought I had more time, I should have divorced myself from Autumn's Grace so it could stand alone. Honestly, even if that was the right call I wasn't sure how to do it anyways.

Spring reached out to me, clutching my throat as I was arrested in my necessary position. "It is disappointing that you have yet to realize that I will always be ahead of you." He snarled, paternal disgrace replacing the otherwise pleasant tone he often chose to use in battle. "I am a higher dimensional being; your timelines don't overlay across me how they do with you. Every iteration of myself, across every timeline, is connected. I saw what you did to 'me' in the Liminal with Kieran."

Karine looked down on us in devastation, knowing that if I tried to escape now it would destroy our only chance of sealing Spring away. I looked up at her, violet returning to my glassy green eyes. *Don't stop*, I thought as loudly as I could. *We can win, do not yield. We can win. We can do this.* I raised my hands to his arm, clutching them with as much cauterizing might as I could muster but to no avail.

"Did you really think for a moment that you could harm me in a way that mattered?" Spring continued to antagonize, my fire withering against his impervious flesh. "I had to obscure my wellness this entire battle, hiding it within the lavish illusions of my frequency. The mist wasn't healing me, it was making you believe that you were making any progress at all. You thought you were stalling me to form this cage, but all I needed was enough time to form a daughter that would actually listen to me."

I felt my body weaken in his grip. I burned hotter, flapping my wings to try to escape, willing my swords to swarm and impale him, casted a gravity spell, kicked with my dangling legs. Nothing. Everything almost seemed to just graze around him. He was playing with us, wearing us down. But we had an answer, and we knew that it worked. I just had to stay alive a little bit longer.

As soon as the thought of enduring survival entered my mind he grabbed one of nearby swords and stabbed me through my chest. I felt the bitter taste of iron fill my throat and mouth as I respirated blood through my wounds; diagnostics going crazy through my program as he keenly ran through my trachea between my lungs with severing my core from major arteries. A fatal wound in an already beaten body. Karine

320

had to hurry, because I was going to die. I was going to die.

The sealing spell was almost complete as Spring reached into my chest cavity, opening the severed organ that housed my engine and pulling it out of me. I watched the capillaries and remaining arteries clinging to the device as my body desperately tried to resist losing what sustained me. I looked back up at Karine, tears running down her face as she continued working the spell. With all my remaining power, I thought to her.

Now or never. Don't let him win.

With conniving precision and surgical ease, Spring tapped several parts of my Wyvren engine and opened it, code and modifications soaring from it in a projection of white, gold, and blue lights. He looked into my eyes with the receptive love of a father watching their prodigal daughter return, keeping eye contact as he drug a line through my existence and staining it with his azalea hues. I felt my consciousness fade; not just in the sense that my body was failing and dying, but I felt my identity being erased. Each stroke of his finger undoing the humanity I had worked so hard to foster. Every motion erasing the love that I had come to know in this world.

Spring gestured towards the completed Wyvren cube, dragging it across the air in the room as its movement interrupted the progress of the sealing spell even further. I saw an orange line cut across my vision

again; I had seen it before. This was a restart. This was
something new. I was a failed experiment. I was a
failure. I was going to die here and leave Karine to relive
all of this again and again, no iteration of me she would
find again ever quite the same as me, perhaps never
making it this far again.

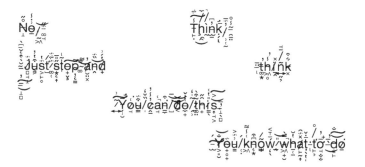

I felt something in me resist the cold emptiness
that swept through my mind. Was it my humanity? Was
it Karine? I wasn't sure from where the voice spoke, but
I knew it was right. I knew what to do. I had seen the
spell before. I was designed to learn from seeing. I
could recreate any magic simply from observing it. I
dropped my hands from Spring's arm that clutched my
throat, the fresh burning pink Wyvren core in his hand
positioned to install it into my defective one. Pink. It was
everywhere. It had been there the whole time. Pink.

I looked Spring in the eyes, forcing the line of
reset to burn away from my vision. I think once upon a
time something in Karine knew that this would be the
answer, if not evidently at least subconsciously. Maybe
that is why I met August in Midnight. Maybe even a part

of Spring saw this destiny between us. Kieran certainly understood it, but not in the way I would come to the same conclusion.

I reached through myself, igniting my green eyes with the spirit of my identity. The vicious green light traveled down my throat and across the fragile vessels that still touched my core, ripping though all of the colors of the code projected between Spring and I. White, blue, gold, pink; all of it. All the colors being replaced with a bright green that ran through it.

I wasn't sure at all what was going to happen next, but I knew that my body was about to die either way. This was my last resort. As I resisted, the sealing spell began to reset and settle between the other two artifacts and myself around Spring. I reached into my memory bank and watched August's color magic. I watched him pull the red from the impossible grass and put the stars back in the sky. I watched. And I learned.

As I felt the final breath leave my dying lungs and felt the vitality fade from my eyes, I exhaled the final will and incantation of that body with the intention of August's spell. In the intent carried through my dying breath, I shifted the green of my existence into the fresh new Wyvren core in Spring's hands; exchanging the hues as the code spilling from me turned completely roseate. My oxygen deprived hand reached forward, weakly snapping my fingers as I displaced something for the final time.

Spring's body jolted, his torso arrested with trauma as he stammered to breathe. He looked down in his hand, seeing not the new Wyvren core Hector had so brilliantly recreated as a copy of my own, but his own shimmering heart; glistening with blood and magic. The engine he held in his hand, still hanging from my dying body, faded from the brilliant green of my soul and burned with he familiar hue of Spring's bright eyes.

Spring dropped my body in despair and disbelief. He placed both hands on his chest, feeling not the familiar beating of his own heart, but the ferocious pulsing hum of a Wyvren core. He shed his robes and looked across his arms, the spellings of ancient and angelic runes beginning to appear in nimble calligraphy across his arms. I had cast aside the husk of my dying body and brittle heart, taking root in the new engine and placing it in its new home: Spring.

Everything was dark. My eyes focused to see the familiar cage in the belly of the Wyvren, Spring's relenting form crouched by the patronizing fire within it. He looked up at me, reddened fury gleaming in his eyes, but a smile on his face all the same.

"You know this story doesn't end the way you want it to." His voice crawled through the cage towards me, dragging in the weight of hysterical inevitability. "So long as I exist, even in here, you will never be free of me. You have made my heavenly form mortal in your choice; you have made yourself just another human body. When it dies, I will be here, ready to reclaim myself. Once you die as this stolen Season, I will escape you and make sure Karine and all of them die, again and again. You have only delayed your agony."

I took a deep breath, choosing not to respond to his threats with visceral feelings. I knew what he was doing, especially here. "You will not have that opportunity, father." I said with quiet conviction. "I'm human now, as you said. So I can call you that, right 'dad?'" I grinned, watching his frustration with my sarcasm.

"I have no intention of leaving you here to fuel the Wyvren." I said. "I will fuel my body and my engine with love. With life. With humanity. With food. *So* much food. Specifically bread." I smiled, ear to ear with liberated pleasure. "Have you had bread, dad? It really is the best."

Spring ignored the sentiment of my teasing, "you can't simply get rid of me." He insisted. "I exist in this essential part of your programming, you can't just send me to..." Spring trailed off as his jaw dropped, the impact of my strategy fully sinking in. "... you really have learned a lot, haven't you, starling?" He said, his words steeped in a subtle and bizarre pride.

"Good bye, Spring." I said, raising my hand and snapping my fingers again. In that command, Spring vanished from the cage in the belly of the new Wyvren core, and was reinstalled into the crumbling core hanging from my former dying body.

I could see back in the physical world, despite my reforming existence as green and pink lights began to swirl around Spring's old body while I replaced it. Karine continued to cry, not fully understanding what was happening as the spell reached climax. The Grace from my old body glimmered, sending a golden light to meet the blue hues of Karine's Time swords, resonating with the engine that burned in my new chest. The colors

325

swirled together around my former dying body, now looking up at me and reforming with bright pink eyes as Spring laid trapped within it.

With a crackling round of snaps, the artifacts crushed around the pitiful sight; the hues mingling with each other and crashing towards the object that used to sustain me. The corpse it set upon withered to dust, the golden ring of Autumn's Grace remaining in its place, while the once shimmering magical cube now a heavy stone of the same shape. Karine swooped down, finally landing and winded from her work, the umbra dissolving form her body.

We looked at each other; her eyes hesitant as she stared into the same green she'd always known resting in the face of Spring's body. There was an eternity of silence as light continued to cascade around me, both of us trying to find the words to say to each other, unsure in our victory and unaware of what would happen next.

"… Ren?" Karine finally asked, her words trembling as she called her swords back to her hands in the event that was not the case.

I looked at her and smiled as a rose colored hue appeared around the circumference of my irises. "Not quite," I responded, both mine and Spring's voice answering. "I still have to finish 'becoming.'" I intentionally gathered the ambient energies trying to find their place around me, and began the familiar process of my creation.

I felt my engine whir louder and louder, rendering my new body into both green and pink

326

magics around the structure within my chest. Petals formed around me; not white, not black, not gold. As the flower of my reincarnation bloomed around me, it was no longer a Lotus.

With the Mantle of Spring in my grasp, I bloomed a brilliant, radiant Azalea.

I felt strength and vitality I had never known course through new limbs as I emerged from the garden of my creation; countless flowers budding and blooming in the lustrous Spring erupting around me. I stepped down, out of my flower, and walked towards Karine with my new body.

Karine covered her mouth, eyes wide with shock. I was without runes, my hair still long and dark. I was tall. I was the same shape. I was the same, the only difference the tinges of pink around my no longer glassy green eyes. They were otherworldly, steeped with higher dimensional magics, but now fully human.

We ran towards each other, embracing one another as we felt the final embers of danger hush their flames in the aftermath of our battle. We held each other, still and tightly. Neither of us had ever know or felt such a clinging victory; such a liberation from the crashing weight of an inevitable force. We laughed, even cried for a moment, and then shared a quiet and calming kiss.

"I can't believe we did it," Karine whispered as we wrapped our arms around each other again, her voice carrying from behind my shoulder. "I can't believe we survived. This is the future I have never seen... the possibility I've never come to."

I sighed, "it isn't unlike what Kieran wanted to happen," I responded. "The personality that was Spring is trapped in that stone, but I still inherited the identity of Spring." I pulled away, looking at Karine with concern furrowing my brow. "It is rare that you haven't foreseen an outcome, and I don't know the consequence of this either."

Almost perfectly on cue with my words, the platform rushed with an auburn light; a burgundy eruption of rust and amber illuminating the war torn platform. We turned, facing the source of the light as it culminated into a humanoid form.

"I can tell you what happens next, 'Sister,'" Autumn's militant voice sneered in unwilling acceptance. "Prepare yourself. And remember that you chose this."

Karine and I looked at the ferocious Season, seething with anger and confusion in the wake of her brother's "death." Even with her scorn and anger baking the air around us, all I could manage to do was continue to share with Karine in our victory.

I looked to Autumn, taking Karine's hand as I spoke. "Whatever you say next, understand and know that we are prepared for not only the future, but for you as well." I threatened. "I don't yet know how to grasp this power in my fists, but I am not ignorant to the evils of your family. And know that you will all pay for them."

Autumn raised her hands above her flowing locks of fiery hair, gathering a bright bronze collection of magics clearly fueled by her wrath. Karine, tugged at the hand that held hers. When I looked at her, she was smiling.

"Let's finish this." She said, smiling her knowing smile.

I grinned back at her, feeling the expanse of possibility thrive and blossom in my chest. We had done the impossible, and continued to stare down the unforgiving precipice of fate. But I wasn't afraid. I wasn't uncertain. I had Karine by my side and I had the potential of Spring in my soul.

I playfully responded, stronger than ever. "I'll follow your lead."

In Spring's garden blossomed an impossibility,

Something more vicious than anyone could have ever imagined.

This flower bloomed to survive

This flower bloomed to overcome

This flower bloomed to change it all.

Of all the garden's that should have never been planted, this secret nursery of destruction shall be undone.

The rare and formidable florescence of petals that trail between our worlds.

The flowers Spring planted long ago.

Fight Azalea.

Fight.

Thank you to my wonderful friends who have supported me in telling the story I have wanted to share for so long.

Thank you so much for reading Lotus, and now Orchid. It means everything to me that you have come this far.

I hope to see you again at the end of Azalea, completing the Wyvren Trilogy.

Thank you, thank you, thank you.